This
Face
of
Evil

This
Face
of
Evil

GREGORY C. RANDALL

WH
WINDSOR HILL
PUBLISHING

ALSO BY GREGORY C. RANDALL

The Cherry Pickers

The Max Adler WWII Thrillers
This Face of Evil
Pawns in an Ancient Game

The Sharon O'Mara Chronicles
Land Swap For Death
Containers For Death
Toulouse For Death
12th Man For Death
Diamonds For Death
Limerick For Death

The Tony Alfano Thrillers
Chicago Swing
Chicago Jazz
Chicago Fix
Chicago Boogie Woogie

The Alex Polonia Thrillers
Venice Black
Saigon Red
St. Petersburg White

The Gypsy King Sci-Fi Adventures
Sector 73

Nonfiction
America's Original GI Town, Park Forest, Illinois

Published by Windsor Hill Publishing, Walnut Creek, California
www.gregorycrandall.info

ISBN-13: 978-1-7365013-1-3 (ebook – Kindle Edition)
ISBN-13: 978-1-7365013-2-0 (paperback)

Cover design by Gregory C. Randall

For my brother Geoffrey J. Randall

The spring before this novel was published my youngest brother, Geoff, unexpectantly passed away. He was sixty-three years old. He was not just my brother but my friend. He left two beautiful daughters, and two beautiful grandchildren. He will be forever missed.

The second horseman of the Apocalypse, War,
watered his mount in a bloody stream, waiting.

1

Berlin, August 1939

For two months, not one day passed that SS-Sturmbannführer Heinrich Schmidt didn't have intense meetings in the chancellery or quick trips through Berlin for more conferences or presentations. Building a killing machine takes time and organization. Finally, during the evening of the third day of a planning meeting in the basement of a nondescript building a block from the Reich chancellery, a dozen exhausted officers and men leaned over long oak tables full of documents and plans. Schmidt, standing upright, slammed his palm down on the table and demanded that his people stop and take a break. Bleary-eyed and tired, they walked away from their maps and notepads, stretched aching backs and shoulders, reached for cigarettes or pipes, and secured their respective military hats. After climbing the forty-four steps from the underground bunker, they squinted and covered their eyes from the intense mid-August sun and inhaled deeply the fresh air of Berlin.

From the guarded exit of the bunker under the government building, they crossed the street to a park. Gathered together, a junior officer said, "It's good to breathe fresh air, sir.

After weeks underground, I'm beginning to know what a badger must feel like."

"And how they smell, too, Klaus," Schmidt said with a laugh.

"I'm sorry, sir. I didn't mean that—"

"Please, Lieutenant. We all are beginning to smell like ripe cheese. It will be better when we move to the front."

In the bunker, the maps and photographs that intimately illustrated the regions of Upper Silesia and the Oder River were spread ten layers deep across the tables. Shown in detail were rivers, streams, and creeks as well as bridges, shallow fords, and almost every building and fortification throughout the region. Their spies and agents had done a thorough job during the last few years, working to supply the Nazi government with critical information about the swath of countryside from the German border eastward and south to Lódz, Poland. There were dozens of such groups for other areas and targets of the impending attacks.

"Are you happy, Lieutenant?" Schmidt asked, blowing smoke into the air.

"I am excited to be involved, sir. Yes, I believe I'm happy."

"That is good; war is never a time to be happy, so be happy now. In a few weeks and then for many months, you will not be . . . happy. Then it will be your duty and honor first. Your personal needs and feelings will be unimportant; in fact, they can get you killed—but you know that. Your training is excellent. Only those with proficient grades, demonstrated skills, and good standing in the *Schutzstaffel* can be part of the LSSAH," Schmidt said, referring to the *Leibstandarte SS Adolf Hitler*, the specialized division that formed the extensive personal bodyguard for the Führer. "I wish I were a member of your group. However, my road is unplanned, and I go where ordered," he added.

The lieutenant noted the ribbons over the man's pocket;

they told the story of the officer's place in the *Schutzstaffel* and in Germany's military. Schmidt had already been an SS officer for more than half of the young man's life.

"May I ask a question, sir?"

"Certainly, Lieutenant. I will answer, if I can."

"It is rumored that you were a policeman in Nuremberg."

"I was and quite proud of it."

"And that you have been in Spain and Poland?"

"Yes, I have. But it is hardly a rumor. Most know."

"What is Spain like? I have always wanted to see it."

"Much less green than our country, I assure you. The people are not as disciplined as we are. They are proud, yes, but are less dependable. As you are aware, while we have helped General Franco with his problems, they are not forthcoming in helping us. That will be remembered."

"Have you met General Franco, sir?"

"Yes, I have. A few months ago, in fact."

"What's he like?"

"Short."

* * *

The planning by the *SS Leibstandarte* for its part in the invasion of Poland was now into its sixth month. The last few weeks had been narrowly focused on the military assignments and objectives of particular battalions and regiments. Schmidt's assignment was straightforward: to follow the advancing mechanized thrust of the attacking division and manage the remaining population left in its dust. The greatest concern—one that he understood completely—were the Jews.

The date for the invasion had been set for the 26th of August. But after moving his people from Berlin to their appointed locations, Schmidt was notified to hold. He was not told why. Nonetheless, he was surprised when it was announced that the Führer had made an unexpected, nonaggression pact with the Soviets. Schmidt was certain that this German-Soviet concordat had something to do with the delay. His regiment was ordered to wait at the border with Poland for new orders.

On the eve of the amended date for the invasion of Poland, Schmidt was asked to sit in on a meeting with the *Sicherheitsdienst*, the state security service in this area of Germany. He was shocked when a soldier in a Polish officer's uniform walked into the room and began to address the assembly.

"Tonight, there will be an incident that will start the invasion," the officer said. "I am leading an assault team in an attack on our radio station near Gleiwitz. With us will be a dozen convicted traitors dressed as Polish soldiers. These *Konserven*, tin cans as you call them, will be excecuted during this assault. They will represent to the world that the Poles can't be trusted. They will be evidence of our justified response. Not that we need a reason to invade this country of swine and degenerates. I am telling you this so your men in forward positions do not react when they hear the gunfire. My men and I don't want to be the first accidental causalities of the war. It would not be good for morale."

The officers quietly laughed at the joke. Nonetheless, each was disappointed that they had not received these orders.

Five days later, on September 1, 1939, the blitzkrieg began by the massive thrust of a million soldiers eastward from positions in Germany, Silesia, North Prussia, and Slovakia. As the invasion advanced, Schmidt and his regiment relentlessly followed. Ahead of them to the east, canon fire and aerial bombardments illuminated the sky with flashes and explosions. Each hour, trucks and columns of horses laden with soldiers and munitions passed them on the dirt roads. On the first day of action, they saw their first dead Polish soldiers. On the second day, the first civilians—women and children—were seen dead in drainage ditches alongside the road. For the next week, it became an unrelenting progression of dead horses, dead enemy soldiers, and dead civilians. Burning Polish vehicles flanked the road and filled the drainage swales. Schmidt's orders were that no Polish civilians be allowed to escape or be left behind to cause trouble. His men, unlike many of the fascists he'd trained in Spain, were better and more efficient at executing these potential threats. Only civilians with German-issued papers could pass; all others were liquidated.

He was also ordered to leave no village standing that might provide cover for potential ambushes or snipers. They torched every village they passed. Across the flat Polish landscape south of Lódz, under the clear rainless September sky, pillars of smoke twisted upward from burning villages and fields. Often, when Schmidt's regiment took gunfire from nearby woods, he ordered incendiaries into the trees to burn out the resistance. They shot the men and women fleeing the flames as if shooting game flushed from a copse.

Each night, a bivouac would be set up, food cooked, a few hours of sleep taken, then move on before sunrise. Not one night, since the start of the invasion, was silent. The concussions of far-off artillery shells unceasingly continued. Overhead, screaming Stuka dive-bombers dropped their bombs just a mile or two ahead of Schmidt's encampments. He was proud of his men and the disciplined German army.

On the fifteenth day of the advance, they came to a ramshackle hamlet northeast of Lódz; it was undamaged and seemed deserted. Schmidt walked along the dirt road that split the village. Wooden structures, a few with glass windows, lined the street. A yellow dog lay on the porch of a house, watching. This was not the first Jewish village Schmidt and his troops had entered; surprisingly, it was the least damaged.

"Lieutenant, take three men and throw grenades through the windows. We will smoke them out," Schmidt ordered.

The explosions threw glass and wooden debris into the street. A couple of the houses began to burn, but there still was no sign of men, women, or children. They continued advancing up the street but were met with no response. Schmidt ordered more grenades. As the men reached the center of the village, a light wind kicked up, spreading the flames to the un-damaged houses.

Schmidt waved to his lieutenant. The man quick-timed it to his captain.

"Yes, sir?"

"Is the village abandoned?"

"Not sure, sir. We still have half the village to inspect. In an hour it will all be burning."

The lieutenant saluted. As he started to turn away, half the man's face exploded, throwing blood and brain matter over Schmidt. The soldier fell. From behind Schmidt, twenty German weapons began firing into the buildings ahead of them. The mechanized half-track, bringing up the rear, opened up with its MG 34 machine guns that ripped through buildings and anything inside. Another German soldier fell. Schmidt took a position behind the half-track, put up his hand to stop firing, and ordered his men to the sides of the street. Three of his men circled behind the buildings and slowly advanced. For five minutes, his men waited for his command. A hail of gun-fire echoed from the end of the smoke-obscured street. As a hot breeze cleared the air of smoke, two soldiers herded a boy and woman up the street to the captain. Schmidt asked in Polish where the other villagers were hiding; neither responded. He calmly removed his pistol and shot the woman in the face.

"*Gdzie?*" he screamed at the boy.

The child, not fifteen, turned and pointed down the street to the last house.

"*Piwnica,*" he croaked.

"Cellar," Schmidt said to his men, then shot the boy in the head.

"Go, before they escape!" he yelled.

The half-track roared up the dirt street, the soldiers running to keep pace. They stopped in front of the last building. In a field of yellow oats, a hundred yards deep, thirty people were running. Schmidt's men opened fire; half instantly fell. The others continued running; within seconds, none remained standing.

"Sergeant, take four men and see if there are any alive. Don't bring any back," he ordered.

As Schmidt walked back to his dead lieutenant, single gunshots, like sharp staccato taps against glass, echoed through the burning village. Schmidt placed the bodies of his dead comrades in the truck and ordered it back behind the lines. He would not leave any of his men behind. The Jewish dead—he left them where they fell.

"Burn the rest of the town and the fields. Leave nothing," he ordered.

Between the burning buildings, the yellow dog could be seen fleeing in panic. It stopped once and turned to see if it was being followed.

2

The beach near Ostia, Italy
June 15, 1943

Max Adler swam with experienced strength through the Mediterranean Sea's swells that washed the wide, invisible beach a hundred meters ahead; he could not remember a blacker night. Unfortunately, the stars overhead did little to improve his mood; while he believed he was invisible, he was sure that every star, as if a spotlight, illuminated him as he breast-stroked through the water. The intelligence regarding beach defensives in this area was sketchy at best; for all he knew, he was swimming toward a hundred Italians manning machine guns. Or worse, the Krauts, all with anxious trigger fingers. His people said this was the best place. If he were alive in an hour, he might begin to believe them. The orders to the captain of the submarine were to land him two miles off the beach of the village of Ostia, row him to within a mile. If there was a village in front of him, beyond the dark expanse ahead, he sure as hell couldn't see it.

The past week had been nuts, plain and simple. He'd flown in the freezing interior of a converted Lancaster bomber from London to Gibraltar, then on to Tunis, and its recently retaken airbase. Then, after three days of waiting in a hot and rancid-smelling tent with a dozen other members of the OSS, he and two others were rowed in a leaky fishing boat to an American submarine waiting a half mile off the coast of Tunisia. No one talked about their respective missions; they didn't want to know what the others were doing and for the most part, didn't care. Their roles were small cogs in the gears of this war, a reason it was called a war machine. Two days later, he thanked the captain for the ocean cruise and slid down the flank of the submarine into a rubber boat with two crewmen who would row him closer to shore. Thirty minutes later, he rolled out of the boat into the Tyrrhenian Sea hoping he was no more than a thousand meters off the beach. Taking one strong breaststroke after another, he remembered the other times he'd entered Rome—Rome before there was a war, this war. None had required swimming into the sights of a machine-gun emplacement. He'd agreed to Ostia because six years earlier he visited the ruins of Capitolium, a Roman port city that two millennia earlier had been the watery gateway to Rome at the mouth of the Tiber River. But that visit seemed like a lifetime ago. Then there were hotels, beachfront cabanas, cold drinks, and welcoming girls. It had been a favorite fascist resort. The war changed that; it was now easier to get shot dead than sunburned on the beach at Ostia.

After fifteen minutes of swimming, his toes touched the sand; he'd reached the shallows. He turned and swam parallel to the beach, hoping to catch hints of any activities, a cigarette being lit, a laugh, a cough. He hated surprises. He also looked for any landmark, something that would tell him where he was, and if he was near where he was supposed to be. The captain of the submarine told him they were "on the spot." He hoped that spot wasn't near a German shore defense. He could hear and feel the surf rhythmically wash up and down the shingle of sand a hundred meters away.

Then, a succession of sharp, brilliant flashes nearly blind-ed him. A fusillade of tracer bullets ripped through the air, not five feet over his head. Shit. He dove, his heavy backpack pushing him into the sand. His mouth filled with grit. The surf broke and rolled him forward. The shore defense could not have spotted him, not a chance. He continued swimming underwater, parallel to the beach. More tracers flew over his head, all erratic, purposeless. Their eerie staccato lights flashed through the water. He doubled up, his knees on the sand, slow-ly raised his head above the surface and listened. Voices, Italian and loud, yelled back and forth. Finally, a voice with authority yelled, "*Stai zitto, idiota. Niente più riprese.*"

"*Ho visto qualcosa.*"

"*Idioti. Fermartevi!*"

Thank God, practice shots. His remedial Italian helped sort out some of it. A final dozen tracers buzzed overhead. What prompted the sudden shooting from the beach puzzled Max as he swam silently away from the rifle fire. Maybe the soldier did see something, a shadow, a ghost, an ex-wife. His swim-mer's arms carried him another hundred yards farther up the shoreline. He hoped with every stroke that he wasn't just ex-changing the last bunker for another guard post. Intelligence said there were no guards, no wire, no mines—just a deserted seaside village. His people were wrong about the guards; the other two could kill him. He slithered up the beach and out of the relative safety of the sea. Hunched over, he jogged up the sand hoping the rising surf and weak tide would wash away his footprints before the morning watch and patrol. He looked back down the beach—no more tracers. It was stupid things like that that could get him killed.

He took a quick look at his watch: 03:35—an hour and a half until the haze of dawn. He continued to move inland amongst the dunes and derelict buildings. Beyond the last low dune, he spotted his first target, the dark shape of a small outbuilding. He prayed that it was not the outline of a fortified bunker. Reaching it, the shadow became an outhouse; a single dark shadow from the aerial photos he memorized. From his rucksack, he removed dry clothes and shoes that had been wrapped in waterproof bags. He carefully placed the smaller bag that held his Colt pistol, two magazines, a knife, and a night compass on the sand. He also found, groping about with his fingers, an orange, some hardtack, and a can of water. He quickly changed his clothes, ate and drank, then stuffed his wet suit into the rucksack. After taking personal advantage of the outhouse, he unceremoniously dropped the bag through the open seat. Snugging the Italian army field hat tight, he walked quickly inland. Fifteen minutes later, as he paralleled the Via Cristoforo Colombo, he estimated he'd walked a mile and a half inland from the beach. Using an Italian-made flashlight, he scanned the road signs, found the one he was looking for, and began the wait for the bus to Rome. The bus, used by local workers, wouldn't arrive for two hours—if it was on time. Rome was fifteen miles away; walking was an option. He decided to wait.

This was the toughest part. He found a spot under a thick clump of white oleander in full bloom and ate another biscuit of hardtack. It was 06:45, the sun above the horizon, when the bus approached, the noise of its gearbox and exhaust breaking the silence.

He walked nonchalantly to the bus stop. Two passengers, an elderly woman and a middle-aged male, also waited. Max fumbled in his pocket for the proscribed fare, ten lire to Rome. At that moment he wished he could shrink his six-foot-four-inch frame by a foot and look the part of a worn-out war veteran. With his two-week stubble, old clothing, and field cap, he hoped he exuded a look of desperation. After seeing the two local passengers, however, with their sunken eyes and obvious effects of two years of war and its deprivations, he knew he was in trouble. He looked too damn healthy.

At first the woman stared at him contemptuously. Then, as if having an epiphany, she smiled. The man she was with looked at Max with a vacant glance and shrugged. The woman cautiously held up her right hand and two fingers; it was the V for victory. Chagrined, almost embarrassed by his easy detection, Max shrugged. The bus pulled to the stop. Max followed the woman and man onboard, offered to help carry her heavy bag. She said something to the driver. The driver looked at this strange worker as Max handed him his fare.

"Cugino. Sta andando a Roma."

Cousin? Rome? How the hell did she know I was going to Rome?

They slipped into seats at the rear as the bus lurched forward. The man leaned against the window and closed his eyes. The woman bent in toward Max and in tentative English whispered, "American, I can tell. Many, so I have been told, have come in from the sea and then gone on to Rome. You, my son, are my first. I won't tell. The sooner these *presuntuoso* Tedeschi go home, the happier I will be. Rome is about an hour away. Say nothing, be quiet. I know most of the passengers—do not talk to them. I will talk for you, if necessary. You are my *cugina*, my cousin. I have just one question—when are you coming to save us?"

"I don't know, mother," Max answered truthfully. "Soon, I hope."

"So do I," the woman answered. "I pray to God that you come soon—before we are all murdered by this stupid war."

The woman, true to her word, provided interference by answering questions from nosey passengers; obviously this was a group that often traveled together. Max was a stranger, and the other passengers did not like strangers. They feared them. Reaching the outskirts of Rome, Max saw the dome of the Vatican in the morning sun.

"Signore, I suggest you get off at the next stop," his guardian angel said. "There is a German barracks near here; often soldiers board. Go. Do the Lord's work."

"I understand. *Grazie, nonna.* And *grazie* to your husband."

"Him?" She pointed at the man. "That lazy good-for-nothing is my son. I go along with him to make sure he shows up to work." She gave Max a big smile. A front tooth was missing. "In fact, he's too stupid to even join the army. Twice he went, twice they sent him home. Such are my troubles. *Buona fortuna, cugino mio.*"

Stepping down to the street, Max waved goodbye to the woman. Through the open window, she again held up the famous Winston Churchill signal. Max would learn that to flash the V for victory sign in Rome could earn you a beating, or worse.

Patting his chest, he reconfirmed the papers in his interior breast pocket. Identification cards, ration cards, a small stack of worn lire, a photo of a cute Italian girl whose name he never learned (he called her Lisa), a package of Italian cigarettes, matches from a restaurant near the Colosseum, and a small pen knife with the name of the shop, Muzio, engraved on its handle. His clothes were Italian as well as the shoes—all had been provided by an Italian workman who had been interned when the British took back Tunis. The poor bastard literally missed the last boat to escape to Sicily. For extra rations and a new set of clothes, the internee handed over his old clothes to Max. Max had them washed, twice. He still wasn't comfortable with the man's underwear, but authenticity was critical, even down to his skivvies.

Twice before the war, Max had been to Rome, each time for just a few days. This was when he worked for his father buying Italian appliances for his family's furniture and appliance business on Maxwell Street in Chicago. The first trip was in the spring of 1938, the next in the summer of 1939. He'd dreamed of going back, to enjoy the city he'd instantly taken to. However, that dream did not include a rubber boat, swimming under machine-gun fire, and sneaking into the Eternal City—all while war raged around him. He also did not foresee his being a captain in the United States Army and a spy for the OSS.

* * *

Chicago, Illinois, February 1939

During the summer of 1938, while on one of his buying trips for his family's store, Max Adler met his college friend, Dominic Fallace at Dominic's parent's villa above the village of Amalfi on the Sorrentine Peninsula near Naples. Cesare and Lucia Fallace treated him like a son during the two weeks he stayed with them. Dominic's sister and brother, still in school in Florence but home for the summer, used him as a sounding board as they practiced their English. By the time Max left for Rome, he had been welcomed into a new family, discovered a profound love of Italy, and had given his promise to continue to learn Italian. It made the events of the following February in Chicago even more heart wrenching.

That cold February afternoon, when Max entered Pompeii's Grotto—one of the better restaurants in Chicago's Little Italy neighborhood—only three of the two dozen red-and-white checkered tablecloth-covered tables had patrons. Young couples sat at two, stealing an hour for themselves. At the third—in the far corner—sat Dominic Fallace. Books and papers were spread across the tabletop; an empty wineglass, a plate stained with red sauce, and an empty breadbasket sat off to one side. Max grasped the chair opposite the man, spun it around, coughing as he dropped his butt onto the seat.

"The sounds of your huge feet precede you, Adler." Dominic looked up and smiled. "Hungry?"

"Famished!"

"Good." He waved to a waiter stationed by the entry to the kitchen.

"*Si, si,* Signor Fallace," the waiter said.

"Spaghetti with meatballs for Signor Adler and two Chiantis."

"Thanks, Mario," Max said. He lit a cigarette. "How's the books?"

"Crushing. If it weren't for my aunt pushing me, I'd come and work for her. Probably make more money in the short term and, most probably, the long haul as well."

"Your aunt and uncle, when will they return from Italy?" Max asked as the waiter returned with the wine.

"Next week. They are still with my folks. I did get a letter. Aunt Renata says they are well. Mother's letter arrived before theirs and told me all about their stay. Considering the fascists Mussolini and Adolf Hitler, shaking the cages of Europe's governments, I'll be relieved when they're home."

Dominic raised his glass. "To my aunt and uncle."

Max saluted Dominic. "To the Rossis, and your parents too."

"Now, if I could get my folks to leave Amalfi. There is nothing left for them in Italy."

"Your brother and sister . . ."

"Still in Florence and old enough to take care of themselves. I've told them to leave too."

"They must make their own decisions," Max said.

Another man, also dark haired and about their age, entered and crossed the room. He took the chair between them. The waiter was close behind, asking if the signor cared for a glass of wine.

"Yes, thank you, Mario," Dwight Loomis said. "God, it's miserable outside."

The three friends had known each other since their first year at Northwestern University. Dominic studied Italian art and history; Dwight studied architecture; and Max, ever the dilettante, studied the law and art, or at least professed to.

"Your folks?" Dominic asked while reorganizing the papers on the table.

"They are good; the stores are doing well," Max told him.

The waiter placed a glass of Chianti in front of Dwight.

"*L'chaim*," Dwight toasted. "To our futures."

The other two raised their glasses.

"Speaking of the future," Max said. "I've booked passage to France. I'm going to Paris. One last trip before all hell breaks loose. My uncle has contacts on art Dad wants for the store, and Mother wants me to talk Uncle Wilhelm out of staying in France."

"Paris? You must be crazy," Dominic said. "With all the madness in Europe right now, you're going to France?"

"France, and maybe Italy. Dom, if I can, I will try and see your folks. However, if my uncle decides to leave, I must help him navigate his way here."

"Be careful. You could get your ass thrown in jail—or worse," Dwight said.

"Speaking of that, I have a great idea," Max said, setting down his glass.

He extracted a folded piece of paper from his coat; its corners were torn. He spread it open on the table. In large black German-style script it read, in English: JOIN US, MEETING OF THE GERMAN-AMERICAN BUND.

"You have got to be kidding," Dominic said.

"You took it down?" Dwight asked.

"Sure. The bastards won't miss it. They're stuck on electric poles up and down Rush Street."

"They are Nazis, for Christ's sake," Dwight added. "And you being—"

"That will make it even more fun," he said. "Like a colored at a Klan meeting."

"Stop it," Dominic insisted. "I won't let you go, or certainly not alone."

"That's the point; you two go with me. We'll be college buddies out to better understand our heritage and politics—good Germans, and all."

"I'm Italian, Ike's Polish, or at least half-Polish, and you're a German Jew," Dominic said.

"It's our word if anyone asks—which they won't. What better way to spend the evening than with a bunch of Nazis and . . . yours truly, the Jew party-crasher?"

"You are nuts," Dominic said.

"Never mind that—it'll be interesting," Max promised. "And besides, it says there will be a guest speaker from Germany—a senior official from Hitler's government."

Dwight sighed. "I'll go—if nothing more than to keep you out of trouble. Besides, could be interesting to see what this master race thinks of Chicago."

"That's my boy. Always out for a new adventure. You?" Max said, pointing at Dominic.

Dominic studied the handbill. "Sure, why not—as you said, it might even be enlightening."

3

Madrid, June 1943

On the society page of the Madrid newspaper *ABC*, the following paragraph was inserted. It was within an article relating the events of a party at the villa of one of Generalissimo Franco's favorite fascist politicians in celebration of visiting representatives of the fascist regime in Italy. The Italian ambassador was in attendance as well as Hitler's Spanish ambassador. The singular paragraph was halfway down from the lead.

> *It is also with some pleasure that I can reveal that Senorita Sophie Norcross also joined the celebration. She is newly arrived from England by way of Lisbon. Her grandparents are Count Franco Conti and Countess Ester Conti of Rome. They are well known to senior officials here in Madrid for their business connections through their industrial operations in Rome. The Contis are longtime supporters of the fascist cause and Prime Minister Mussolini and have more than once met with Generalissimo Franco here in Madrid. Senorita Norcross arrived wearing a dark black evening dress that stole the hearts of many*

of the men at the party and the enmity of some of the women. It is important to note that Senorita Norcross arrived in Madrid under the shadow of a political cloud and without her British passport. Rumors abound about her recent anti-British comments that may have contributed to her abrupt departure, some say expulsion, from London. Her father, the past ambassador to Italy and a loyal supporter of Prime Minister Winston Churchill, refused to answer any questions about his daughter. England's loss is Spain's and the cause's gain. When asked how long she was staying in Spain, she replied, "Not long. I miss my grandparents in Rome. Point of fact, I miss everything about Rome." We wish her well.

The night of the chronicled celebration, Sophie Norcross stood off to one side of the elegant marble-clad ballroom and did everything to avoid the son of the Italian ambassador to Spain. The diplomat's son reeked of a cologne that, when stewed with a peculiar aroma that emanated from the pomade he'd used to flatten his unruly and quite curly black hair, roiled her stomach. She had tried twice, unsuccessfully, to lose the man who stood six inches shorter than herself. Once by passing him off to one of the Spanish ladies that arrived with the military officers, the second time to a young Spanish officer— that one seemed to be working out. Unfortunately, like a bad Spanish peseta, he kept coming back, this time with a reporter. She stalled as long as she could, talking about innocuous subjects until the reporter lost interest and drifted away to talk with an old dowager who seemed to be thrilled by the attention of the younger correspondent.

"Roberto, I am leaving," Sophie finally said to the ambassador's son. "I have a long day tomorrow and the train for Marseille leaves tomorrow at midnight. If all goes well, I will be in Rome in three days. Then again, these days, nothing ever seems to go according to plan."

"You will be missed. It was a pleasure to see you again after all these years," Roberto said as he bowed. "May I escort you back to your hotel? My car is available."

Sophie smiled graciously. She had met the man at a summer party fifteen years earlier at her grandparents' villa in Rome's San Sebastiano district. She vaguely remembered him; he was a boy then. He obviously remembered her. He had not changed. He had grown from a small knob of a blossom into a short, obnoxious, and pretentious fop.

"I wish I was going with you; I miss Italy so," he said. "Being stuck here makes one feel like they are in a sweltering prison. The food makes you choke; I long for the finer things in Rome. And don't even start about the wine—good God and Christ, mouthwash is better."

She understood the real reason he stayed in Spain—to avoid being drafted and given the opportunity to die for his country in some God-awful part of the world.

Sophie steeled herself for the week's travel. The train would head east and cross through the Pyrenees, then hug the French coast to Vichy Marseille, then cross the Italian border to Genova. From there, after a transfer, she would reach Rome in a day. All this assumed that the Allies wouldn't drop a five-hundred-pound bomb on her head somewhere along the route. Much of the travel would be at night.

The truth, obviously not disclosed in the planted article, was that her father still loved her, her British passport was securely locked in the family safe in Kent, and that when she reached Rome, she was to meet an American OSS agent. The previous fall, she'd spent three months with the American at the secret Canadian spy training facility Camp X. She had found the man intriguing, funny, and, for a Jew, quite the libertine. She assumed that his route was a lot more treacherous than her champagne and caviar jaunt in a comfortable train car across the underbelly of Europe. She needed a cover story, a big cover story, and Spain was it. Her goal in Madrid was simple—acquire the proper papers and gain notice and passage from Spain to Italy; these could only be obtained through the Italian ministry. She knew that when you are the publicly disgraced daughter of one of England's most prominent diplomats, it is hard to keep a low profile—this charade was intentional. To travel alone, especially a woman traveler, would increase the jeopardy and exposure. Nonetheless, she must return to the home of her mother and grandparents in triumph.

She took one last sip from her glass—a fine Spanish Amontillado sherry. All of these were the trappings and pleasures of being a spy. Then again, being exposed, arrested, and imprisoned—or worse—were distinct and undesired options.

As she turned away from the ambassador's son, a commotion rose from near the entry to the ballroom.

"Damas y caballeros, Su Excelencia el Jefe de Etasdo, Generalissimo Franco."

General Franco, in full uniform, strolled into the ballroom. Men and women bowed and then began to clap; the sounds of appreciation filled the room. During the last five years— since his fascist Nationalists' victory over the communist-led Republicans—Franco had secured and strengthened his position as dictator of Spain. He'd also kept Spain out of the German-Italian war that now engulfed the rest of Europe. In many ways it was a victory. He had more than enough battles of his own against regional factions, Catalan fighters, and communists. Sophie had been warned to be careful. To become an opponent of Franco was to join the more than two hundred thousand that had been murdered by the regime since the end of the Civil War. She took a step back and pressed herself against the wall. She needed to leave, now. Slowly weaving her way stealthily through the crowd, she eventually reached the rear door.

"Leaving, Senorita Norcross?" a dignified man in a dark gray uniform asked, a cigarette in his hand.

She recognized the German military attaché for the Vichy government; she could not recall his name.

"Yes, Senor. I have an early train. I am going home to Rome," she said.

"Colonel Allard, at your service," the attaché said as he saluted her and bowed. "Rome, a wonderful city. I miss it dearly."

"I grew up there, but I wouldn't know about its current condition. I am more concerned about my grandparents; that is why I am going."

"And you will have to cross France," Allard added.

"Of course. I understand geography, Colonel. It is either by train or by swimming. I prefer the train. An Italian boat on the Mediterranean has little chance of survival."

"One could fly," Allard said.

"I'd prefer not to be mistaken for a pigeon and shot down. No, Colonel, I am fine with the train."

"I understand. Be careful, and a word of caution—make sure your papers are in order. Travel can be difficult these days."

"Thank you," Sophie said. "Our embassy here has made sure they are in order."

"Is that the British embassy or the Italian?"

"Tsk-tsk, Colonel, so rude. Then again, you are German. And besides, that is none of your concern. But if it will help to end this tiresome conversation, it is the Italian embassy. Would you like to talk with the ambassador? He is a close friend—let me take you to him." She turned and located the ambassador; the man festooned in a dark dinner jacket and red, white, and green sash was talking to General Franco. Colonel Allard also noticed the conversation.

"That's quite all right. Have a safe trip, Senorita Norcross."

"I will, and you as well, Colonel. I also suggest that you, too, keep your papers in order." She abruptly turned and walked through the door and down the stairs, past a line of limousines to an older car that waited at the end of the queue. "*Vamos*," she said to the driver.

Since the conclusion of the Spanish Civil War, and during the intervening five years, the Spanish welcomed a relative internal peace. Nonetheless, retributions and vendettas continued. The walls of prisons in Madrid and Barcelona continued to be scarred by the firing squad's bullets.

Late the next evening, Sophie boarded the train for Barcelona at the Atocha train station. From Barcelona she would take the Marseille train, transfer again to the Milan train, and then on to Rome. Taking her seat in the first-class car, she was surprised to see Colonel Allard. Her first thought was to ignore the man and return to her small cabin. But it would only put off the inevitable.

"Colonel, such a surprise. I assume you are returning to Vichy?" Sophie said.

"No, I am going only as far as Barcelona—meetings. Then, if they go well, on to Marseille. The advances in North Africa by the British and Americans are disturbing, but I'm sure that these are things that don't concern you."

"Colonel, this ghastly war is all about politics, and I stay away from all that. If you will excuse me, I need to settle into my cabin. It will be a tiresome trip."

"Please, Senorita, if you need help or assistance, please ask."

Sophie nodded to the man and left for her cabin. She spent the rest of the night and early morning there, only asking that the porter bring her water. Late the next afternoon, as they approached the mountains to the north and west of Barcelona, she had decided enough was enough. She was hungry, and not surprisingly, Colonel Allard was sitting in the dining car, an empty seat opposite him. She sat.

"The steak is good, a little tough, but the sauce is serviceable," the colonel said.

"The wine? Is it serviceable?" She looked at the bottle on the table.

"My manners, I'm sorry." He pointed to the waiter and Sophie's glass. It was quickly filled.

She sipped. "Serviceable," she said.

He smiled. "Serviceable, the word for the day. Yes, barely."

The Republican resistance, albeit crushed across Spain, still had active true believers amongst the native Catalonians. They had not accepted capitulation, and it was one of the last regions to fall in the brutal advance by Franco's Nationalist army. When opportunities were presented, these Catalonians took advantage of them. In the mountain pass above the village of Cervera, midway on the rail line between Mantresa and Barcelona, they struck.

"What the hell," Allard yelled, as the train screeched to an abrupt stop, the glasses tipped, the bottle fell to the floor. The German, his Luger held close to his side, rose and headed to the rear of the car. Sophie followed. The passengers stared out the window into the dusky evening, the mountains still lit by the setting sun. A woman stifled a scream when the heavy footsteps of the guards on the roof boomed through the car. The only other sound was the steam being released by the locomotive, three cars ahead. The car door slammed open and a panicked conductor pushed his way down the aisle of the carriage.

"What's the problem?" Sophie demanded.

"The engineer says it's bandits. They've blocked the tracks ahead. We have seen this before. Now that the war is over, the traitors have turned into bandits and murderers."

"What do they want?" Allard said.

The conductor shrugged. "What do bandits always want? Money or hostages for ransom." He squeezed past them, adding, "I suggest you be prepared. I am told they are not happy with Italians or Germans."

"Damn, in two hours we would have been in Barcelona," Allard said, staring after the overwrought conductor who continued through and then out the rear door of the dining car.

"In one hour, we might be dead. I'm going to my cabin; I will be right back," Sophie answered.

Two minutes later, she returned. She had changed into pants and a jacket; in her right hand she held a Beretta pistol. Allard looked impressed.

"One must be prepared these days. Travel can be dangerous, I've been told," she said.

They passed through the last two cars of the train and stepped off the rear platform. They walked along the gravel of the rail bed to the army officer in charge of security.

"What is the situation?" Allard asked.

"We don't know, sir. There is a barricade ahead. The engineer is concerned about explosives under the rails. My men have not seen anyone on either side of the valley. Maybe they are waiting for darkness. We will carefully push forward and then make a run for it. They may have sabotaged the track ahead or loosened the rails, but we won't know until we try. Sitting here, we are nothing but targets."

The officer turned and began to jog toward the front of the train, presumably to talk to the engineer. His head, not ten paces from where Sophie and Allard stood, exploded. The sound of a rifle shot, echoing across the valley, immediately followed. The officer crumpled to the gravel. More shots followed the first. Sophie and Allard slipped between two of the cars and listened as bullets struck the train and shattered windows. From the sounds of the impact, they were flanked on both sides.

"We need to move! I'm going to the engine," Sophie said. "You take over the troops. Keep them firing into the hills; let no one run."

Sophie sprinted to the cab of the locomotive while bullets hit the metal panels of the rail cars ahead and behind her. In the locomotive she found the engineer and the fireman crouched behind the thick iron panels of the engine; neither moved when she climbed in.

"On your feet," Sophie ordered.

"They will blow us up," the fireman said. "This has happened before."

"Have you seen this before?" She pointed her pistol at the man. "Get this train moving, or it will be the last thing you see."

Neither man budged.

"Now, or I will first shoot you in the leg."

The two men slowly stood, then both instinctively ducked after a bullet whizzed through the cab.

"If you don't move us right now, we will all be dead," Sophie shouted.

The return fire from the soldiers on the train continued. The rebel gunfire never slackened.

The engineer engaged the gears, and the train slowly gained traction and speed. The pile of railroad ties across the tracks was five hundred feet ahead. When the insurgents saw the train moving, they increased their volleys. How many men on the train were hit, Sophie didn't know or, at the moment, care.

The locomotive slammed into the makeshift barricade; the long, sweeping cowcatcher and defensive iron grillwork tossed the debris aside. The train pushed on amidst a final barrage of bullets. The fireman, hit by a bullet, spun away from the open door. He clutched his shoulder; blood oozed through his fingers.

Sophie took a quick look and smiled.

"*Es sólo un rasguño*," she said.

"Scratch? *Scratch?* I am bleeding to death like a stuck pig," the fireman said.

She ignored him, secured the pistol near her, and helped shovel coal into the firebox. The fireman rummaged for a towel, which he stuffed under his shirt, and then sat in the corner of the cab. He glared at Sophie for several minutes before passing out.

The train, with its dead and wounded, screeched to a jarring stop in the village of Manresa. Sophie walked back to the dining car. Sitting in the same spot at the table where they'd had dinner not an hour earlier sat Colonel Allard, the front of his shirt bloody. He looked up at her, smiled, mumbled something she didn't understand, then slowly lowered his head and died. The local police chief arrived shortly after being informed of the attack on the train.

"How many dead?" he asked, in a matter-of-fact way.

"Four—the captain and two soldiers, and this German officer. The fireman is being taken to whatever you call a hospital," Sophie said. "Aren't you going to send someone to go after them?"

"Why? They are most likely gone. You are lucky. Three weeks ago, twenty Nationalist soldiers were caught on a troop train and shot dead along the tracks. It could be the same scum for all I know."

"So, you are going to do nothing?" she asked.

"*Señora*, I am going to fill out the forms and send them to Madrid. If they wish to do something, they will do something. Me, what can I do? This war has killed hundreds of thousands. I do not intend to be added to the bloody pile just as we have peace—such as it is. You are going into Barcelona. Thousands have died there—the aerial bombings, the executions by both sides, the depravity. One was my brother. Therefore, whoever they are, I don't fucking care. I have a wife and kids. Someone has to stop all this craziness."

Seeing Sophie's glare, the chief continued, "You all can go to hell. I hear your train's whistle. I suggest you board. There is no place for you to sleep in this town, and only God knows when the next train will arrive. *Adios, senorita. Vaya con Dios.*"

An hour later, the train pulled into Barcelona. After a reasonable dinner across the street from the train station, Sophie reboarded another train and in the dead of night crossed into France. Two days later, after traveling only at night, she reached the Central Train Station in Rome. The train was full of German officers and soldiers. As she left the train station in a taxi, a siren began wailing; the last time she'd heard that sound was in London. Here, people just looked up and then went on with their business.

4

Rome, June 15, 1943

Max walked through the narrow streets of the Trastevere district, the smells from the bakeries reminding
him that he'd only eaten an orange and a hardtack
biscuit since his last meal on the submarine. He bought a loaf
of bread and gulped a cup of espresso; memories of Rome
washed over him. His immediate destination was an apartment on the far side of the river, near the Via G. Zanardelli. A
short man in a black uniform, reeking of garlic and cigarettes,
stopped him as he began to cross the Ponte Garibaldi.

"*Documenti, per favore!*" he demanded.

Max looked down on the man; he was at least a foot taller. He fumbled intentionally inside his coat and extracted the
worn package of documents. He handed the folded identification card to the man.

The policeman stared at the documents, then Max, then
the two loaves of bread wrapped with a newspaper.

"You are Max Kline, from Cortina. You don't look Italian,"
the policeman said.

"My parents, Catholics," he said in mangled Italian, "fled
Austria during the Great War. They took residence in Cortina;

I was born there."

"Why are you in Rome?"

"To work, Officer. I need work. I have a chance at a position in a bakery. I am late; I need the job. Please." Max extended his hand for his papers. "Here, take this." He handed him one of the loaves.

"*Grazie*—however your Italian is awful. I might consider you a spy, maybe a German spy?" The little man smiled. "There is a reward . . . for spies."

"I've spoken German since I was a child. I apologize for my poor Italian. I am learning. I will try my best."

The policeman closed the identification card and handed it back to Max.

"You be careful, young man. Someone might be mistake you for a German—the resistance would love your head on a stake. Then again, I might like the reward. Go—and again, thank you for the bread."

An hour later, Max wound his way through the Ponte district to an alley a block from the Tiber River. The address was what he'd committed to memory. A panel of buttons and names was secured next to the door at the side entry to the building. As he pushed the button next to the name *Longoria*, the wooden door burst open, and three boys spilled out. Each waved a wooden sword, and all wore paper hats; they yelled and laughed. Their voices echoed down the alley. When they saw Max, standing to the side, they instantly stopped. The tallest looked at Max, then marched up to him and aimed his sword.

"*Tedesco?*" he asked, using the sword as a pointer.

"*Italiano*," Max answered.

"Sure, sure, and I'm Mickey Mouse," the bold one answered.

The others laughed. The door latch clanked metal on metal and the door opened. A man stood in the open entryway.

"*Si?*" Then he looked at the boys. "Scram."

"I have come to fix the plumbing," Max answered.

"Plumber? You a plumber? Bullshit," the youngster said, again pointing his sword.

"Si, si, it is in here, follow me." The man moved out onto the top step and looked at the boys. "You get lost. You are nothing but trouble; I told you to scram."

"We are going to make the Germans leave," one of the other boys said, puffing up.

"You will need bigger swords to do that," Max said.

"We will get them." The boys then clacked their swords together and fought their way down the alley to the main street beyond. Max pushed past the man and walked into the apartment.

"I'd hoped they would send someone who at least looked Italian. That way, to the stairs." The man led Max deeper into the dark apartment building. He appeared old; he was small, wiry, and bald. His skin was tightly drawn to his face, almost like a weathered cadaver. "You will stick out like a tall cypress on a hill."

"I've been called a lot of things, but never a tree," Max said.

After three flights, they came to an apartment door, and the man pushed it in. Max followed him down the hallway.

"You can sleep in there; I expect you are tired." The man pointed to a threadbare couch in a small alcove. "I have food and wine; you can stay the rest of the day. Tomorrow, you have an early meeting with the priest. He will take you to your permanent residence from there."

Max handed the man the loaf of bread. He took it without saying thank you.

"Your name?" Max asked.

"Babbo Natale."

"Okay, I get it. No names."

"I don't know you and you do not know me. If I'm caught

with you, I go straight to Regina Coeli prison and then a date with the firing squad. I prefer my freedom. The fascists and the Germans are cracking down—their spies are everywhere. So, I suggest you get some sleep; you will leave early in the morning. And that tall kid, the one who called himself Mickey Mouse, his name is Pietro. He will be your guide. When you get to the priest, you will pay him a hundred lire."

"That's a dollar, American."

"Don't tell him that; he'll triple it. The food and wine are in the kitchen. I'm going out. And don't drink the water from the spigot."

Early the next morning—an hour before the sun crested the Quirinal Hill to the east—Max quietly opened the front door. Standing in the dark alley was the boy; he was smoking. The boy nodded to him and held out his hand; Max passed him the money. They walked casually north to the Tiber River, and then climbed down a worn and rickety wooden stairway to a rowboat secured to a mooring post. It was next to the pathway at the base of the floodwall that enclosed most of the Tiber River in this portion of Rome. For a month, since Allied bombing of Rome, all lights had been ordered off, and the city was still dark. Windows and storefronts were draped; from ten thousand feet, the city, and its dark Seven Hills, were lost in the expanse of the Italian countryside.

As Max rowed, he looked past the kid and saw the ghostly shape of a fast-moving scull appear at the bend in the river. It emerged from the shadow under the Umberto I Bridge.

"Don' say a word; we have a visitor," Max whispered.

The narrow hull and its single rower effortlessly glided across the glassy surface. The rower's back was to them. Max quickly moved their boat out of the way, paused, and for a long moment remembered the day, seven years earlier, that changed his life.

* * *

Berlin, Germany, August 1936

From the embankment of Berlin's Langer See, the German crowd screamed over and over the cadence, "*Deutschland, Deutschland, Deutschland . . .*" Six long and narrow rowing boats, nine men in each, raced on the surface of the canal, forty-eight oars striking the water. Again and again, they beat to the time of the ninth man in the stern, their coxman. The Germans, from the embankment, yelled the name of their country, drowning out the roars of the international crowd. Three of the boats battled forward and back for the win—Italy, Germany, and the United States—all foreshadowing the world and the war three years later. Max Adler stood among his fellow American Olympians, all yelling their own cheers to the Americans in the farthest boat. The day before, Max had finished out-of-qualifying for the medal rounds in two swimming events. If he had been granted, by the Olympic gods, one second to be split by his two events, his fortunes at the Berlin Olympics would have changed. Now he was one of the crowd, not a contestant.

The American rowing boat, from the University of Washington, beat the German rowers by less than two meters. Above the canal, on the deck of the building called Haus West, Adolf Hitler stood along with other German dignitaries in support of his rowers. The crowd, on both sides of the Langer See, was a mixture of Americans, Italians, Germans, British, Hungarians, and Swiss. They milled about after the race, the Americans celebrating, the others moaning over their countries' losses.

"Quite a race," a tall man said as he walked up to Max. Max, at six-foot-four inches, stood only an inch taller. The man was lean, thin faced, and athletic. He, like the others on the Olympic team, wore a sports coat, tie, and white straw boater's hat. He was not an athlete.

"Yes, it was, Mr. Jones," Max said. "I've watched our Northwestern rowers a few times on Lake Michigan; it's a lot of work. Quite a race."

"You put your time in the pool; I'm sorry about missing the finals."

"The honor is in the competition."

Zebadiah Jones intently looked at Max and smiled. "Bullshit, and you know it. You are here to win; we are here to win."

"There's that too," Max said.

"Today's the last day. We are heading out tomorrow; be ready. The train leaves as scheduled. It's in your paperwork—do not miss it. You, of all people, do not want to stay here in Germany."

"That is not your problem, Mr. Jones. I was born in Berlin. My folks left ten years ago. I'm Chicago raised, Midwestern through and through—American as you. I won't miss the train."

"The closing ceremony is tonight; I want you there."

"Gladly. Anything to poke a stick in the eye of that paperhanger."

"I'd suggest keeping it down a little. German ears are about."

Max smiled then leaned into Mr. Jones. "Fuck 'em."

Max had planned his afternoon adventure since he'd qualified for the Olympic Team. This was his first time back to Berlin since his parents and he had fled. For permission to leave Germany, his parents were forced to sell everything to the Nazis: the house, the store, even most of their furniture. Max's grandparents had died before he'd been born. His mother had said, more than once, she was glad they had not lived to see what was happening to Germany. Only his uncle Wilhelm, his mother's brother, was alive. Wilhelm moved to Paris four years after they left Berlin, just as it became difficult for a Jew to live in Germany. After Adolf Hitler became chancellor and dictator, any Jew with sense and money fled Germany. The cost of their freedom was everything they owned.

He believed his safest costume, on the streets of Berlin, was his double-breasted Olympic jacket with its embroidered shield-shaped red, white, and blue patch. His white boater hat set him immediately apart from the conservative residents of Berlin. After checking the hallway in the dorm, he casually took the rear service stairway to the street. Then, after boarding and unboarding a series of trolleys—a process described in detail by his mother—and keeping an eye out for one of the team monitors, or worse, one of the German agents he suspected were following members of the American team, he went to the main Berlin train station. Using his best Berlin German, he bought a return ticket to the Berlin-Grunewald station in the western borough of Charlottenburg-Wilmersdorf. His destination was the *Nachbarschaft* neighborhood, where his family lived when he was a child. If caught, he'd have a hell of a time explaining this escapade to Mr. Jones—and an even harder time to the Gestapo and the Nazis. It was best not to get caught.

Sitting amongst the Sunday travelers, he tried not to make eye contact with the other passengers. They all knew who he was, or at least that he was an Olympic athlete—maybe not which country, but certainly one of the thousands from around the world taking part in the greatest event that Germany, Nazi Germany, had hosted. Max watched the woods flicker by as the train wound its way through the Grunewald forest. Berlin's development had, over the last fifty years, expanded outward and westward into the surrounding forest. New neighborhoods had been built that were now the homes for the rich and successful businessmen of the Reich. And now, due to the expanding Nazi economy, many houses were under construction among the older buildings. Two decades earlier, his parents' neighborhood was home to many of Berlin's famous Jewish families. Some, like his parents, immigrated to England and America from their beloved Berlin when it became apparent that Berlin no longer loved them. His mother told stories of cocktails at

Max Reinhardt's home celebrating his early films, and the film actresses and actors they had known. These movies were Reinhardt's entry into Hollywood when the Jewish director found that he, too, was no longer valued in his homeland.

After leaving the train at the Berlin-Grunewald station, Max sat on a bench one block from the station to see if he'd been followed. After ten minutes, he saw no one suspitious and began to walk to Richard-Straus-Strasse, the street where he'd lived as a child. Memories flooded over him; childhood memories that made up almost half of his life; memories— some vague, some sharp—of a happy child. He passed the playground where his father had pushed him on the swing—it still hung there as if waiting for him. Then past the tavern where they would have Sunday dinners. Then down neat and orderly streets, with block after block of mansions that Berlin's businessmen built as monuments to both themselves and their success.

There were the memories: Looking at a mirror, dressed in a jacket and tie, short pants, and polished shoes with his mother standing behind him crying. And then on the front porch as his Jack Russell terrier, Rolfie, was led away by a friend's son. His two suitcases also on the porch, because that was all he was allowed. The ocean leaving Bremen harbor and the seagulls flying overhead. His father secretly showing him the suitcoat he wore every day and the one hundred gold pieces that had been sown into pockets inside its lining. He remembered being seasick and the dolphins swimming alongside the ship. Memories, some pleasant, many sad, but even to this day, ten years later, he remembered the neighborhood. He had three hours before he was required to be back at the dorm for the closing ceremonies.

It was a pleasant Sunday afternoon; immense linden trees shaded the street. On the opposite side of the street, nannies pushed prams and walked their charges. Neatly trimmed hedges hid the front gardens of most of the houses. Even the birds, calling and shrilling to each other, welcomed him home. Halfway up the block, he stopped at a house—the *Haus* in the framed picture on the piano in his parents' living room—and wiped his forehead with his handkerchief. The house, two full stories high, with a steep roof line that reminded Max, as a child, of the prow of a dark wooden ship, rose above its own yew hedge. Today, it still stood proud. The windows of the second floor, with their diamond-shaped leaded glass panels, reflected the sun. Whoever lived there now kept it well maintained. He would dutifully report this to his father.

Hearing a harrumph behind him, he stood to the side as a full-figured woman scurried past. She stopped, turned, and studied his face. Then, as if she recognized him, she snorted and started to say something, then stopped, turned her head away as if remembering, then looked up the street. She harrumphed again, then hurried on. Max watched until she stopped at a house three down from his own, opened the gate, took another long look at Max, then slammed the iron gate behind her. Her head, with its large straw hat and feather, bobbed above her hedge, then disappeared.

"And it's good to see you, too, Frau Schimel. It has been a long time. Mother does not send her regards," he said, with a laugh.

With the slamming of the gate, an expectant stillness filled the neighborhood; even the birds stopped their trilling and cooing. Nothing stirred; no cars passed. It was as if a thick fog had been draped over the street; sound just stopped. Then, in the direction of the train station he'd left a half hour earlier, a far-off wailing began. The wailing became a klaxon siren that shattered the quiet of the borough. With each passing second it became louder and more searing, as if the horns of hell were ripping the peacefulness out of the Grunewald—a high, then low, then high mechanical scream that shook Max's soul. It was a sound deliberately intended to pull terror up from one's belly. He looked toward where Hagen Strasse crossed Richard-Strauss-Strasse and watched a black police car careen onto his street. Two army trucks followed, their dark gray-green sides emblazoned with swastikas and flags. No longer buffered by buildings and foliage, the klaxons increased in volume, until they almost forced him to cover his ears. He was caught; he would be arrested and charged with being a spy. He had failed, but at least he had once again seen his house. He wished he could have told his parents. It was too late to run; fear now filled the air; he waited like a condemned man.

However, the police car passed him and then the trucks. They skidded, brakes squealing, to a stop—three houses down and nearly across from his old home—in the middle of the street. Ten soldiers dismounted and waited as two black leather–clad Gestapo agents exited the lead car and started yelling orders. Another German officer, wearing a black uniform, stepped out from the car's rear seat. Four of the soldiers took positions on the street near the trucks; the others followed the two agents through an iron gate and into the front yard of a house obscured by hedges. Shocked by his good fortune at not being the raid's target, and not wanting to move and call attention to himself, Max watched. The soldiers, in turn, watched him.

Then came the splintering of a door and the yelling and screaming. Within moments, the soldiers reappeared through the gate dragging four men and women toward the trucks. One soldier held two terrified and screaming children under his arms. More soldiers appeared, pushing more men and women ahead of them with their rifles. When the first group reached the back of the last truck, one of the prisoners punched one of the soldiers in the nose; the soldier staggered back, blood streaming down his face. Then the man reached into his boot, pulled out a pistol, and shot the soldier point blank in the chest.

He swung the pistol toward the other soldiers and fired again, missing them. The shooter, almost Max's age, spun around and ran down the street, followed closely by a woman. When the pair was a hundred feet from the truck, a volley of gunfire crackled. The man turned and fired at the same instant he was struck by bullets that knocked him to the cobblestone street. A second volley struck the woman; she fell next to the man. Neither moved. Max watched the two die, their blood flowing between the cobblestones. A child broke away from the group at the truck and ran toward the fallen couple, screaming in Yiddish, "*Muter, tate! Muter, tate!*" Seeing Max, the child abruptly turned and ran toward him; he wasn't sure what he should do. The child, a girl maybe eight years old—only a few years younger than he was when he'd left this street—wrapped her arms around Max's leg.

"Please help, please help. Don't let them die," she cried in Yiddish.

Max looked again at the two fallen Jews. None of the soldiers made a move to help them. He looked at the child; all the strength in her tiny body tightly held him. "That's okay, child, you'll be fine," he answered in Yiddish.

Breaking away from the loading, the black uniformed officer walked directly to him. With him were two soldiers.

"Let the Juden scum go," the officer said in German. "You don't want to be involved, friend. This does not concern you."

The child had buried her head in the cloth of Max's slacks. The soldier grabbed her by the arm and wrenched her away. She screamed in pain.

"Stop," Max yelled. "Leave the child alone."

Max tried to pull the girl back from the hard grip of the Nazi. The child again screamed.

"Who the hell are you to talk to me like that?" demanded the SS officer. "She's nothing. She's filth. Stay out of this."

Max looked at the officer. He'd seen hundreds of Wehrmacht and Wafen SS officers during the last two weeks, more than enough for a lifetime. This one was different. His uniform was exceptionally well made, the boots polished to a high gloss, and his face mature, older than most he'd seen. However, unlike the officers enjoying Hitler's Olympics, this one carried a Luger and he was pointing the weapon at him.

That's when Max saw the death's head emblem on the man's cap, and the SS insignia on his collar, and the three pips on the left collar.

"Leave her with me. She's nothing to you," Max said in German.

"What are you going to do? Stop us?" the SS officer said, surprised. "These are traitors to the Reich. We have our orders. Do not get in our way."

The child screamed again as a third soldier joined them. The new soldier pointed his rifle at Max; the other soldier jerked the girl away.

Max was six inches taller and fifty pounds heavier than the soldiers. He took a step forward, ready to knock the man to the ground and rescue the child.

"Don't try it," said the officer. "I would hate to have you shot for interfering with Reich business." The man studied Max. "American? Olympian? Now why would you be here?"

Max was not prepared for this confrontation. "A friend from home lived on this street. He asked me, if I had the time, to stop and look around. Then tell them what had happened to their old home."

"And which one was theirs?" the officer asked, looking up and down the street.

"The one there," Max said, pointing at the house next to his old home. It was owned by a member of the Krupp company when he lived here.

"Ah, so you are a spy," the SS officer said with a grin. "You speak German well. Yes, my friend, I think you are a spy."

"No, I'm not a spy . . . I'm just an athlete."

"I understand, but you need to be careful. Someone less understanding might come to a different conclusion." The officer turned to the soldier. "Throw the child in the back of the truck and remove those bodies. Be quick."

The soldier dragged the screaming child toward the truck.

Powerless, Max watched the truck back down the street. It stopped short of the two bodies; four soldiers threw the lifeless couple into the back. There were more screams from inside. Another soldier swept up the weeping child and tossed her into the back of the truck as if she were a large doll.

The SS officer looked Max up and down. "An American Olympian; interesting. It is strange to see you out here. What is your name?"

"Max Adler."

The officer removed a small notebook and made an entry. He looked again at Max. "I suggest you go back to your dormitory; you will miss the final ceremonies. They start soon."

"What did they do?" Max asked.

"They were born. They are Jews. They have been plotting against the fatherland and stealing from us. They are Jews. They are nothing; it is an internal matter of state business. Tonight, the Olympics are over. You must return to your team."

One of the Gestapo agents yelled at the soldiers to get back in the truck—they were late.

"Hauptsturmführer Schmidt, we must go," one of the two soldiers standing next to them said.

"I will be right there," Hauptsturmführer Schmidt said.

"I'm a—" Max started to say.

"A fool?" Schmidt interrupted. "Yes, you are a fool. And I suggest you shut the fuck up before you say something you will regret."

He paused and again considered Max.

"Well, fool, today's your lucky day. If you want to come

with us, I can gladly find you a seat. I wish you wouldn't. The paperwork is more than I want for today."

Max said nothing.

"Good. We have other collections to make. Accordingly, I suggest you go back to America and celebrate Jesse Owens's victory and the rowing. It will be one of America's last."

With that promise, Schmidt climbed into the rear seat of the sedan and waited as the other Gestapo agents climbed in. Then, together, the vehicles thundered down Richard-Strauss-Strasse.

The child's screams haunted him during the closing ceremonies. He couldn't look at any German without seeing the soldiers, the Gestapo, and the SS officer in the black uniform.

The next morning, they gathered near the buses that were to take them to the train station. Max tried to avoid Mr. Jones. He failed.

"Where were you yesterday afternoon, Mr. Adler? I saw you return just before the start of the closing ceremonies. One of my men tells me that you took one of the trolleys. Now where would you be going in the middle of a Sunday afternoon, Mr. Adler?"

"I took the trolley to the train station to go out and back from the Gruenwald. I wanted to see some of the countryside around Berlin. My family was from there."

"Nice story—bullshit, I'm sure. However, now, I've no leverage here; we are done. You can do what you want. But if you miss the train and the boat, you are on your own. And you, sir, being Jewish and here in Germany . . . I suggest, Max Adler, that you do not miss the train."

"I won't. I've seen enough, Mr. Jones."

5

Rome, June 15, 1943

The skiff pulled to the side of a wooden dock that extended out into the Tiber River. Pietro jumped out and secured the boat. They climbed the narrow ramp that led up to the Prati district on the north bank of the river. Behind the Chapel of the Holy Family, Max tapped gently on the rear door of the stucco building built against the church's back wall. A priest opened the door.

"Father Conti?" Max asked.

Father Guido Conti was fifty-eight years old and the older brother of Sophie's mother. He was six feet tall, a touch to the portly side, and sported a thick beard that was now in the process of turning from summer brown to winter gray. The priest looked the American over, smiled, and stood to the side. "Please come in. No need to announce to the neighbors my visitors—there are enough rumors. Or so I've been told." He looked at the boy, Pietro. "You hungry?"

"Yes, Father."

"Go down that hall and ask the woman there to feed you breakfast. You have one hour, then you can take this gentleman to the Popolo house."

"Yes, Father." The boy walked quickly down the narrow hallway.

Max's Italian often resulted in conversations that rolled over him. Father Conti repeated what he told the boy in English, then added, "They are in there; we will be brief. They are important people and they may be missed. Ask them your questions. They will probably tell you lies, then they will leave. You will follow."

Sitting in the rectory's cramped living room were three men. Max did not know any of them, just their names from a short list that he'd memorized while in London. All three were obviously not happy to be here. Max cared less—he needed to find the physicist. He knew two were socialists who would do anything to throw out Mussolini and the fascists; the other was a communist who would do anything to throw out the socialists and the fascists. Father Conti did the introductions. Max nodded; the names matched four of those on the list in his head.

"These gentlemen teach at the university. When word reached them about your wanting to find Professor Massimo Cattaneo, they let me know that they knew him."

"And?" Max asked.

"And what?" Father Conti answered.

"Do they know where he is?"

Max listened as an intense conversation began between the priest and the men from the university. It was loud and confused. Fingers were pointed. One stood then sat when the priest said something. He knew they were professors; however, it was never verified. Two minutes later, Max literally threw up his hands and walked out of the room. The priest followed.

"What?" the priest asked.

"They know nothing. Sure, they know the professor, but he has been missing for three months . . ."

"I know that."

"Am I correct? Did they say he was working in his lab one morning? Then he abruptly collected his papers, placed them in a leather valise—this is according to students who were there—stood up, said goodbye, and walked out of the lab. And he has not been seen since?"

"Yes, that is what they said. Two confirm that story. And it is the same story, repeated over and over. There is a rumor that if anyone helps us find Professor Cattaneo, they will be allowed to go to America after the war is over, no questions asked."

"Yes, I heard that. Might as well sell tickets," Max said. "The line will be out the door and down the street. As with most rumors, not a chance in hell."

"I am sorry. I was told they had information. I also told them not to believe the gossip they hear. I did tell them—you heard—that if there is proof of Cattaneo's location, there may be a reward."

"That and a cup of espresso," Max added. "Father, please take down all their information. I will add it to what we have. At some point all of these rumors and clues might actually come together and lead to something."

"Is this man worth the chance of you being caught and probably shot?" the priest asked.

"Father Conti, just collect the information, and avoid telling them anything more. And I cannot tell you why I must find this man. Just know that he is important, to me and to the United States. You asked why I am here. This man, Professor Massimo Cattaneo, is well known in the American science community. I am not privy to who he is or why the Allies want him. I am here to find him and get him out of Italy. The sooner, the better. It's that simple."

"My niece tells me that you are friends of Cesare and Lucia Fallace," Father Conti said. "They are old friends of mine. Cesare's brother Tomas and I went to seminary together. And

Lucia comes from an old Jewish family living in the Trastevere district. I stop in Amalfi to visit when I can. How are they?"

"Father, it can be a small world. The last I heard they are well, but that was more than two years ago. Yes, they are the parents of a friend of mine, one of my best friends from college; he's dead now."

"I knew Dominic—great kid. Such promise; he had a big heart."

"Yes, he did, and he was a true friend."

* * *

Rome, the Campo Marzio District
Max and his new young friend and guide, Pietro, left Father Conti's church and cut through the streets back to the Tiber River. Reaching the Ponte Regina Margherita, they mixed in with the citizens that filled the midday crowd crossing the bridge.

At the Piazza del Popolo, Max looked up an alley and saw a wall of posters with Il Duce's mug plastered as high as a man could reach. A boy, not much older than Pietro, was slathering black paint in bold Xs across each face of the dictator. From beyond, a whistle blew, and two fascist policemen rushed the kid. He was quicker and bolted between Max and Pietro and out into the Via del Corso. Max saw the smile on the kid's face. It's all a game; a game until they shoot first and whistle later.

However, unlike the delinquent, Max saw apprehension and even fear in the faces of the Romans. They didn't look you in the eye; they kept their heads down, moved quickly, even furtively. The war still baffled Max. Millions had died—how many more until its end? Pietro said that his uncle was in Russia somewhere at a place called Stalingrad. Mussolini had sent thousands of Italians in support of the German troops. The kid did not know where Stalingrad was, only that his uncle was dead and buried there.

Pietro left Max at the door that hopefully led up to an apartment. The boy waved, walked away, and disappeared around the corner. Max knew he was within blocks of the apartment where he'd spent the previous night with the man with no name. Nonetheless, in this labyrinth of alleys and narrow lanes, there was not a chance in hell that he could have found it. He climbed the stairs to the door marked 4D and softly knocked. Beyond, there was the scraping sound of wood chair legs on a wood floor, and the unmistakable click of a large-caliber automatic having a bullet chambered. Then the shuffling of leather shoes.

Max knocked again, two knocks, then four, then two. The door opened an inch.

"Yeah, what do you want?"

"To find the height of Niagara Falls."

The door opened and a wiry weathered man, holding a Colt pistol, blocked the hallway. His smile displayed the gap of a missing tooth on the left side.

"Who in the tom tit are you?" the man asked. His accent was Cockney, an English articulation that Max learned to recognize at Camp X. "Your name?"

"Adler—who else would I be?" Max answered.

"The fucking bishop of Rome, sweetheart. I have no clue as to what you look like, but from your height you won't last long here—too easy to pick you out of a crowd. But that's your problem, mate. There's some food and wine in the kitchen." He stood back from the door and waved Max in with the pistol, then looked back down the hallway and closed the door. He slipped a thick timber across the door.

Max walked to the back of the apartment. The man said, "That room on the left is yours; make yourself at home."

At the small kitchen table, the Englishman set down the gun and dished out a plate of spaghetti.

"The sauce is thin," the man said. "We got plenty of pasta,

but no tomatoes. The wine's not half bad."

"Who are you?" Max asked, hoping for the right answer.

"Me manners, damn sorry about that. I'm Albert Kent, First Lord of the Admiralty. I'm working here to make ends meet." Kent pulled a pipe out of his pocket and began to stuff it.

"Well, Admiral Kent, I will need a few things. Did MI6 fill you in?"

He lit the pipe and blew smoke rings. He then leaned back in his chair and watched Max eat. "Good, eh?"

"No, it is awful. But I learned that you eat when you can. Quantity over quality. There is a war on, don't you know."

"Really? I thought I fucking missed it. Salt helps."

"Salt wouldn't help this. I requested for a dress SS-Obersturmbannführer uniform, and not the field-type dress. I will need it during my time in Rome. And an SS field officer's uniform as well."

"You are an arrogant and naïve son of a bitch. Nazi SS uniform? Why not a staff car and a driver?" Kent answered.

"Can you drive?"

"Me? Absolutely, and a good mechanic too. And we have a car."

"A regular prim and proper British spy. I assume you speak German."

"*Fick dich*," Kent said. Took a long draw on his pipe, then a good swallow of wine. "The uniform is being made—Sophie said you were tall. But there will need to be a fitting. We had to blow up a cleaner's shop near the German officer's quarters. Afterward, we scrounged a lot of pins, patches, and even some material for additional uniforms. Your disguise, and I get the creeps just saying this, will be ready in a few days. It is more than enough time before you attend the party at the Conti villa in San Sebastiano."

"What party?" Max said as he scraped the plate with a

piece of bread.

"The party that celebrates the return of the count and countess's granddaughter to Rome. It will be at the villa two nights from now; you have been invited. I have no fucking idea why, but people told me to tell you. There's an invitation on the table there."

"What time does the tailor open?" Max said as he lit a cigarette.

"She opens when I knock on the door down the hall; it is better to keep these things close. Having a German uniform in your possession is a capital offense. The sooner you have it, the sooner she doesn't and is all the happier with me."

"What kind of organization do you have?"

"A close-knit group—five solid men, and the ability to get a few more. In the garage under the apartment is a motorcycle and a black sedan. Very German looking. It's always a risk, but you must act like them to scare the shit out of the fascists. I'm amazed that we haven't been buggered yet. But it's there."

"These men, do they speak German?"

"Three do, but with Austrian accents. The others are Italian and French. One speaks Yugoslavian. It's a mixed bag."

"You?"

"Italian and German and can pass as a Frenchman."

"Do you know why I'm here?"

"The story is that you are here to find a professor at Sapienza University. And once you find him, get him out of Italy in one piece. I am to help as much as I can. Everything I do beyond that has to be cleared by her."

"I'll talk to her about that."

"Good luck, I've known the lass a long time. I hope that you stay on her good side."

6

Chicago
February 1939

In the early evening drizzle, the three friends took the ele-
vated train to Lincoln Avenue and walked the two blocks
to the hall listed on the leaflet. Outside its entrance, a squad
of men in brown uniforms stood at ease in the rain, their hands
clasped behind their backs. They wore short ties, Sam Browne
belts, and red and white armbands. A dozen red, white, and
black Nazi flags, as well as the German-American Bund's ban-
ner, stood upright in stanchions behind them. Flanking the
row of German flags and banners were red, white, and blue
American flags.

"These guys are serious," Max said, as they made their
way past the line of brownshirts. Every man scowled as rain
dripped off their narrow patent leather brimmed caps tightly
strapped under their chins.

In the crowded lobby, long tables piled with papers and
pamphlets lined the walls. Women dressed in traditional dirndl
skirts and blouses attended each table, handing out flyers and
cards. Posters and Nazi flags hung on the walls and from the
ceiling rafters.

A full-cheeked man, in suede lederhosen, long socks, and sporting a substantial girth, hurried up to the boys.

"Welcome. Siegfried Hamel's the name. All my friends call me Siggy," he said, a smile on his flush face. "You're new. I can tell by the looks on your faces, and I know everyone. A lot to see and take in, isn't there? Please—make yourselves at home."

Siggy stuck his hand out and energetically shook theirs.

"Information about our summer youth camp in Wisconsin is there, and the dates for future rallies are at that table with Heidi—she's my daughter." He pointed to a cute blonde girl at a nearby table. "And, before I forget, if you are planning to go to New York for next week's important rally at Madison Square Garden, let me know tonight. I can reserve for you a seat on the train. Your names?"

"Klaus. Klaus Bruin, and these are my friends Conrad and Alex," Max answered, to his friends' surprise.

"We heard about tonight's rally, saw the posters," Max continued. "It sounds exciting—we couldn't wait to come. I want to hear about the doings in Germany—my folks are from there. Sorry, Siggy, we can't go to New York, even though it's tempting."

A poster hung above the crowd; it promoted the German-American Bund rally in Madison Square Garden the following weekend.

"Wish I could as well," Siggy said. "But business keeps me here. Many are going—Herr Kuhn is leading the rally. He's been to the Führer's rallies in Munich and Nuremburg; he's modeling the New York rally after those events. I've seen the newsreels."

Max asked Siggy about the guest mentioned on the handbill.

"He is a brilliant speaker and very close to the inner circle in Berlin," he answered. "Herr Schmidt is touring the Midwest on a break from his duties. It's not often we get visitors from the fatherland—if you know what I mean." He laughed.

Max smiled.

"Look around—there's sandwiches and cold beer. We should start right on time."

"Congenial bunch," Max said as they walked from the hall-way into the main hall.

"He reminds me of Charon at the gates of Hades," Dominic replied. "All smiles and the like. Siggy's the guy taking the coins before you climb on the boat that takes you to hell." He turned to find that Max was no longer with them. He was at the table talking to Siggy's daughter.

"Come on, Klaus," Dwight called to Max. "We need to get good seats."

"Conrad, Heidi is telling me about the camp in Wisconsin. She says it has a pistol range and a lake for swimming and boating. She's going to show me some photos."

"Klaus, you can socialize later," Dwight answered.

Max smiled at the girl and mouthed the words "later" as his friends pointed him toward the main hall doorway.

"Quit making this into a joyride; these guys are serious," Dominic whispered.

"That's why it is so funny. They do take it seriously," Max replied. Standing at the rear of the entry hallway, talking to Siggy, were two people. The man was severe—his face taut, with a thin mustache; his dark pinstripe suit was impeccable. Even from thirty feet, Max could see the Nazi pin on his lapel. It was also a face he knew. He tried to remember from where. However, it was the woman next to the man that seriously caught his attention. Black hair fell to her shoulders. Taller than the man, elegant, and athletically trim, she wore a gray suit over a white silk shirt. The look was topped by a black fedora-like hat. A ten-inch red feather, stuck in the brim, bobbed when her head moved. She, too, wore a Nazi pin on her lapel.

"What do we have there?" Max said, tilting his head.

"Stay focused," Dominic said. "And from her looks, she'd eat you alive."

"Let me think about that for a minute," he answered.

"Good God, Adler," Dwight said under his breath. "A shar51looking woman in a skirt—is that all it takes?"

Max felt himself being pulled into the hall.

"Come on, lover boy," Dominic added and then pointed toward a row of seats halfway from the front stage.

Two uniformed Chicago cops stood next to one of the doorways. One laughed with a man in a brown uniform identical to the men outside; the other cop was stuffing a sausage into his mouth. Neither cop seemed concerned about any of the people in the half-full room. German music played over the loudspeakers keeping the crowd agitated and entertained. By the time the music changed to a march, the hall was almost full, and everyone was standing and clapping. At the sound of a drum roll, the color guard marched into the center of the room, immediately followed by a double file of honor guards. They were the brownshirts from outside—every man was soaked. They advanced to the stage and took flanking positions. As the drumming increased, ten men walked onstage and took their seats. Multiple banners, with German script, hung high over the stage. At a signal from the stage, the drumming ceased.

"*We Remain Comrades*, and *Triumph and Will*," Max translated. "And that one, *Strength Through Unity*. Endearing, don't you think? Catchy." Max saw the couple from the lobby take seats on the opposite side. The woman interested him. Maybe it was the hat. The man, he kept trying to attach a name to the face.

"Shhhh—and pay attention. You are the one that wanted to come," Dwight hissed. "If they find out you speak German, they might have serious questions for you—ones they ask in an alley."

More men, carrying American flags, marched to the front

of the stage and dropped them into stanchions. As if a signal, the music stopped. A thin-faced man with a gray goatee, also in a brown uniform, walked to the lectern and asked everyone to stand for the reciting of the Pledge of Allegiance. To the trio's surprise, everyone posed with their right arm thrust outward in the manner of the Nazi salute.

He then went through housekeeping issues concerning memberships and current enrollment, even the cost of dues and newspaper subscriptions. After the thin-faced man left the lectern, a heavyset man, also in uniform, strode to the center of the stage. As the audience stood and applauded, he acknowledged the crowd, and shouted, "*Sieg Heil.*" The room shook with echoes of: "*Sieg Heil, Sieg Heil, Sieg Heil.*"

"Full-throated SOBs, aren't they?" Max muttered, leaning into Dominic.

"My friends and comrades, welcome. To those who don't know me, I'm Fritz Kuhn, the Bundesführer of *your* German-American Bund."

More applause interrupted his speech. ". . . I want to thank the *Ordnungsdienst* standing before me for security, and a special welcome to our new friends of Germany gathered with us tonight." Kuhn turned to three men sitting on the stage and saluted them with a Nazi heil. "I also want to acknowledge our associates from New York who have joined us." He nodded and saluted the couple; the feather in her hat bounced as they stood and waved. "We have a glorious future ahead of us, and the great things happening in our fatherland show us that future. Unlike this forsaken land, where our collective and racial heritage is being polluted and destroyed, our Führer is leading us to better understand how we can change this future—an American future—and return to what is right and just."

More applause.

"Comrades, thank you, thank you. I will keep my remarks short."

That brought a smattering of clapping, mixed with laughter.

"Yes, yes, I understand. Like you, I, too, want to hear our guest. Berlin has chosen Herr Schmidt to assist with its relationships with foreign associations, such as our beloved German-American Bund. Herr Schmidt has traveled far and wide, helping and aiding our leadership here as well as in New York. His goal is that we all work together to achieve the great ideals begun in the fatherland. So, without further delay, I introduce Herr Heinrich Schmidt!"

The applause was rich, with loud welcomes and huzzahs, followed again with the repetitive cadence of "*Sieg Heil.*"

Heinrich Schmidt, in a dark business suit, strode to the podium and passed his eyes over the cheering and adoring crowd. He raised his hands to both acknowledge the crowd and to ask for quiet

"My comrades in this great struggle, I want to thank Bundesführer Kuhn and the German-American Bund for inviting me." He paused and waited as the audience took their seats. "I have come from Berlin, where they are proud of what you are accomplishing here in America and for the future that you now hold in your hands. I salute you."

More applause, louder than Kuhn's, followed.

"Let me tell you a story about how the Jews control every aspect of your lives, even here in this great country, even in this city."

"That man is scary," Dwight whispered to Max. "These Americans are children playing dress-up games. That man, dolled up and looking respectable in a suit, gives me the creeps."

"No shit," Max whispered back, as they applauded with the crowd. He looked at the woman, then the man standing next to her, and then to the stage. Bingo—Berlin. The man on the stage was the officer who was in charge of the SS squad that abducted and murdered the Jews on the street where he once lived. The man in the suit was the American Olympic team monitor, Zebadiah Jones. What the hell?

"And then we saw how members of our family—our German family—were being treated in the Sudetenland, Austria, and now Poland. It is our honor and duty to help them—"

Still stunned, Max whispered back to Dominic, "Yes, my parents told me about their help in Germany. I've seen it—the fear, the arrests, the beatings, the thugs in the street, the stolen businesses, the disappearances."

"Quiet," Dominic said. "I'm trying to listen."

Schmidt spoke for another fifteen minutes. ". . . and now we will act. We have cast off the yoke of England and France. Now we can, and will, move forward. We have returned our beloved Vienna and the Führer's homeland, Austria, to the German fold. We again claim the right of every nation to determine its own path, and to lead others down that righteous road to a new future under National Socialism. You are leading that fight here in America. You must take back those rights lost to the communists and the Bolsheviks, and most especially the Jews. You are the leaders of a purer and stronger future for America."

"We need to get out of here. The crowd is on edge," Dominic said. "These people believe his crap; that man is more than scary. Come on, Max."

"Wait until we all stand," Dwight said. "We'll leave through the side door."

"Hold on, fellas," Max said. "Just a few more minutes." He looked over the crowd to Jones and the woman. The feather on the hat bobbed in cadence with the clapping.

"No, Max—we leave now," Dwight said.

"So, my friends and comrades," Schmidt continued. "March with us, fight with us, and most importantly, win with us. Our Germanic legacy will be your legacy."

At that, Schmidt clicked his heels together and saluted the

crowd. The roar of *"Sieg Heil"* again reverberated through the hall and out into the street. On the stage, Schmidt and Kuhn shook hands; others also joined in the congratulations.

"Now," Dwight said, and he stood.

Max, as he followed Dominic, watched Schmidt cross the stage, shaking hands. The speaker acknowledged his American comrades with a sharp nod of his head.

"I agree, that's enough fun," Max said and followed Dominic.

The three pretenders put on broad, fawning smiles, and quickly navigated their way through the excited crowd. The lobby, with its cluttered tables, was congested with energized brownshirts and Bund members. The woman with the feathered hat, alone and without her partner, stood to one side, smoking a cigarette. Max noted that she was keenly watching the crowd. Then one of the brownshirts walked up and aggressively started talking to her. She was doing her best to ignore him.

"Get lost," Max heard her say. "That uniform doesn't give you the right to annoy me, boy. Keep it up, and I promise you, you *will* be sorry."

"Come on, doll. After this is over, I know a great place for a drink."

"You are not old enough to drink. Go get some warm milk," she said.

The brownshirt took the woman's arm. Max saw her wince from the pressure. Another lout joined his comrade, took the other arm, and laughed.

Walking up to the three, Max said, "You assholes, leave the lady alone. Can't you see that she wants nothing to do with you Neanderthals?"

Dominic grabbed Max's shoulder, slowing him. "We need to go."

"One second," Max said.

The first brownshirt turned and glared at him. Adler's trim, lanky form stood a half-foot taller. In contrast, the jackboot's uniform stretched over his belt. The buttons on his blouse looked as if they might explode.

"Get the fuck out of here. This does not concern you."

"Yes, it does," Max said evenly. "See, comrade, she's a friend of mine, and I do not appreciate my friends being man-handled by dim-witted morons."

Max took the lout's hand and squeezed it until he released the woman's arm.

"We are late," Max said to the woman.

"And you were redundant," the woman said, looking at the brownshirt. "Dim-witted moron?"

The first fascist looked up and studied Max's face. He re-leased his grip on the woman's arm.

"We need to go," Dwight said. "Now!"

"Shall we?" Max said.

"Thank you," she said to Max. "That fool has been bother-ing me since we arrived this afternoon from New York—how-ever, it seems I have found a knight errant." She put her hand on his arm.

The crowd in the lobby had thinned. The four headed to-ward the doors leading to the street.

"We are going for a drink," Max said. "Would you care to join us?"

She smiled again; it was a smile that Max swore he'd never forget.

"I appreciate the offer, but my partner is coming. Maybe some other time."

"I'm Klaus Bruin," Max said as he looked at the approach-ing Jones.

She smiled; her red lipstick shimmered in the overhead lights of the hallway. "Sure you are," she said.

Just as Jones reached them, another brownshirt dressed in

a wet uniform planted himself solidly in front of Max.

"I know you," the man said, jamming a finger into Max's chest. "You're Adler."

"Haven't a clue what you're talking about," Max said, trying to press by. "I'm leaving."

Standing with his thick jackbooted legs apart and his left thumb hooked through his leather belt, the man didn't budge from Max's path.

"No, you are not. I know you. We went to the same high school. You were class president, a prick—and a Jew."

7

The German Embassy, Rome
June 18, 1943

SS-Obersturmbannführer Schmidt tapped on the door to the library. Inside, sitting comfortably in leather chairs, were Generalfeldmarschall Albert Kesselring, German ambassador George von Mackensen, and SD-Obersturmbannführer Herbert Kappler.

"Heinrich, come in, man. There's much to talk about," Kappler said. "There's wine on the table; sit there."

"Thank you, sir," Schmidt answered. He passed by the wine and took a seat opposite Kesselring.

"Was your trip comfortable?" Kesselring asked.

"These days travel is never comfortable, Field Marshal. I spent a few days with the family. It had been too long. But I made it."

"Where are you staying? I was told that you passed on the accomodations here at the embassy," Kappler said.

"At the Hotel Minerve—I've stayed there before. It is comfortable and close to many fine restaurants."

"Excellent hotel. I've attended a few events there over the years," Ambassador von Mackensen offered.

"I am a soldier, Ambassador. Parties bore me. I'm hoping that the sooner we complete our work, the sooner I can return home. I miss my family."

"Well put, Schmidt," Kesselring said. "Work, yes. There is work to do. Kappler?"

"Schmidt, you are here to continue your work moving the Jews out of Rome and Italy. You have the experience and the skills. I've read your file—excellent work. I also understand that you have brought some of your people with you—even better."

"Thank you, sir. However, aren't we overstepping our welcome with the Italians?"

"Yes, overstepping might apply, but in this case it is more of anticipation than overstepping. There are significant changes coming to Italy and especially Rome during the next few months. You have the clearance, so here are some facts. During the next few months, the Allies will invade Italy. Some believe it will be here near Rome to cut Italy in two; others say to the south where our defenses are weak. Even a few say Sicily and then mainland Italy. In any of these scenarios, the end result is that Italy will be invaded. In addition, we do not trust our Axis friends—Mussolini is holding on to power with the slimmest of margins. There is significant confusion in his ranks, and with the defeats on North Africa, the Italian army has ceased to exist as a fighting force. So, many of the Führer's primary demands must be accomplished as soon as possible."

"I am not surprised," Schmidt answered. "I will begin the restructuring needed to begin to collect the Jews. I will have for you my transportation needs within the week, as well as—"

"That is not the primary reason why you are here, Major Schmidt," Kesseling interrupted. "I have received special orders from Berlin this morning, orders that specifically, for the short term, add to your mission here in Rome."

"Really? I was not aware of any pending change."

"Sometimes the Reich has greater needs than the removal of Jews, and this is one of them," Ambassador von Mackensen said. "Field Marshal?"

"Schmidt, you are to locate and arrest Professor Massimo Cattaneo. You are to bring him here where he will be detained and questioned. Then you will escort the professor to Berlin where he will be turned over to the proper authorities. After that, you will return here to resume your original orders."

"This man is that important? Who can be that important? I have work to do, important work."

"I understand," Kappler said. "And when this is over, the Jews will still be here. All I know is that this professor is a physicist, teaches at the Sapienza University, and is a close friend of Enrico Fermi."

"Who?"

"Enrico Fermi. He is a Nobel Prize winner and escaped to America just before the beginning of the war."

"What was the prize awarded for?"

"His work is with neutrons and radioactivity. He now teaches at Columbia University in New York City—the school you attended according to your file."

"That was more than twenty years ago. You said neutrons and radioactivity. I assume that the Riech is interested in this man, Cattaneo, because of this involvement?"

"A good assumption, Colonel. Yes, we wish to make sure this man and his talents do not fall into the hands of the Americans. That is all that Berlin has told me. I am sure there is more, but we are not entitled to know everything. Your orders are to find him and bring him here."

* * *

Chicago, the German-American Bund Meeting
February 1939
The voices in the lobby of the Northside meeting hall went instantly quiet. Two uniformed bund members moved in behind

Max. One was the thug who had bothered the woman. More brownshirts gathered behind their comrades. All were eager for something to start.

"Yes, men, this prick is a fucking Jewish spy—Max Adler. He's a Bolshevik and a communist. And those two," he added as he pointed at Dwight and Dominic, "must be his commie friends."

"I don't know what you're talking about," Max said, as he tried to elbow his way past the man and toward the front door. The two New Yorkers stood a few paces away, watching. Outside, the rain fell in windblown sheets across the brick-paved street.

"You two get out of here," Max said.

"Not a chance; we won't leave you," Dominic said.

Heidi walked up to Max. "You, a Jew?"

Max looked at her and didn't answer.

"A Jew?" she repeated.

"Yeah, maybe. Why?"

She spat on him, spun on her heels, and pushed her way back into the crowd.

"See, Jew boy, even nice girls don't want to be around you," the brown-shirted classmate said, laughing.

Turning back, Max said, "My friend, let this go. Everything is cool."

"Friend? I ain't no friend of a fucking Jew. We don't appreciate spies—especially kike spies."

The jackboot nodded toward Dwight and Dominic.

"You fellas got two seconds to get out of here," he said. "We have a lesson for kike Adler."

Before either of his friends could move, hands grabbed Max from behind and pulled him through the doors and out into the rain; two held Max as their comrade swung a fist. Max jerked his head back; the blow glanced off his cheek, knocking spit and rain through the air. Two more brownshirts joined in.

They punched Max in the ribs and kidneys, forcing him down to his knees and to the sidewalk.

Max rolled forward, dragging the attackers down with him to the pavement. Max was the first up and put three quick jabs into the face of his accuser. The man stumbled back, his nose broken, blood spraying from a cut lip. Max continued the attack. Someone in the crowd pushed the thug back toward Max, who put two right-hand body blows to the man's ample midsection. The man gasped for air. As Max turned, someone blindsided him, stunning him. Reeling, he staggered back.

Behind Max, Dominic and Dwight had their hands full throwing punches and avoiding kicks. The animal frenzy of the mob increased. It collapsed in on the three, forcing them to retreat and stand back to back. A rubber hose arced through the air and smashed against Max's shoulder; the pain was searing. Then a blow caught Dwight at the back of his neck; he stumbled.

Dominic, seeing an opening, reached in and grabbed both of his friends, pulling them out into the street. His hands, cold, bloody, and wet, almost lost their grip. Max looked back into the wild-eyed crowd and saw the two policemen standing against the building, out of the rain, watching. *Why don't they stop the fight?* As they finally reached the curb, a thrown brick caught Dominic just above his right ear. The impact knocked him to the ground. The side of his head bled from the ragged cut carved by the brick.

Max, bloodied and on one knee, saw Dominic lying on the pavement behind him. Dwight, to his other side, held up his fists, readying himself for the next surge. The Nazis charged and renewed the attack.

Max knocked the first to the ground and then spun to help Dwight. Max suffered a hard fist into his back above his belt. The pain from his punched kidney was excrutiating, and he lurched sideways. Dazed, he fell backward. Then, regaining his feet, he threw fists and elbows at two thugs kicking Dwight; they both fell to the sidewalk. Other brownshirts stepped in to take their place. Dominic, sprawled on the wet street, still hadn't moved.

Max again pressed the attack. The blows came fast and furious; most struck air. Then the crowd backed away.

"I suggest you get away, friend," a familiar voice said to Max.

Max saw that it was Siggy. The bund member had Dominic by the underarms and was dragging him away from the brawl.

"Take your buddies and go," Siggy yelled.

Through the rain, Max saw Dwight swinging wildly at anyone who came near him. A hose caught the side of Max's face; he again went to one knee.

"Halt!" a voice shouted from beyond the circle of fighters. Then a piercing whistle cut the air. "I order you to stop."

Adler's high school classmate tried to rein in his kick, but it still caught Max's thigh. The others stopped immediately. They stepped back from Max and Dwight.

Max, still on one knee, heaved heavily. He could feel his face swelling; his clothes were soaked and his jacket lapel was torn. He saw the bloody hands of Dwight. Siggy, next to the prostrate Dominic, tended to their friend. Above the taunts of the crowd, a forceful voice—experienced in giving orders—demanded everyone to stand down.

"Who started this?" Heinrich Schmidt said as he pushed his way through the rabble.

No one answered.

"Is this how you respond to a question from an officer of the fatherland? Again, I ask, who started this?"

Max's classmate rose and stood at attention.

"It was me, sir," he said and pointed at Max. "That man's a Jew and a spy. We were teaching him a lesson."

Schmidt glared at Max; there seemed to be a moment of

recognition. Even though almost three years had passed, that afternoon in the Grunewald was still fresh and sharp in Max's mind.

"Lessons are only taught when orders are properly given. We are not a rabble, and you are fools trying to settle grudges with fists and clubs," Schmidt said, not disguising the disgust in his voice. "There are proper times for proper actions, and this is not one of them. In Germany, you would be disciplined for not following orders. I can only imagine how things are run here."

He turned to Kuhn.

"I hold you responsible, Kuhn. Your men have turned an evening of triumph into a cheap boxing match. I am very displeased."

Schmidt glanced away; he was looking for someone. He stopped when he saw a man holding a notebook. The reporter was scrunched under the protection of an umbrella. After Schmidt caught the reporter's eye, he turned back to the men surrounding Max.

"And to you, gentlemen, I apologize for the actions of these soldiers. They were acting without orders."

Before Max could stand and take a swing at Schmidt, the German spun on his heels and reentered the hall, leaving the crowd confused. Collectively embarrassed, they began to quickly disperse.

Dwight took Dominic from Siggy. Dominic began to slip in and out of consciousness. Max signaled for a taxi.

"This is bad, very bad," Dwight said. "I saw this on the farm when my uncle got kicked in the head by a cow. Like Dom, he went in and out of consciousness. He spent the rest of his life barely aware of anything."

"Where's the nearest hospital?" Max asked the cabbie.

They made it to Cook County Hospital in less than ten minutes. Max and Dwight, each with an arm under Dominic, carried him into the emergency room. There, Dominic completely collapsed.

"Where?" Max yelled as they entered. "Where?"

A nurse pointed down the hall. She ran ahead of them as they carried Dominic; they went into a room with a single bed. "There," she said, as more nurses and a doctor arrived.

"You're lucky they didn't crack *your* head," Dwight said to Max. "You'd be a prize."

"My guess—they wanted to impress the crowd. And we were the object of their affection."

One of the nurses ushered them toward a small room off the main corridor. "What happened?" she asked.

After Max told her, she returned to Dominic's room. Helpless, Max and Dwight watched as they worked on their friend.

"Dom's in a bad way," Dwight said. "Right now, we're all he's got until his aunt and uncle get home."

Max paced the waiting room, rubbing his hands together. His head spun with guilt and hurt from the hoses and fists. *My fault, my fault, all my fucking fault.*

The two dozed on the hardwood chairs in the waiting room. Shortly after eight the next morning, a nurse came and escorted them to an office on the third floor. There, a doctor waited behind a large desk.

The storm had passed during the night. Winter sunlight now streamed through the east-facing window, throwing a cold light through the doctor's office. Diplomas and photos lined the walls, a wall of books flanked the doorway, and family photos stood in frames on the middle shelf of the bookcase.

"Gentlemen, I am Dr. Rosenbloom. Have a seat." He gestured to a pair of leather wingback chairs facing the doctor's desk.

They did as told.

"Mr. Fallace's injury is extremely serious," he began. "There is a massive hematoma on the interior right side of his skull.

It's pressing against his brain like an inflating balloon inside his head. His skull is also cracked where he was struck. We have tried everything to reduce the pressure. Unfortunately, we are limited to the technologies we have at our disposal. I have drilled three small holes in the skull, and that allowed some reduction of the swelling. However, it is impossible—even with X-rays—to see if we are having any lasting effect. Only time will tell—are you his family?"

"No, just friends," Max said. "His immediate family, an aunt and uncle, are returning from Italy. They will not arrive home for another week."

"There's not much more I can do right now," the doctor continued. "We must wait for the swelling to subside before we can see any effects."

"And those are?" Dwight asked.

"Full recovery to something far, far worse. The results can be like those of a stroke, with paralysis and speech problems—there is a chance of his dying."

"He could die from this?" Max asked.

"It's possible. We are trying to do everything we can. As I said, only time will tell."

The doctor studied the two young men. "Tell me what happened. From the looks of you two, and the bruises on Mr. Fallace, it looks like you were in a fight."

Max began to explain, but after getting to where they started to leave the rally, he stopped. He couldn't go on. Dwight finished.

"I still have family in Germany—it is so difficult to get them out. There's quotas, and sponsors are needed," the doctor said. "My parents came to America forty years ago after another of those cyclic pogroms that wash over the supposed civilized people of Eastern Europe. I wish I could help my family escape. It is difficult—even our government won't help. You two go home and get some sleep. The nurses tell me you've been here all night. There's nothing you can do. Stop by later, during visiting hours, and tell the nurse you're here. I'll bring you up to date then."

Max sent a telegram to the ship Dominic's aunt and uncle were on, the Italian Line's *Rex*. He explained as much as he could in a short message. Their response was quick, expressing their hopes and offering prayers. Once they arrived in New York, they would catch the first train. They would be home in a week.

For the next two days, Max and Dwight exchanged bedside responsibilities. There was no change in Dominic's condition; he remained unconscious and unresponsive. The swelling had subsided but, according to the doctor, the damage, such as it is, was done.

"Time is our hope and friend," the doctor offered.

Dominic's aunt and uncle, Renata and Anton Rossi, returned. The family moved Dominic to a convalescent hospital near their restaurant. Max and Dwight continued their daily visits, each time hoping that their friend would raise his head, speak, even just acknowledge their presence.

"Damn fascists. Even here, thousands of miles away, they find a way to hurt my family," Anton Rossi said.

Max received a telegram from Lucia and Cesare; they thanked him for his telegram.

"Lucia and Cesare are heartbroken, but there is nothing they can do but pray," Anton said. "They sent their son here to America to prosper, and now he lies in his bed, a vegetable."

"He will get better," Max offered.

"Yes, with God's help. My wife prays for that, and she lights candles in the church."

Ten days after the fight, and against all their prayers, Dominic's death came as his heart slowed until it stopped. Dr. Rosenbloom said afterward, "There was too much brain damage. We tried everything."

After the doctor left, Max said to Dwight, "It wasn't enough, Ike. They could have tried harder."

"They did, and you know it," Dwight said. "I know you won't believe me, but it's better this way. I know—I just know it."

After Dominic's funeral, the Rossis invited everyone back to the restaurant for a reception. Max was still upset for his part in his friend's death. Nothing Dwight said would soften his mood.

"I killed him—it was my fault," Max said to an older couple.

The woman put her hand on Max's cheek. "No, son, the Nazis did this with their evil. Not you."

The man, almost as tall as Max, added, "Your mother and I saw this in Berlin—this is no different."

Anton and Renata approached. "Max, can you introduce us?"

"God, my manners," Max said. "Renata and Anton Rossi, these are my parents, Rose and David Adler."

"We appreciate your being here, thank you," Renata said. "Dominic spoke fondly of you,"

"He was a good boy and a great friend to Max. We are sorry for your loss. We will miss him," David said.

"Thank you."

"It was still my—"

"I will hear no more of that, Max," Renata said. "How were you to know?"

"Going to the rally was stupid and pointless. I know their hatred," Max said.

The waiter brought a tray with glasses of red wine.

"To Dominic," David said, and held up his glass.

Max stared at his glass and then at his friends and his parents. "To Dominic Fallace, the best friend a man could ever wish for."

They stayed at the restaurant until the afternoon shadows gave way to evening. The Rossis hung the *CLOSED* sign and a note on the door. As the crowd thinned, Max's parents again offered their respects and left in a taxi. Max watched as would-be diners stopped, read the note, and then walked away. Everyone in Little Italy knew what had happened, and they understood the pain the family felt.

"I am going to make us some dinner," Renata decided. "That's what Dominic would say: 'Stay for dinner; have another glass of wine; be happy.'"

While Renata was in the kitchen, two men entered through the front door, ignoring the sign.

"Sorry, we are'a closed," Mario, the waiter, informed the pair as he pointed to the sign.

Dressed in dark suits, white shirts, dark ties, and gray fedoras, the men ignored the waiter and walked to the table where Max, Dwight, and Anton sat. The taller of the two held up a badge and looked directly at Max.

Ignoring the badge, Max spoke first. "Mr. Jones, what are you doing here at my friend's funeral? Haven't you put us through enough? I saw you at the Bund meeting. I was stunned. So, go, get the hell out of here—you, you, Nazi!"

"Max Adler, I am FBI Special Agent Zebadiah Jones, and this is Special Agent Louis. We are from the FBI's Washington, D.C., office. Do you have a few minutes to talk?"

"You were head of security for the American team at the Olympics. The FBI? That's a damn lie. You and that woman are Nazis—I saw you talking to them at the hall, all chummy. They even introduced you."

"We were undercover. And I was also undercover in Berlin during the Olympics. The German-American Bund is collapsing after the fiasco and riot in New York's Madison Square Garden last week. We are chasing down the stragglers. I offer our government's and my personal condolences for your friend."

"Jones, we buried our friend today, and all you offer is condolences. I don't believe you're FBI. You and that cute piece of candy on your arm are Nazis," Max said and stood. "And, if you are who you say you are, why do you have to do this now? The police were no help. In fact, I think they were sympathetic to the thugs. You stood there and did nothing. So, tell me why the FBI is involved?"

Louis looked at Jones.

"I was there to observe," Jones said. "Can we talk?"

"Sit, sit," Anton said, looking up at the agents. "Do you gentlemen want some dinner? There's plenty."

"Thank you for the offer, but we need to go." Jones nodded to his associate.

"Who was the woman?" Max asked.

"She is of little consequence, Mr. Adler. She is an associate. Our roles were simple, to watch and observe," Jones replied. "The fight was sudden and now sadly fatal."

"You could have stopped it," Max said forcefully.

"I told you why we couldn't. We were there to observe the German, Mr. Heinrich Schmidt. We belive he is a colonel in the SS. He was the headliner—he has been on our list of people to watch. We believe that he is more than a just a speaker from Germany. We lost Schmidt when he entered the United States in New York. We were lucky to find him at the rally."

"So, he's under arrest?" Max asked.

"No, he's good at avoiding us, and after the fight, he slipped away. We spotted him a day later at New York's Grand Central Station; he was about to take a cab directly to his ship. Our New York office questioned him, but he carried diplomatic papers. We are glad to have him gone."

"That's it? That's all you did?" Dwight said.

"That's all we could do. We are certain that he is a spy. But since he only met with the Bund that night and, as far as we could ascertain, with no one else, there was little we could do. And he had a stack of diplomatic papers that complicated an arrest."

"And our friend is dead," Max said.

"Yes. As I said, I'm sorry."

"With your background," Jones said, nodding toward Max, "we were surprised that you were there."

"My background? Are you watching me now?"

"The way things are in Germany, we are watching as many as we can who have emigrated from Germany. Ask your parents. We have talked with them. And your time in Berlin with the Olympics; it increased our interest."

"My parents had nothing to do with this. Why are you bothering them?"

Jones ignored the question.

"A Jew at a German-American Bund meeting—that surprised us. Why were you there?"

Dwight interrupted, "It was a lark, something to do. It was stupid—we know that, now. Curiosity—nothing more."

"Curiosity killed the cat," Jones said.

"That's one of the most insensitive remarks you've made since you sat down," Max said, rising from his chair.

Dwight put a hand on his friend's shoulder.

After a moment, Jones said, "I apologize. Yes, it was insensitive. Did either of you have any contact with Schmidt before that evening?"

Max paused and looked at Jones. "In Berlin; I saw that man in Berlin. At the Olympics, the day of the closing ceremonies. He was arresting Jews. I tried to intervene."

"You tried to stop him?" Jones asked.

"Yes. It was brief and brutal. I've told no one about it."

"It was the afternoon you disappeared?"

"Yes."

Louis jotted something in his notebook.

He asked if Max would walk outside with them.

"Just a few more questions," Jones said.

"Sure, why not," Max answered. He looked at Dwight.

"Just you, Adler," Jones said.

Max followed the agents out onto the sidewalk. He lit a cigarette.

"What now?" he asked.

"Your parents told us that you are going to visit an uncle in Paris after you go to Italy to see Dominic's parents. Why?"

"It is the least I can do. I need to return Dominic's personal items to his family. They are heartbroken. I was already going to Europe—a buying trip for the store. I've adjusted my itinerary to go to Naples before Paris. I leave in a few weeks."

"It's strange to be going to Europe, where there is so much . . . trouble," Jones said. "Why?"

"You know why. The boat arrives in Naples, near where Dominic's parents live. I have a ticket to return in a month."

"On the SS *Conte di Savoia*?"

"How the hell did you find that out?" Max responded, then reflected. "Yeah, I know, you're the FBI."

"Are there other reasons you're going to Italy?"

"There is a radio manufacturer outside of Milan. I want to see their latest models."

"Others go to Florida or California; you go to Europe— maybe Germany?"

"They don't make radios and produce art in Florida. Mr. Jones, this is business. You of all people know that. I've been there three times since the Olympics. All business—even clocks from Switzerland."

"Berlin?"

"No. Just the one time. It was enough."

"A Jew traveling in Germany and Austria isn't too popular these days, even if American. It's a foolish adventure. It could get you arrested or killed," Agent Lewis said, speaking for the first time.

"Who was that woman you were with?" Max asked.

"She is a member of another government's intelligence organization."

"She's a spy?"

"She is a friend and an agent, but that's all. And she is gone—she followed Schmidt. We expect that he's probably back in Berlin now."

"I wouldn't send a dog to chase that man."

"I'll tell her that when I see her."

Max thought for a moment. "Is she single?"

"None of your business since you will never see her again."

"They said he'd be a handful," Agent Louis added.

"Who told you that?" challenged Max.

"Your parents."

"Why are you here, Jones?" Max asked.

"There's a lot happening in Europe right now. Germany has taken Austria and Czechoslovakia," Jones said.

"Yeah, the stupid Munich Pact agreement and the Anschluss last year. Hard to even trust the British now."

Jones ignored the remark. "As I was saying, there's a lot going on. We need eyes and ears, nothing fancy. Just a sense of what's happening; it's hard to believe what we read in the newspapers."

"You are asking me to spy?"

"Nothing military or political. We want to know what the people are thinking about Mussolini and even Hitler. Someday this might be important."

"Like if a war starts; I get it. And how will I communicate all this critical information to you? If I agree."

"Just send letters to your mother. She will pass on anything that is interesting."

"You have my parents involved?"

"They came to us, Max Adler."

8

Rome, Antico Caffé Greco
June 19, 1943

About a block from the Spanish Steps, Max sat at a small table in the rear of Antico Caffé Greco; he nodded and acknowledged the two German officers sitting across from him. In fact, he took too much interest in them; they acted uncomfortably. He was dressed in a conservative suit and black tie. His look was disconcerting. Shortly they stood, put money on the table, and left; at the door one turned and glared at him. Max had learned that, to gain suspicion, act suspicious. His staring confused them. His appearance probably added to their paranoia; who was spying on whom?

He sipped the rich coffee, now priced beyond what the normal Roman could afford. He glanced at his watch for the fifth or sixth time; she was late. He had been there for twenty minutes—all was prearranged. She would come into the narrow café. She would not be alone; maybe her grandmother would be with her, maybe a friend. They would ignore each other, yet smile, then part. It was all a bullshit act to see if either had been followed. The real meeting would be that evening at the party welcoming Sophie back to Rome.

Out the front window, above the curtain, a large feather danced. It was impaled on a gigantic buff-colored straw hat—always feathers. He followed its course along the window to the door; an elegant older woman preceded the hat into the restaurant. Sophie's grandmother, Max assumed. He understood where Sophie had inherited her grace and style. Both air-kissed the maître D, who then walked them to a table directly across from his. Sophie tried her best to ignore him; he did his best not to step up and kiss her.

Gloves were placed on the table, napkins adjusted, sugar brought, and two cups of rich dark coffee arrived, all without a word said between the Contis and the waiter. When the cakes arrived, Sophie's grandmother smiled and quickly finished hers. As the countess finished her last bite, Sophie looked up at Max and flashed a smile. It was one of those "I have a secret" smiles, the corners of the lips just lifting for a moment. He returned the smile with a slight Teutonic nod. It was in keeping with the room's expectation that he might be a senior German official of some kind, especially if they saw the previous pair of Germans leave. Paranoia is a useful tool when used properly.

Max pointed to his cup and the waiter returned and refilled it. He then said, "Sachertorte," his accent unmistakable. The waiter scurried away, knowing. Sophie looked up and shook her head from side to side, then slowly inflated her cheeks. Max nodded, looked around the room, then winked. The countess set down her fork, finished her coffee, then leaned toward her granddaughter. Sophie nodded in agreement, took a handful of lire from her small purse, and slipped it under the saucer of her own coffee.

Max's cake arrived as the two women stood; Sophie looked again at Max and again puffed out her cheeks. He took a large forkful and slowly put it in his mouth. She shook her head and followed her grandmother out the cramped café.

Through the open door, Max watched the black Fiat pull to a stop directly in front of the door. The two women, with the aid of the driver, climbed into the rear seat and left.

The waiter returned to the table. Max, using his index finger as a lure, asked the waiter over. "Who was that woman?" he asked in Italian with a thick German accent.

"She is the granddaughter of the Count and Countess Conti," the man answered. "She has been coming to Caffé Greco for as long as I've worked here, more than twenty years. The other is her grandmother. The countess has been having coffee here since the last century; they are very good customers. They are important people here in Rome, very important."

"Thank you," Max answered.

"And you are, sir?" the waiter asked.

"An interested person."

"Well, Mr. Interested Person, be very careful about the Contis. They have friends in very high places, and to fall out of favor with them would not be in your best interests. I am pleased that they know my name—Henri."

"I would suggest, Henri, that you be careful about what you say about people, including your friends. You may not know who you are talking to. *Verstehst du, Freund?*"

His German stunned the waiter; the man went white. He turned and cleared the tables near Max and went to the front of the restaurant. Max left a few minutes later and as he passed the waiter, nodded.

* * *

Naples and Amalfi, Italy
June 1939

After the incident at the Bund rally and the death of Dominic that winter, Max went to Europe. His business travels early that summer of 1939 initially took him to England, then the night ferry to Paris. He spent two days with his uncle Wilhelm, his mother's brother, trying to convince him to leave France and go to Chicago. His uncle adamantly refused.

"The Nazis won't make it ten kilometers into France," Wilhelm said. "Between the army and the Maginot Line, we are as safe as anywhere in Europe, maybe more."

"That's the point," Max answered. "There is no place safe in Europe. You haven't been back to Berlin in fifteen years; you don't know what it's like. What *they* are like."

"I talk with people, refugees and those like me, who've fled Germany. I will tell you this, Hitler doesn't need the trouble all this will cost. And besides, the British and French have given him what he wants. He should be satisfied."

"He won't stop until he has everything. He is like a glutton at a table of rich hams and sweets—he will never be satisfied."

"He has had Austria for a year; it is his home, after all. I'm sure he'll be happy now," Wilhelm said.

Max left Paris frustrated. He hated to write the letter to his mother telling her that Wilhelm had decided to stay. He did tell her about the palpable anxiety that permeated Paris, the full trains that went south, and the thousands of refugee Germans, Austrians, and Poles he'd seen at the station. Almost all were Jews. He traveled with them south and took a steamer from Marseille to Naples.

Standing on the wide Neapolitan stone pier, he studied the crowd gathered to welcome the passengers from his ship. The clattering iron wheels of dozens of baggage trucks, pushed by stevedores, added to the din. Passengers jostled behind Max. He heard *scusi* a hundred times as reunited families hugged and kissed. Two people stood out: a lovely woman elegantly dressed in a smart flowery red and blue dress and, in contrast, standing next to her, an erect and full-figured jovial-looking man dressed in a dark-vested suit and black fedora. He held a sign that read *Signor Adler*.

Smiling and taking a deep breath, Max walked up to the woman.

"It is so good to see you again, Signora Fallace. And you, too, Signor Fallace," he said.

The woman placed her hands on his shoulders, pulled him down, and kissed him on both cheeks.

"Max, did you grow some more?" she asked with a huge smile, then turned to Signor Fallace. "Where are your manners, old man? Take his bag."

"Not necessary, Signor, I can carry this," Max said. "I travel light. If I need something else, I will buy it."

"Typically American. Dominic was like that," she said. "He would come home and not carry more than one suitcase. He . . ."

The signora turned to her husband; a tear left a thin line on her makeup.

"That's okay, *amore mio*," he said. "Let's get this young man to the car. There are many miles to go before we reach the house, and I don't want to be on the roads after dark. The fascists drive like crazy men."

Marveling at the sights and smells, Max followed the pair through the people and baggage carts. Vendors hawked their trinkets to the tourists. Men carried trunks and luggage on their backs like mules. Small children weaved their way in and out of the legs of the departing passengers, many holding out a hand for a coin or two. Watching all the chaos and not paying attention, Max stumbled.

"Are you okay?" the signora asked.

"Yes. I'm fine. Maybe it's the solid land after the two days on the sea," Max said.

"Prosecco and a good dinner, that is what you need."

The drive through the chaotic waterfront of Naples dramatically changed to one of quaint, quiet villages constructed of stone and stucco. Reaching the base of the mountains that split the Sorrentine Peninsula, Cesare pointed east toward the great volcano Vesuvius.

"Max, now that's an evil bitch," he said. "Temperamental as a woman, but a thousand times more dangerous. Beyond that low hill is Pompeii, the Roman city destroyed two thousand years ago during one of her fits."

They turned off the main road to Salerno and began to climb the mountain behind Castellammare. The complaints from the Fiat grew louder at every grade change. The road zigged and zagged. Max's stomach protested as it had during the first days at sea. Nonetheless, the countryside amazed him. Great trees in thick groves of gray and dark green covered the steep hillsides; acres and acres of vineyards filled the valleys. When he asked about the trees, Lucia answered, "Lemons, but they won't be ripe until winter, and those others, the gray ones, are olives."

Magnificent views of the Tyrrhenian Sea could be seen between the groves. Then they would disappear as Cesare drove into dark, verdant canyons. He turned eastward at a T-intersection hanging a hundred feet above the sea. The sign pointed right to Positano and left for Amalfi. Max took a deep breath and offered a silent prayer for his stomach.

"Max?" she said, leaning forward from the back seat. "Thank you for being our son's friend. He loved you like a brother."

Max wanted the Fallaces to be angry, to rebuke him for what he'd done to their son. "If I hadn't—" Max began to say but was cut off by the signor.

"It was not your fault, my boy. I know these fascist animals. They are evil, and even though it may have been unintended, they killed him like they have killed thousands here in Italy. And that madman in Germany is no better."

"Signora Fallace, I loved him too . . ." Max tried again.

"Please, call me Lucia," she said, interrupting him. "Signora Fallace was Cesare's first wife. Me, I'm a latecomer, the black sheep of the family. I'm the Jewish aunt no one talks about."

Cesare swerved to miss a truck. She explained that her family name was Levi, and that she had met Cesare more than thirty years ago in Rome where he had moved after his wife died.

"Whenever the Fallace family mentions the Signora, they usually mean his first wife," she said. "Even after almost thirty years, and three children, I'm still on the outs. Maybe being Jewish and from Rome has something to do with it; Rome is the far side of the moon to them."

"I'm sorry we didn't have time to talk last summer," Max said.

"It was crazy, everyone home, you and Dominic, the children. I will never forget," Lucia replied. Cesare slammed his fist against the steering wheel, the noise of the horn blasting at a car pulled over to the side of the road. A black-uniformed man, standing next to the vehicle, lifted his arm with a rude salute.

"Fascists. They think they own the road," Cesare said.

Max listened as she told him her father had been a baker in a small shop in the Trastavere in Rome. She lived in Rome until she was eighteen years old.

"Yes, it was about the time the socialists took power here," she said. "I remember my twenties as being difficult—little food and great unrest. However, being a baker's daughter, even a Jew, wasn't too bad."

She tapped Max lightly on the shoulder.

"Max, you have grown more handsome." Holding tight to the dashboard, he turned a shade of pink.

The road pitched steeply down to a narrow strand of rocky beach. On one side the buildings climbed to the hilltops; on the other, the sea caught the evening reflection of the sun as it neared the horizon. At the next intersection, Cesare turned left and drove up through the village of Amalfi. In the darkening gloom of the June evening, the headlights played out in front of the car as they climbed up out of the village. Cesare parked at the foot of a high stone wall.

"I'll have the boy move the car to the garage," he said to Lucia.

He pointed to a stairway built into the side of the wall.

"Now we climb."

He remembered the climb, it wasn't too difficult; clearly, Lucia and Cesare were accustomed to it. Max had to stop and take in a breath. Whether it was the climb or the unfolding view as he went higher, he wasn't sure. Reaching the terrace, a young boy met them and reached for Max's bag.

Lucia said something in Italian, and the boy smiled.

"He will place it in your room; it is the same as last year," she said. "Maria has prepared a wonderful meal. We tend to eat late this time of year."

Max walked to the edge of the stone terrace with its views to the south. The lights on the far shore began to show, and the great curve of the Bay of Salerno was lost in the mist of the Mediterranean Sea.

"Beyond those hills is Salerno," Lucia said, pointing east. "A rich and beautiful city. We will have lunch there maybe to-morrow, or the next day."

"I didn't know there were places like this anywhere in the world," Max confessed. "Chicago, a few days in New York, and, as a child, Berlin are the only cities I've really known. Sure, I've stopped in Rome and Paris for a few days, but they are cit-ies—busy, loud, dirty. For a year, I have dreamed about coming back here. This is heaven."

"Sometimes during a cold winter, you might change your mind, or when the summer reaches over one hundred degrees," Cesare said. "But right now, yes, my boy, it is heaven. Please sit. I had forgot that you are originally from Berlin?" He pointed to an arrangement of chairs and lounges.

Max retold them how his family had fled Germany for

America when he was eight years old.

The central living room opened onto the terrace. In the doorway appeared a stout woman in a white dress and red apron. She brandished the biggest wooden spoon that Max had ever seen.

"Maria says that dinner is ready," Lucia said. "Max?"

She offered him her arm, and as they walked together through the doorway, he realized that now he had finally found Italy.

Two days later, the Fallaces treated Max to lunch at a restaurant on Salerno's historic waterfront. After a lunch of seafood pasta and a crisp Soave, they strolled along the harbor, passing hundreds of fishing boats, tramp steamers, and even a few luxury yachts, two with red German flags. The swastikas shook in the late-afternoon breeze; they were the first Max had seen since arriving in Italy. Later, they stopped at a café along the waterfront for a glass of wine.

"I never tire of it," Lucia said, gazing out over the water. "Each movement of the sun changes its temperament. Today she is warm, welcoming, but expectant. Summer, with its heat, is coming."

Max watched her gracefully swirl the wine in her glass. He had never met a woman so sure of herself, beautiful, and strong.

The sound of drums and cymbals broke the spell. From the far end of the embarcadero he could hear the songs of the marchers. The fascists, dressed in black, marched in loose formation. Lucia leaned in and translated the words.

"They sing Mussolini's political incitement *Il Giovinezza*." Reaching the area in front of the restaurant, they began the song again. "*Come on, comrades in strong ranks, let's march toward the future. We're audacious and fierce phalanxes, ready to dare, ready to dare.*"

"The phrases go on and on," Cesare said. "They sing about

vengeance and retribution, and revolution. We Italians are famous for our songs."

"Will this lead to war?" Max asked.

"My boy, I think this war was started years ago," Cesare said. "It will soon become one not fought with rough songs, but with bombs and bullets. I fear for Italy."

The bumpy ride back to the house, in the cramped Fiat, was like a dream to Max. The private cruisers with their abominable flags wouldn't extinguish the memories of this day. Later, on the villa's terrace, they shared a glass of wine from Cesare's own vineyard. Glimpsing a movement at the open doorway, Max turned and saw a beautiful girl standing there.

"Max, I forget myself; I want you to meet someone," Lucia told him. In German, she said, "Judith, you can come out."

The woman, demure and about Max's own age, stepped out onto the terrace. He could see that she was anxious and furtive. She glanced about, like a cautious puppy, toward the sea and then the edge of the terrace, then back at Lucia.

"Please child," Lucia said, again in German. "Come and sit. This is a friend of my son's—Max Adler."

Max stood as the young woman approached.

"Max, this is Judith Rothman," Lucia said, continuing in English. "She is staying with us in the guest house up the narrow trail behind the house. She has kept to herself while you've been here; she's shy." She turned to the woman. "Sit there. Judith is the granddaughter of one of my oldest friends. Sadly, Ruth died four years ago. Two years later, her daughter, Judith's mother, also died—both from cancer."

Lucia continued. Judith had fled Berlin and managed to reach Switzerland where a mutual friend came up from Milan and retrieved her. She was staying in a village on Lake Como. She spent last winter with this friend in Milan and then traveled south to Salerno.

"The Nazis have declared open war on the Jews. She was

lucky to escape with her life," Lucia told Max.

All at once, Judith broke into tears and hid her face. Lucia comforted the young woman as great sobs wracked her body. Max could tell that this was not the first time.

"Soon after Judith was born, her father, a great German patriot, died from wounds he'd received in the Great War. During the last five years, she and her mother lived in constant fear as the power of the Nazis grew. Her mother had to sell her small tailoring business to a German—no Jews can own a business in Germany now. When her mother passed away, Judith was adrift. I wanted to go and get her, bring her to us; but travel papers are hard to get for Jews. She stayed with friends—then last winter *Kristallnacht* came. They burned down her apartment building and brutally killed the landlord with clubs; he was a well-known Jew. Moses was a quiet man whose greatest dream was to see Jerusalem. Years ago, during a visit with Ruth, he and I talked about Palestine. I had been to Jerusalem; he wanted to know everything. Moses was truly a lovely and devout man."

Judith took in a great breath and slowly let out a sigh. Max felt her emotions.

"I am glad that Judith's mother and grandmother hadn't lived to see what happened," Lucia continued. "The Germans are now arresting Jews, communists, trade unionists, and even the outspoken Christian and Catholic clergy."

"Hitler is fulfilling his pledge to rid Germany of the Jews and dissenters," Max said, not hiding his disgust for the German leader. "My parents are in contact with friends and relatives."

"I hope they all can get out. There is no future for Jews in Germany," Cesare said.

Lucia's houseboy briefly poked his head out the door and said something to her. She excused herself to attend to household matters.

Max gently touched Judith's shoulder; she jumped as if she had been shocked.

"Are you okay?" he asked in German.

When she heard Max speak German with a Berlin accent, she smiled.

"Oh, please—sorry, but my English is not so good. I try to learn, but they forbid us from going to school or take classes. May I practice my English with you before I go?"

"Certainly, but where would you go? It's pleasant here."

"Yes, it is. I will try to go to Palestine to fulfill Moses's and my mother's wishes. I know it will be difficult with the British stopping and turning around everyone, but I will try, even if I must jump from the boat and swim the last thousand meters. This ring was his." She released the upper button of her blouse and showed Max a simple ring on a chain. "I intend to leave it in the great synagogue in Jerusalem. He would appreciate that; it's my mitzvah for him. He can watch me place it on holy ground from heaven."

"He will, I am sure," Max said. "Can you tell us what happened?"

"Max, there will be plenty of time later," Lucia interrupted as she returned. "I have more chilled wine and some delicious bread the boy brought up from the village. There are also some tasty cheeses. Let's see what we can do to cheer up Judith. She is safe here. Safer these days than anywhere else in Europe."

The appetizers and wine lasted until the cook signaled the dinner was ready. Then more wine and plates of pasta appeared.

"I may be Jewish," Lucia said. "But Italian tomatoes flow in these old veins."

"They are nice old veins," Cesare said, with a wink.

"Aren't you concerned, even a little?" Max asked Lucia.

"Yes, I'm concerned. According to the prophets, I'm one of the chosen people. A lot of good that is doing us now.

Now we are chosen for the camps and slave labor. At least in this country, most Italians have a tolerant and accepting attitude. Most, except for that fat strutting monkey Mussolini. I'm afraid of what he'll do to curry favor with that Austrian madman—he will be a puppet. But I'm as Italian as any in this country. The Levis have lived in Italy for four hundred years. I have lived here with Cesare; in Rome in my family's apartment; and at Cesare's farm east of here in the Campania. I'm bonded, for better or worse, to the Fallace family. My children share the blood of this land with all Italians. No one can tell me I'm not Italian."

9

The German Embassy, Villa Wolkonsky, Rome
June 19, 1943

SS-Obersturmbannführer Schmidt walked through the lush gardens of Villa Wolkonsky. His interests were the roses—they reminded him of those his wife grew in her garden in Schwabach. The villa was known for these roses. In fact, before the war, garden parties were held as an excuse to admire and smell them, especially in May. The villa was now the German embassy and had been since 1920. An elegant if not typical Roman structure, the villa was built in the early nineteenth century. The Germans improved not just its appearance but its security as well. As Schmidt walked to the edge of the largest bed, a peacock crossed his path. Beyond, Wehrmacht soldiers stood near the sandbag and machine gun emplacement at the street entry. He had personally inspected the four other placements that surrounded the triangular-shaped property with its enclosing brick wall. While not the best solution, it was adequate.

Slashing through the property, garden, and into the building itself, was a portion of the aqueduct built in AD 52. That structure had brought water to this portion of Rome from a reservoir more than fifty miles away. It now made an interesting architectural feature of the garden. The embassy's location, to the south of the tracks that led to the Stazione Termini, placed it almost in the geographical center of Rome.

Schmidt had been offered the use of one of the guest rooms on the upper floor. While tempted, he preferred the privacy of the Grand Hotel de la Minerve, a block from the Pantheon. He was not concerned about his safety; he'd seen too much of war to be worried about what might happen to him. His responsibilities were to carry out the orders of his superiors; his rank and relative independence were more than enough of a reward.

"Obersturmbannführer Schmidt," a young officer said. He stood behind the colonel at attention.

"Yes, Klaus," he answered.

"The Generalfeldmarschall wishes to talk with you."

"Do you know why?"

"No, sir. He is with the ambassador in the library."

"Tell them I will be there shortly."

"Yes, sir."

The young lieutenant walked quickly through the garden back to the villa. To be so young and have the whole world in front of you, Schmidt thought. It had been like that for him, those first years after leaving his post as a policeman in Nuremburg and joining the party, the Nazi Party. His language skills, especially English, allowed him privileges within the Schutzstaffel, the SS. His time at Columbia University gave him insights into the Americans far beyond his peers, and his solid German education rounded out the man. He was older than the young cadre of officers within his command here in Rome, a command that he had not requested. Nonetheless, his skills in moving cargo and managing those in charge of this logistical nightmare were well known. That was why he was here in Rome. He was to organize the systematic removal and relocation of the Jews of Italy to specific camps in Germany and Poland where they would be properly processed.

As he walked back through the garden to the villa, he heard the long blast of a train's whistle from the rail yards not a third of a kilometer to the north. Sounds, like smells, will trigger memories.

* * *

Drancy, Outside Paris
July 1942

Like chiseled teeth, the steeples of small churches punctuated the gray sky over the French village; they stood white and sharp. From his vantage point on the narrow wooden observation bridge high over the train, SS-Sturmbannführer Heinrich Schmidt watched both the landscape of the rooftops and the scene below with detached professional interest. The screams of the women and the cries of the children echoed and filled the air between the wooden boxcars already crammed with Jews to the point of suffocation. Schmidt, holding a clipboard, acknowledged then noted the numbers signaled to him from his officers near the railcars below. Massive Alsatians, controlled by soldiers holding chain leads, barked and lunged at the men trying to shield their families from the dogs. Often, with encouragement, they bit a hand or a leg, drawing blood. The processing was successfully moving ahead as it had in Lódz, Kielce, and Lublin.

Yes, Poland had educated his soldiers well, exceptionally well. It showed.

Schmidt's recent work in occupied Poland had garnered praise and advancement. He required thoroughness and discipline, and it was evident in his men. They followed orders with dedication and unflinching duty.

In time this scourge, this vermin, will be eradicated, he thought. *Then the future will be free of these meddling fools. This race that, for a thousand years, has held the German people in its tight financial thrall.*

His soldiers continued to drive the men and women to the railcars after being unloaded from the trucks that had transported them from the Vélodrome d'Hiver in Paris. These

French Jews were no different than the Jews in Poland. They begged, screamed, and even tried to escape. His men shot any who attempted to run. The clipboard Schmidt held listed the Jews' names and their origin. He was not surprised that many on the list were German and Polish names—Jews who had bribed their way out of Germany and even Poland. They had schemed to survive and paid to live. Now they were caught—served them right.

A soldier approached Schmidt. By the cut of his German uniform and his insignia, he was one of the new French recruits that the SS included in its growing ranks of French nationals. The tricolor patch on his arm designated this distinction.

"Sturmbannführer, this train is full," the man said after saluting. "It will leave in one hour. There will not be another until late tonight. Do you want us to hold the remaining Jews here until the next train?"

"How many?" he answered in French.

"About two hundred. Four truckloads."

"Can you count?" Schmidt asked.

"Yes, sir."

"How many railcars are there?"

Without looking, the soldier said, "Twenty."

"Then put ten more Jews in each and return to the Vélodrome and prepare to collect tomorrow's shipment."

The man looked at the crowded rail cars. Three out of ten Jews would be dead in two days. He smiled. Of course, then there would be more room. He saluted and left to carry out the order.

Schmidt nodded approvingly. His men learned their trade well. It was difficult to learn the proper way of soldiering and fighting. But they had executed his orders and followed every command. He was proud of them. Germany would also be proud.

Just two years earlier, on September 15, 1940, and a year after the Blitzkrieg, Schmidt had celebrated his fortieth birthday in a Polish baron's estate confiscated by the SS. For the next eighteen months, he'd moved with a core group of officers from post to post throughout central Poland. At each location, he'd been instrumental in establishing Jewish ghettos. Only once, during the late summer of 1940, and at the invitation of then SS-Sturmbannführer Kappler, the new military liaison in Rome, had he left his post in Poland. He'd returned from Rome a month later. He did not abide these "Jewish pens," as he thought of them. But he also knew the ghettos were the best way to keep the undesirable Jews together until further arrangements could be made. In time, these rich Polish lands would again be Germanic. Ethnic Germans, displaced during the previous twenty years by the Poles, had already begun relocating to central Poland, chiefly in the regions around Lublin.

"Someone has to manage the farms vacated by the Jews," he remarked to another officer one evening. "We cannot leave these lands to go fallow when our country needs wheat and potatoes. These factories are excellent and far safer from possible aerial attacks than those in Germany."

By the end of 1941, thousands of ethnic Germans who had fled Russia and other recently reoccupied lands had relocated to central Poland. Now called *Volksdeutsche*, they received apartments, farms, and even furniture often confiscated from the Jews.

Now, after two years of occupation, France required his skills and expertise gained from managing lists and shipments of human cargo in Poland. His primary concerns, for the moment, were the assurances of the availability of railcars and locomotives. His direct orders, signed by German Reichsführer-SS Himmler himself, aided the acquisition of these freight cars for transportation.

Schmidt's teams had spent three months developing the programs and routes required to move more than three hundred thousand French Jews and Eastern European Jewish refugees to Germany's concentration camps: first to Drancy, France, for processing, then to Auschwitz in Poland. He was thankful to be left out of the actual development of the concentration and extermination camps. He could see that these were professional dead ends for his career, no matter how necessary they were. Even he had trouble associating with the camp officers when they attended Schutzstaffel functions. The smell of death clung to them like the acrid smoke from a fireplace. No amount of cleaning could remove it.

As other officers in his command learned the skills necessary to carry on his work in France, Schmidt's hope was for reassignment to Italy. His expertise would soon be needed in Rome, and his fluent Italian would be helpful. He'd studied Julius Caesar's conquests as well as the Roman Legions and their discipline techniques for governing soldiers. A firm hand wasn't required to make men comply with a leader's will; it was demanded. There was no gray area between discipline and orders; commands were to be carried out immediately and without hesitation. This had been proven in Poland, in the Low Countries, and now in France. Rome itself would be another matter as he found during that short month he was there. The Italians and their internal squabbling within Mussolini's government confused the German command stationed there. The Italians fought reasonably well in North Africa but were now on the verge of losing everything to the British and American advances. Schmidt would require the men under his command not to falter.

From the bridge he could still hear the muffled screams from the railcars, but they were soon lost as the train accelerated out of the rail yard. Clothing, children's toys, and discarded pieces of luggage littered the gaps between the rails. He lit a cigarette and watched as beggars and scroungers emerged from the wooded slopes beyond the rails and began to pick through the debris.

10

Via di Porta, San Sebastiano District, Rome
June 20, 1943

The Conti villa stood in a quiet tree filled neighborhood referred to as the *Parco San Sebastiano*. It was just south of the Colosseum, and midway between the Stazione Termini and Ostiense train station. The neighborhood was also hidden behind the two-thousand-year-old Aurelian Wall that extended for kilometers east and west along the southern part of Rome. Many of the splendid villas inside the San Sebastiano neighborhood were examples of Italian craftsmanship, royal titles, and old money. One of the finest was Count Franco Conti's—affectionally called *La Follia Vitruviana*, not in derision but out of jealousy. It was a magnificent mixture of marble, butter yellow stucco, carved stone, and red terracotta, all of which had now, one-hundred and fifty years after its completion, fallen into a physical state—not unlike Italy itself—of threadbare delusional grander. A garden, now stripped of its famous sculptures, surrounded the villa. Its fountains were dry, the roses sad and anemic, and the hedges in need of trimming.

Along the base of the building, and below the first floor, a dozen windows provided light and air for the servants, the kitchens, and storage areas. The edifice was a reminder of an age long gone, now lost to nostalgia, fables, and dreams.

The main floor was for entertainment with its ballroom, living rooms, dining hall, and library; on the second floor were the living quarters. The topmost floor held abandoned furniture and the ghosts of the Conti family and other past owners, long forgotten. However, the basement hid a secret that the Contis didn't fully appreciate. Since the ascendance of the fascists twenty years earlier, the basement and subterranean areas of the villa had returned to being clandestine places of intrigue, conspiracies, and anti-fascist actions. It was a location where those wanted by the fascists could find a moment's rest before they were secreted out of Rome.

During the construction of the foundation for the house, in the latter part of the eighteenth century, a dry cistern was discovered. The cistern was sizable, more than large enough to hold tens of thousands of liters of water—a forgotten reservoir for a forgotten Roman villa that once stood on the site. This stone and plaster tank was connected to a channel, now also dry and abandoned, that had provided fresh water to the neighborhood. This tunnel connected north and south to an expanding labyrinth of more tunnels and catacombs. It was presumed that this was part of a system of underground aqueducts that supplied water to Rome's great bathhouse, Terme di Caracalla—whose ruins now stood just a few hundred meters to the north of the San Sebastiano neighborhood. The Contis—the villa's current owner for only the last fifty years— knew about the cistern but not about the supporting network of tunnels and passageways. However, the Roman resistance did, and for the last four years had used the Conti villa as a way station, their own Roman Underground Network. As a curious child, who spent her summers in the house, Sophie Norcross knew of their extent and significance.

* * *

Two vehicles followed the narrow gravel drive to the Conti villa. They drove past the impressive front marble entry and parked near the rear stairway. The black Fiat Torpedo 2800 sedan was led by an armored vehicle. The mid-June evening was warm and dry.

Sophie Norcross stood at the top of the stairway with her grandparents, the Count and Countess Conti. Prime Minister Benito Mussolini impatiently waited for the driver to open his door, and then hurriedly crossed the gravel to the base of the stairs. Another man, in uniform, followed. They arrived at the same time the count reached the bottom step. The count raised his arm in salute and then extended his hand to the prime minister.

"Welcome to our home, *Eccellenza*," Franco Conti said.

"It is always a pleasure, Count," Mussolini said. "This is General Ambrosio; he is my new chief of staff."

"General." Conti nodded his head. "It is a pleasure to see you again. Please, upstairs."

The countess and Sophie turned and preceded the men as they climbed the stairs. When they gathered in the hallway, Franco Conti introduced the women.

"Countess, it is a pleasure to see you again; it had been too long," Mussolini said. "And you, Signorina Norcross, it has been what, fifteen years since we last saw each other? I believe your father was ambassador then. When you see him, give him my regards—I miss our dove hunting trips."

"Your memory is correct, Your Excellency," Sophie said. "But it may be closer to twenty years. It was soon after your appointment as prime minister. I believe it was at a party my grandmother had here at the villa. I was just a child, but I remember it well."

"Countess, we can always rely on the memories of children," Mussolini said as they turned into the library. "I'm sorry that I can't stay for the party this evening. It is good to welcome you back to Rome, Sophie. Other matters demand my attention."

"We understand," Count Conti said.

They gathered in the library, Il Duce and Ambrosia to one side of the long central table, the count and countess to the other side. Sophie took a seat between her grandparents.

"I understand how busy you are, Your Excellency," Sophie began. She looked directly into the eyes of the Italian dictator. "I will get right to the point. I have been asked to play the role of the negotiator by my father and the government of Great Britain. Italy has always been close to the hearts of England, and these past four years—since the entreaties of Lord Halifax and conversations with Count Ciano in the spring of 1940—have pained us greatly."

"And us as well," Mussolini said. "Hundreds of thousands of Italians dead or captured, billions of lire squandered. My people have suffered terribly. We have lost in North Africa, Russia, and I fear what will happen here in Italy. Hitler, the fool, will not listen to reason."

"We understand," Sophie continued. "I have been asked to relay this simple message: Agree to an unconditional surrender and you and your family will be protected. Italy will be spared."

"Protected? How in God's name can you protect me and my family? There are spies everywhere; the Germans control Italy. Even now there are members of my own party, damn them all to hell, that are turning against me."

"We can safely remove you from Italy; take you to Tunis or even Egypt."

"It is the king you must convince," Ambrosia injected. "He has the people's allegiance."

"You stay out of this, Ambrosia. The king is a worthless old fool," Mussolini said. "The man, a relic from the last century, can screw himself. I am the power in this country, not some doddering king. It is me you will negotiate with. And you, Ambrosia, are you the king's man? Are you the fox in my coop?"

"No, *Eccellenza*. No, I am yours to command," responded Ambrosia.

"Do you see the fawning I must put up with, Sophie? Sometimes I feel as though I am on an island."

"There is little time; even you can see this," Sophie said.

"So, the invasion is imminent? Where? Rome, Calabria, Sicily? What can I do to stop this? The Germans control the country. You will do what you must."

"That is why a separate peace would ensure the fewest dead. Your people will know what you did to protect Italy. We will do what we can to protect you."

"And can you protect me from the communists? The Germans want a puppet; the communists want me dead."

"We can and will protect you and your family," Sophie said.

"Duce, you can't do this. The king must be involved," Ambrosia said.

"*Eccellenza*, the real power lies with you," the count added.

"Think of the children," the countess said. "You can negotiate a peace that will allow the party to survive. Allow the citizens of Italy to survive."

Mussolini stood and slammed his fist on the table. "I will not negotiate with a pistol to my head. And as soon as we leave here, you, Ambrosia, will run to your master and tell him everything. I fear Italy will burn. I will remain in power, help the Allies, provide a buffer to the Germans."

"We are far beyond that, Il Duce," Sophie said. "This is offered not as a list of options that you can pick and choose from. There is only one item on the list: capitulation."

"I will not be forced into this."

"*Eccellenza*," Count Conti said. "We have been friends a long time; we marched together in Milan, remember? My company supported you in those dark days when there was no money, no future. Wasn't it my contacts with the industrialists that provided the power and the money that helped you to force the king to name you prime minister? And now I ask you to help Italy, to save Italy."

"I have the support of the people!"

"The Italian people have grown tired of hunger, of war, and of the Germans," Sophie said. "And the Americans care less about you and those that support you. This is the only chance you have to control your own destiny."

"I am Italy. I am the present and the future of Italy. Don't you see this?"

"I see what I see," Sophie said. "And right now, there are half a million Allied soldiers ready to march across this land. You will be forgotten, hated because you had a chance to stop the war that will butcher your homeland. There is no time."

"There is always time."

"Not for you. I must know your answer in two days. Arrangements then can be made to protect your family."

"I will not be led about like some dog on a chain. Two days? I will give you my answer now . . . never! We are through, Count; it is only because of our friendship that I don't have you arrested for sedition. It is you who should be concerned about your place in Italy. When I heard that your granddaughter had returned, I was happy for you. I was told of the things she said in England, the articles in the papers, her support for the Fascist Party. I knew they were lies."

"You have two days, no more. Do you understand?" Sophie said.

Mussolini, his face red with rage, stormed out of the library; Ambrosia followed. The Contis heard his heavy jackboots march down the hallway, then stop, then start, then stop.

"He's lost," the countess said. "Franco, help the man leave."

* * *

As the vehicles with the prime minister and his chief of staff came around the corner of the villa, they passed the first guests arriving for the party. Max Adler, in his SS officer's uniform, stood on the steps. Seeing Il Duce leave the villa was confusing. He turned back to the steps. Valets stood at attention at the bottom, one to welcome and assist guests arriving by car, and the other at the top to confirm the guests' identities. Max Adler was announced as SS-Standartenführer Max Stoltz.

He would tell people, those few with the courage to ask, that he was from Berlin, and a friend of Signorina Norcross. There were no other SS officers at the party; in fact, no other German officers of any rank or department had been invited. A few Italian officers in uniform stood to the sides talking to the guests—they were close friends of the Contis. Father Conti entertained an entourage of priests and monsignors hovering over the large table of meats and other treats. There was a shortage of most anything edible in Rome, so they wanted to take advantage of the spread—before they went back to their usual parochial rations.

After Mussolini left, the Contis entered the ballroom. Standing next to them was Sophie. Sophie's mother, Chiara Louisa, grew up in the villa, attended school nearby, and met the British ambassador to Italy, Sir Edward Norcross, during a party when she was twenty-one. Sophie, born a few years after their wedding, spent summers running through the gardens, exploring the cellar, and sliding down the banisters. Her winters, when her parents returned to England, were spent on an estate in Kent.

"Father," Father Conti said to Count Conti, "this is SS-Standartenführer Max Stoltz. He has been helpful with some problems my parish has been having procuring food for the children. He had heard of you and your work for the war effort, both here in Italy and Austria. He wished to thank you personally."

Max stood at attention and snapped his heels, bowing to

Count Conti then to the countess. "I am pleased to meet you, Count. You are talked about in Berlin, sir. The expertise that you have shared in aeronautics is greatly appreciated."

"And, Standartenführer," Father Conti continued, "this is my niece, Sophie Norcross. She has just arrived from England. We are glad that she has returned to the family."

Sophie extended her hand and leaned close to Max's ear. "A pleasure. Aren't you laying it a little thick? Children? Berlin? Really?"

"You look familiar," the countess said, studying Max. "Have we met?"

"We have not, Countess. I'm sure I would have remembered you. And besides, this is the first time I've been to Rome."

Before the countess could answer, the small band began to play a waltz. The Contis took a step back and greeted another couple that had just arrived. Father Conti led Max away.

From behind them, Sophie said, loud enough to be heard by her grandparents, "Not so fast, Colonel. You promised me a dance the last time we were together. I intend to collect that promise." With that she took Max's hand and walked him out onto the dance floor. Max, dressed as one of the most feared and evil men in Europe, felt naked. He held the gorgeous Sophie Norcross in his arms knowing that she'd just compromised him and placed them both on somebody's list to be assassinated, or worse.

"What the hell are you doing?" Max asked as soon as the tune changed to one better suited to closer dancing. "The room has eyes. Any of these could be resistance or Gestapo—you choose."

"I don't care, Colonel Stoltz. I missed you."

* * *

Camp X, Ontario, Canada, July 1942

"Good morning, my name is Alfred Nobody. Welcome to

Camp X. Take your seats. I will be brief. We have much to do and little time to do it." The man wore a Canadian army uniform; there was no rank sown on the sleeves. "Since I am Nobody, and none of you wear any identification, this will be easy. I will refer to you all as assholes, since by its nature an asshole is a void found in the bum, which means it is not really there. It fits all of you to a T. None of you are here, none of you will know where the others are from, and I assure you, none of you will know where you are going or what will happen to you."

Max Adler looked around the small, barren room. Outside, the February temperature hovered around eight degrees. Inside, the temperature was warm enough to keep water from freezing, just barely. On the front wall was a large blackboard flanked by empty shelves. There were no windows. The one door from the hallway had a glass upper panel that was woven through with wire to reduce or eliminate the danger of splintering glass. Four pictures hung on the rear wall. The first was the king of England, the second Franklin Delano Roosevelt, the third Winston Churchill, and the last, though Max did not recognize him, was the Canadian prime minister, William Mackenzie King. The three countries responsible for the personnel at this training camp were Canada, England, and America. The respective flags stood in the corner on stanchions.

"At this training facility, the goal here," continued Nobody, "is to turn you mild-mannered so-and-sos into killers, assassins, saboteurs, and spies."

"Aren't killers and assassins the same thing?" a woman's voice asked from the back.

"Ma'am, a killer gets in the face of his victim—he stares him in the eye 'fore he sticks the knife through his ribs. The assassin waits for the right opportune moment and from a hundred yards shoots the son of a bitch. A killer has the chance of being killed; the assassin gets another notch on his belt. None of what we do here is pretty, but the reason for my team's existence is to make sure that you survive to fight another day. I do not want to waste the time and the money to train you and the first day you are on the street, someone wraps a wire around your neck or shoots you from a hundred yards. Get it?"

"Yes, Mr. Nobody."

"I can't hear you . . ."

"Yes, sir, Mr. Nobody."

At lunch, Max sat at a long table with two other Americans—no last names were exchanged. A strange concoction of beans, rice, and sausage had been ladled onto his plate. A slice of thick bread was dropped on top and a cup of coffee was stuck in his free hand.

"This is not half bad," one of the Americans said. He told them to call him Bob.

"Yeah, a lot better than that crap they gave us at Camp Richie," the other said. "Now that was some kind of inedible garbage; I believe they were experimenting on us."

"You were at Richie?" Max asked. "When?"

"Late last summer, three months, just after it opened, then two months—"

"I suggest, gentlemen, that you do not say another word," Mr. Nobody said from behind them. "One more and both of you will be back with a frontline unit waiting to go into whatever godforsaken shithole they want to send you. There may be a time and place for these conversations and fuzzy reunions, but today is not one of them. Talk about your mother, your girlfriend, your car, the size of your wanker, but do not talk about who you are or where you've been. Got it, mister?"

"Yes, sir. Got it, Mr. Nobody," Bob answered. He went back to his beans and rice.

Max hadn't eaten since he'd boarded the train in Buffalo, New York, almost twenty hours earlier. When he finished with his serving, he and Bob went back for more.

"You had two helpings? I can't believe it," the other man at the table added. He said to call him Joe. "You must be hungry or desperate."

"My drill sergeant," Bob said, "told us that a soldier must eat when he can, sleep when he can, and piss when he can. There will be times when you can do none of those things, so be prepared."

Max studied Bob and Joe; he'd pegged them for enlisted men. But that was the reason for the anonymity. They were here to learn, not pull rank or shirk. And Nobody was right: either pay attention, or when the time was right—and it would come—kiss your ass goodbye.

The woman who asked the question about killers and assassins sat down with the three men. Her presence was a shock to Max.

"Good morning, ma'am," Joe said.

"Don't 'ma'am' me, soldier," she sharply replied. "I may be old enough to be your sister but I sure as hell am not old enough to be a ma'am. Call me Fi—that's all you need to know. Isn't that right . . . Max?"

Max's smile was broad and warm. He'd not expected the woman from Chicago and the Nazis Bund meeting to drop her fine, firm butt on a chair next to him in the middle of nowhere Canada. He looked to the ceiling and murmured a prayer of thanks.

"Well, Max?"

"If you want to be called Fi, that's fine by me. And even though we spent a not-so-pleasant night with a ballroom full of Nazis a few years back, I still remember that we were never formally introduced. So, Fi, I'm Max. Pleased to meet you."

"And I'm Fi, short for Sophie. The strange things that the tides of war will leave on the shore."

"Which am I, Fi? Flotsam or jetsam?"

"I'm going with flotsam."

"Training will be fun," Max added. "Especially the part

about self-defense and close-in combat."

"Such a Boy Scout. We will see."

* * *

Villa San Sebastiano,
June 20, 1943
Max walked Sophie back across the ballroom to a chair next to her grandmother.

"You dance divinely, Colonel Stoltz," the countess said. "Sophie says that she knows you—how can that be?"

"Countess, I was in Spain while she was there, a liaison between the Reich and Generalissimo Franco. I was leading a training group. I met your granddaughter at a ball not unlike this one. I enjoyed her company, and I was honored to receive the invitation through your son, Father Conti." Max bowed. "So, if I may, I will excuse myself."

As Max walked away, he heard the countess say to Sophie, "Well, he is our guest; it is the least you can do. Show him around. He's such a handsome young man."

Sophie took the officer's hand and steered him toward the open door of the terrace.

"Why was Mussolini here?" Max asked.

"And hello to you too—I missed you. Did you enjoy your cake?" Sophie answered. Then looked him in the face. "And why Il Duce was here is none of your business."

"If my ass is on the line and my job has the chance to be compromised, it is definitely my business. And the cake was delicious."

"There are bigger things going on; it's the nature of our business. You know what you need to know."

"And if the roof falls in?" Max said.

"Make sure you are not under it," Sophie said. "I can handle it. Did you find Cattaneo? My uncle has his people looking."

"I suggest we don't talk about it here. Nice house. Care to give me a tour?"

An hour later, after she'd shown Max the upper floors, the library, and the kitchen in the basement, she led him to the far end of the second floor.

"My room. I spent many summers here before I went to school," Sophie said as she backed him across the room with her hands to his shoulders.

There, with moonlit views of Rome and the Colosseum through the windows, she slowly undressed him, slipped off her yellow gown, and made love to the man she'd been sent by her bosses in MI6 to watch.

11

Via dei Prefetti, Rome
June 23, 1943

Max stood on the roof of the apartment building, the smoke from his cigarette drifting about in the hot evening air. It was twelve days since he'd entered Rome. His mind wandered to heroic armies and pillaging hordes that had marched into this city; he'd sneaked in like a rat holding close to the dark edges of the alleys. The city was pensive and quiet, too quiet.

He had been told, before leaving Tunis, that Sophie Norcross was being sent to Rome to make it a joint American-British operation. That was hard to do, since only Max knew the operation's true orders. British intelligence had a cursory knowledge of the seriousness of his operation. Max believed that Sophie was here for other reasons as well. This was not a game of show me yours and I'll show you mine. She would, he hoped, in time, show him hers. And while what she did show of hers in the villa was more than delightful, he hoped that there would be more. He dealt in information and was coming up short on every front. And, most curiously, why was the prime minister of Italy, Il Duce himself, at the villa three nights earlier? There was nothing in any plan or order that he'd received that included the fascist dictator.

Max's own operation was simple: find and secure one of Italy's greatest physicists, Massimo Cattaneo. He was then to encourage the man to leave Italy, and if that failed, kidnap him. He also knew that Cattaneo would have been the probable winner of the Noble Prize in physics in 1940. The physicist would be both a scientific and political trophy. However, due to the war, the Noble Prize had not been awarded that year, or for the past three years.

Since his arrival, Max had received no additional information about his target. What he did know was memorized. He also carried a group picture of Cattaneo and other Italian physicists at the awards ceremony. It was the only photo of Cattaneo anyone had. Cattaneo taught at Sapienza University in Rome and was a close friend of Enrico Fermi, the 1938 Noble Prize winner in physics. All Cattaneo's other Italian associates had fled Rome and were now working somewhere in Britain or America; their locations were well above Max's paygrade. Cattaneo never left Rome. Cattaneo told friends at the university that his mother was ill, and he needed to be with her. An associate, who escaped through Cairo and asked for asylum with the British, said that Cattaneo hated the Germans and what they were doing. But as long as his mother was ill, he would not leave Rome.

Max knew who Enrico Fermi was; the world knew who Fermi was. He was the leading theoretical physicist in nuclear energy and its potential for human use. Max also knew that after being awarded the Prize in Stockholm, he and his wife went to New York City and applied for American residency. This was probably due to the new racial laws in Italy imposed by Mussolini and the fact that Fermi's wife was Jewish. It wasn't a stretch for Max to add up these facts and conclude that Fermi and the United States wanted Cattaneo for Fermi's team. A team that most probably was looking for a way to use nuclear power to win the war. And Max realized that if he could figure that out, he was certain that the Germans were also in the hunt as well.

When he returned to Washington, D.C., after completing his training at Camp X in Canada, Max was called to a meeting with his commanding officer, Colonel Zebadiah Jones, and OSS Director General Bill Donovan.

The war had been good for Zeb Jones since his days as a babysitter during the Olympics. He moved from the FBI to the army, and in 1942, into a position in Donovan's Office of Strategic Services, a new spy organization set up soon after the start of the war for America.

"Captain Adler, you have only one goal—get Cattaneo out of Italy and into our hands," Jones told him after the meeting with Donovan and Fermi. "If you can't get him, make sure no one else can use him—and that includes our Allies." Jones's comment surprised him, but Max was army now, OSS, and would follow those orders, written or not. His OSS cover was that he was there to help already placed British and American intelligence assets collect logistical information about the Italians and the Germans in and around Rome. After twelve days, he was no closer to finding Cattaneo than the morning he walked out of the sea.

Max asked to go in alone. Jones said, "Not a chance. Your Italian is awful. You don't know the city, and even though you look like a German, they will probably see through you. Sophie Norcross will do more to save your arrogant and inexperienced ass than any American I can attach to this operation. She is fluent in Italian, is in fact half-Italian on her mother's side, grew up in Rome, knows almost everyone, and has developed and employed spy-craft skills that you barely understood during your time at Camp Richie and Camp X. Her commander believes in her, and this is her third operation behind enemy lines. Most don't last their first. You, Max Adler, don't know jack shit."

Max knew all this; he'd trained with her. They had a friendly rapport that bordered on the next step in many male-female relationships. He was then abruptly removed from Camp X, met with his boss in Washington, then stuck in a C-47, and sent to England. They met three times during the planning stages of the operation, then he found himself in the back of another C-47 flying into North Africa.

He was told that Sophie would travel to Rome through Spain. She was also arriving under the specter of being unceremoniously thrown out of England for activities that, if she were in Germany, would have led to her execution as a spy. The British were just slightly more forgiving, especially since her father was a prominent diplomat and past ambassador to Italy. They just confiscated her British passport, her citizenship, and publicly denounced her just before she fled to Spain.

Now twelve days into his orders, he had not met one person who had had contact or even the smallest bit of information about Cattaneo or his location. And outside of the pleasant dalliance in her childhood bedroom, he'd not seen Sophie during the past few days. According to Father Conti, his niece had been seen at several fascist social events at other villas around Rome. Max, a little put out by the news, was hiding out in a grim, hot third-floor apartment halfway between the Spanish Steps and the Pantheon.

His flat mate, Albert Kent, fellow spy, was an expatriate and English. The man worked for MI6 and cheated at gin rummy. Late one afternoon, Max was given a note. It was the first contact he'd had with Sophie since the ball. The first line in her short message was cryptic: *How high is Niagara Falls?* It was a line they'd agreed to months earlier. The note instructed him to meet a man with information about Cattaneo. Without the opening question, he would have disregarded the instructions.

After dinner, Max slipped out of the apartment and walked through the dark streets. Reaching the designated restaurant, he watched and waited. The unusual summer fog, thick and wet, had drifted up the Tiber River from the Tyrrhenian Sea. He killed his cigarette and entered a nondescript Roman restaurant with large windows that faced the narrow street. It was three blocks from the Spanish Steps. Sophie's note was simple: sit at a specific table, at a specific time, in this restaurant, wait twenty minutes, then step away to the men's room. Upon returning, he would find a small book of poetry at the table; it would be old and worn. The courier would not see him, and he would not see the courier.

While he waited, Max ordered a bowl of thin soup and a glass of red wine. At 8:20 p.m., he rose from the table and pointed to the *bagno*. The waiter shrugged his shoulders. Five minutes later, he returned to the table and found only the *conto*—his bill—nothing else. Through the window, he saw two men in dark leather overcoats and hats. They were questioning a third, obviously nervous, man. The Italian agents pressed in on the man, undoubtedly sensing his jumpiness. One agent's finger was pushed hard against the man's chest, thumping it repeatedly.

Max dropped the required lire on the table and walked out into the fog. Ten feet from the three, he stopped and in his best German said, "Fritzy, is that you? You old dog."

Both agents whirled around and glared at Max. They were not as surprised as the courier; he looked like he wanted to pee in his pants.

"Fritzy, it's Freddy from school, in Berlin. Come, man, you must remember me?" Max said and continued to walk casually toward the three men.

The agent on the left said, "*Si fermati proprio lì.*"

Max had no intention of stopping, guessing that his German momentarily threw them off. He was hoping that neither spoke German.

He was now two steps away.

"You should have written. I would have met you at the station."

Then, abruptly, he switched to his faulty Italian.

"Did you bring the book of poetry I asked for?"

The courier, still stunned by Max's sudden appearance, began to reach inside his coat. One of the agents reacted by pulling out a pistol. Max recognized it as a Beretta semiautomatic.

Again in German, Max continued, "Fritzy, are these men bothering you? Please, gentlemen, please, put those toys away. Fritzy, Fritzy, don't you remember me?"

At that, Max clocked the first agent across the face with the pistol he had drawn out of his own pocket as he left the restaurant, hiding it snugly within the folds of his coat. The man collapsed to the pavement. The other agent tried to raise his pistol; Max put the barrel of his pistol two inches from his nose and screamed, "*Nein! Getta la pistola.*"

The mixture of German and Italian confused the courier. He stood frozen.

"*Ora!*" Max ordered.

The pistol clattered to the pavement.

"On the ground," Max said, to the agent. He relieved the unconscious man of his weapon. He gestured with his gun to "Fritzy," who picked up the second agent's pistol.

"Don't move!" Max said to the second agent, who now lay prostrate on the wet stones. "You are being watched. Move and you are dead."

Then, to the messenger, "Fritzy, we go, *now*."

"Fritzy" did not have to be told twice; he ran toward the corner. Max was fast behind him. They ran a half-dozen more blocks before the whistles started. Max directed them into an alley, then toward a door. He knocked once, waited, and then knocked again, twice. The door opened, and he pushed Fritzy past a man holding a double-barreled shotgun. Then they went down a dark hall, dimly lit at the far end. There, in a small candlelit room smelling like old garlic and olive oil, two men sat at a table.

"You weren't supposed to bring him here," Albert Kent said.

"Couldn't help it; this idiot was stopped by the secret police. They should have sent someone who wouldn't piss in his pants when he was questioned."

Max turned to the courier and held his hand out.

"Fritzy, the book," he said in Italian.

Still stunned by what had happened, Fritzy wasn't buying it. He slowly raised the pistol he'd picked up from the street and pointed it at Max.

"I'll be damned. Would you look at this—he does have balls," Albert said.

Max quickly grabbed the short barrel of the pistol and twisted it away from the man's shaking fingers.

"You must remember to click off the safety if you're going to point it at a man. Now sit!"

Fritzy did as ordered. A glass of wine was pushed his way; he hastily drank it. A spot of wine coursed down his cheek and held on his chin, covered with a four-day stubble of beard. He brushed it away with his sleeve.

"Well?" Max said.

Fritzy looked in turn at his rescuers.

"Thank you," he said in Italian. Even Max could tell from the accent that the man was not a Roman.

He produced the worn book and handed it to Max. Without looking at it, Max put it in his pocket.

"You were lucky; those were *segreti*, the secret police," Max told him. "A little dense, but dangerous assholes all the same. Were you the best they could find?"

"The original courier was arrested and shot three days ago," the courier said. "I came from Milan in his place. Hell, I don't even know Rome, and they send me here. Thank you, again."

"No problem, but if I ever meet your superiors, I'll tell them they're a dumb bunch of stupid fuckers to have sent you."

The man smiled for the first time. Yellow teeth, one broken in front, filled his mouth. He tried to comb his black hair with his fingers.

"Here's the deal, Fritzy. These gentlemen will give you a chance at a bath—and Lord knows you need one—a shave and a new suit of clothes. Tomorrow, you will be a businessman from Milan on your way back to that lovely city and your communist buddies. My guess, they will mistake you for a capitalist, and shoot you when you get off the train. I have faith in these boys; they will take care of you. Right, Albert?"

"Jolly right, we will. The sooner you are gone, my friend, the happier I'll be."

"And with that, Fritzy, good night," Max said.

"It's not Fritzy, it's—"

"Don't even say it. I don't want to know you, and I sure as hell don't want you to know me. So, as we say in the old country, see you on the other side."

"The other side of what?" Fritzy said.

Max looked at Albert and rolled his eyes, then lightly nipped the brim of his hat in salute and walked down the hall. After a quick check up and down the alley, he disappeared into the rain.

When he reached his apartment, the small piece of a toothpick he'd inserted in the doorframe lay on the floor. He put the bag with spaghetti and what might be called meatballs down on the floor and pulled his pistol. He checked up and down the hall. No door was cracked, and not a sound vibrated from the floors below. Positioning himself off to one side, he tried the door handle; it turned. He slowly pushed the door open and waited for the sound of gunfire or worse. Nothing. He counted silently to four.

"It's clear," Sophie's voice carried into the hallway.

He walked into the apartment. She, too, held a pistol. He walked to her and gave her a kiss on the cheek. Her eyes hadn't left the open door.

"I'm alone, no tail," Max said.

"I suppose you were out on a date."

"Yes, with a madman from Milan."

He took the book of poetry from his coat pocket.

"I believe this is for you. And you have something for me?"

"A note from my uncle. He has a lead on the physicist."

He held out the book. But she had to tug it from his hand. Then Max rapidly spun on his heels and aimed his pistol at the man in the corner.

"And why is that asshole here?" he demanded.

12

Colonel Zebadiah Jones sat in the worn cloth chair in the corner of the apartment. An automatic pistol sat on his lap, a glass of wine on the small table to his right.

"Colonel?" Max asked. "Is it about Cattaneo? I've been looking for two weeks. There's been some rumors, but nothing concrete. And Rome is a big city."

"No, it's not the physicist. Bigger things underway."

"Invasion—yes, I get it. It's obvious and it's probably even more obvious to the Germans."

"A forgone conclusion," Jones said. "In your case, even bigger. Your girlfriend has been holding out on you; I just found out."

Max looked at Sophie, who stood in the middle of the room glaring at Jones.

"What the hell do you mean by that?" Max said.

"It seems that she is here to negotiate with the local dictator," Jones said, sipping the wine. "Something about saving his ass if he signs on with a peace treaty or something. All hush-hush, all so British proper. Get the glory, save the Empire."

Max turned to Sophie. "Is this true? Is that why I saw Mussolini at the villa?"

"Really, you ask me this while you are trying to kidnap a

man here in Italy to help you make an atomic bomb? Were you going to share that with me, with us?"

Max looked past Sophie to Jones. "She's got you there. She is a spy, after all. A good one, I think you said. I'd be lost here without her, you said."

"I found out that Hitler doesn't tell his partners in this war anything either—that was Il Duce's biggest complaint," Sophie said. "He wasn't included in the decisions. So, is this the road we are on—neither side trusts the other?"

"It's stupid, Jones. You know it and I know it," Max said. "Even you don't know what's going on with Fermi. Sure, it's the big picture, but the detail—nada, nothing. The Nobel guy wants his guys and we are sent to find him. I don't give a damn what Sophie does with Mussolini. If it helps save a dozen lives or a million, it's all good. Shit, Jonesy, you don't tell me anything. My friends die not knowing why. It's war, I get it. Besides, I haven't eaten a decent meal since yesterday's breakfast. There's a bag in the hall with dinner, and there's enough for all of us. If you get it, I'll open more wine." He pointed to Jones.

They ate in silence, until Max asked, "Why you? Is there a problem with the radio?"

"The radio is fine; your reports are clear. This information I need to tell you in person."

"So you've told me. My guess is that the Germans will shoot Mussolini," Max said.

"That is his greatest fear—his own fascist party turns on him," Sophie said.

"So, what is this information you need to tell me?"

Just as Jones started to talk, there was a tapping on the door, the pattern of knocks correct. Sophie and Jones took positions to cover Max. He opened the door; Pietro stood there. He moved quickly into the room. Max looked down the corridor, then closed the door.

"Colonel, this is Pietro. He's my personal assistant and gofer. He was the one who brought the message from Father Conti to meet with the professors from Sapienza."

The boy saw the bottle of wine on the table, picked it up, and drank what remained.

"I have information," Pietro said in Italian, then spotted Sophie and Jones. "Who are they?"

"They are okay," Max said. "Friends of mine."

"What happened? What information?" Sophie said, also in Italian.

"Max, she's cute, he looks sketchy. I'd watch out for him," Pietro said.

"Out of the mouths of babes," Max said.

Pietro studied the two, then looked at Max. "I got two kids who watch the university—they are waiting for the guy you want. This morning, I was there to find out what they seen. Big commotion, then some German soldiers walk down the steps from the university with two guys—they were two of the men who were with you last week at the church. They looked scared. They put them in a big black car, *una bella Mercedes*, and left."

"Do you know where they went?" Sophie asked.

Pietro looked again at Sophie and smiled. "No, they go too fast. They also have posted guards around the university. Don't know why."

Jones lit a cigarette, then walked across the room as Sophie told him what Pietro said.

"You have an idea why, don't you, Jones?" Max said.

"Maybe," Jones answered. "Three weeks ago, a mid-level paper-pusher in London's intelligence communication branch was arrested by MI5. They had been watching the guy for two years. They fed him information and observed how it eventually ended up in Germany. The name of your guy, Cattaneo, showed up in one of the last bits they identified. It was in a message sent here to Rome, to the German embassy." Jones looked at Sophie. "It's obvious that your people tend not to be sharers, but this was important enough to pass on to us; maybe because you are involved."

"The Germans are aware of Cattaneo?" Max asked.

"Looks like it," Jones said. "I don't know any more than you do, Max. But I've been told to tell you to pull out the stops and find him—it can't be any clearer. If the invasion comes, it may become impossible. And it was strongly emphasized that this man must be found before the Germans get him."

Pietro saw the bowl with the remaining spaghetti.

"What's left is yours, Pietro," Max said.

The boy grabbed one of the forks and dug in; in seconds, it was gone. Pietro whispered *thank you* in Sophie's ear and quickly left.

"You trust him?" Jones said.

"Yes, he's too simple not to trust," Max said.

"What's the real reason you're here?" Sophie asked.

"Whether you know it or not, and I assume that you suspect it, there are other Allied agents in Rome. Their jobs are to collect information and pass it on—troop movements, logistical information, trains moving south. We even have a man in the German camp that passes on what Kesselring has for breakfast. I am here to meet them."

"Our orders have changed?" Sophie asked.

"No. In fact, if you run in to someone you know from home, I want you to go the other way. You are to find Cattaneo, then immediately contact us. I will let you know how to proceed. There are people waiting for that call; they will get him out. The best way is by boat."

"We have people looking. As I said, he's a ghost," Max said. "For all we know, he's dead—or worse, the Nazis already have him."

"Do what you can," Jones answered. "Believe me, this man is critical to the war effort, and that's all you need to know."

Max lit a cigarette. "There's something else, something critical. You wouldn't risk everything to come here unless it is important."

"Yes, and you won't like it. Washington has learned that a particular German officer is now in Rome. He was seen at the train station in Milan on his way here. He ran Jewish extermination teams in Poland and the Ukraine, Paris deportation operations in France, and we assume that he will oversee doing the same here in Italy. We believe that he is close to Himmler and may have the ear of Hitler. Here in Rome, it's probably SS-Obersturmbannführer Herbert Kappler. And Max, he is someone you know, SS-Obersturmbannführer Heinrich Schmidt. I believe he is the officer you met in Berlin during the Olympics, and I know he was the man in Chicago at the Bund meeting. We want you to wrap this guy up. OSS wants to squeeze him. He seems to be lax in his personal security. Some of our sources believe he thinks he's invincible."

"You want us to kidnap a senior SS officer and sneak him out of Italy?" Max asked. "Maybe we should grab Kesselring at the same time. Good God, Jones, I get Cattaneo. But this guy? Really?"

"He knows enough to have a serious impact on the war. That knowledge is key. And to have him out of the picture would help too."

"We could just shoot him," Sophie offered. "Unfortunately, there's a thousand others in line behind him. He'd be missed for less than a day."

"Can you get both Cattaneo and Schmidt?" Jones asked.

"I have no idea; I need to find Cattaneo first," Max said. "Let's say I get them. Then what?"

"We will give you a location where you can drop them," Jones said. "It will be somewhere along the coast. If you get Cattaneo, move him first. Don't wait to get both."

"I won't leave my grandparents; I told that to my boss,"

Sophie said. "He understands. I will remain here to be an asset providing information. And besides, my grandfather is one of the few who can talk to both political sides here—a conduit between the fascists and the communists. It's also the reason why Mussolini came to the villa. Trust is hard to find these days."

"Max is the leader of this little party," Jones said. "I want to make sure that both of you understand how serious this whole operation is. Cattaneo is critical to the war and your grandparents are critical to the peace afterward. I can't order you, but this Mussolini thing has to stop."

"Max said you were an ass; now I'm beginning to see it. Look, Zeb, you and I have worked together off and on for more than four years. I'm a field agent—that's what I do. We've lost agents in Brussels, Paris, and even Berlin. When our agents are caught, they aren't shipped off to some concentration camp or shot. The Nazis like to use the guillotine—efficient, terrorizing. I fully understand what's at stake. Yes, I will try to talk to my grandparents about the future of Italy, but I don't like it. Hell, they probably already understand. They are both eighty-two years old. I'm not sure how much influence they have left."

"Just see what you can do. Try to make them understand," Jones said. "Sophie, your parents understand—in fact, much of this operation is your mother's idea. She still believes her parents love Italy more than fascism."

"Damn you, I know what my parents want. They aren't exactly thrilled about my profession, but they understand that we are at war. Anything I can do to make it shorter, that's why I'm here."

"Your father is an important liaison between British SIS and American OSS," Jones said. "He knows more about what you're doing than you do. He is the reason I'm here. Your mother gave me this. You are supposed to give it to your grandmother—she will recognize it. Use it to convince her to help."

Jones reached inside his shirt and pulled out a chain. On it were two pieces of gold jewelry.

"This is the cross your mother has worn since your family left Italy. I'm sure you recognize it. You are to give it to your grandmother and ask for all the help she can give."

"And what's that other?" Max asked.

"My St. Christopher medal."

13

Rome, the German Embassy
June 30, 1943

From the café across the street, Max watched as another Mercedes pulled into the short turnaround and stop in front of the German embassy's gates. A manned bunker flanked the near side of the drive and commanded a view up and down the street fronting the northern side of the embassy. Two guards stood at the gate. This time, Max's luck won out. As the driver quickly walked around the car to assist his passenger, the Mercedes' rear door swung open and Heinrich Schmidt exited. The braid and medals on his black uniform flashed in the afternoon sun. He extracted a cigarette from a case, tapped it on the roof of the automobile, and then, with a silver lighter, lit it.

Across the street, four boys, who had been playing a sidewalk game, stood confidently in a straight line and at attention and waited for Schmidt to acknowledge them. Seeing them, they all saluted with a stiff right arm. Schmidt smiled and touched the tip of his right black-gloved hand to his cap. Then, unexpectedly, the four boys spun around, bent over, pulled their trousers down, and mooned the man. Max smiled at the theater, but mostly at the look on Schmidt's face. The officer threw his cigarette to the stone paving, crushed it, and walked stiffly through the gates of the Villa Wolkonsky. The driver of the Mercedes backed up and drove away.

Max waited for an hour, then left the café and took a stroll around the embassy complex. He was dressed as an old man, carrying a cane and walking with a pronounced limp. Often, he would turn and look to see if he was being followed. However, at the moment, he was certain there were not enough German spies and their handlers in Rome—yet. Axis and fascist surveillance resources were thin. They would strengthen over the summer—of that he was certain. The fascists in Rome were said to have an anti-spy apparatus, but it was weak and easily bribed. The true believers were German, not Italian. And now, after Jones had added this Nazi officer to his list, he still had to find Cattaneo.

"Signor Max, a woman gave this to me. She said she was the maid to a woman you know," Pietro said and handed Max a small envelope.

Inside was a simple note. *How high is Niagara Falls? The obelisk, the Pantheon fountain, tonight 8:00.*

* * *

That evening, Max sat in a café not fifty feet from the obelisk. The crowds were thin; the heat of the last day of June was beginning to dissipate; two lovers sat on the edge of the fountain and watched the Carabinieri stroll across the piazza on their rounds. A restaurant across the square was filled with German officers. Everything about this meeting concerned him. He felt a tap on his shoulder; he jerked and almost yelled. It was Sophie.

"How did you—"

"I came in through the back door. Finish your drink and follow me," Sophie said.

They wound their way through the tables. "Unlike that place full of Germans, only Italians eat in this restaurant. It seems there was a serious bout of food poisoning a few months back—it only affected the German soldiers. Nothing was proven, but now no German eats here."

"A form of chemical warfare?" Max asked.

"Chemical weapons are outlawed."

They walked out the back door and into the alley.

"Follow me," Sophie said.

He did. They wound their way through the passageways. At some turns they could see the massive dome of the Pantheon. She was leading them in a circle around the ancient Roman building.

When they reached a small piazza in front of a church and hotel, she said, "Sit here and give me a cigarette."

He lit it for her, then they both sat on a small stone bench in the far corner of the square. Another obelisk sat in the piazza's center; it was sitting on the back of an elephant.

"Bernini sculpted that. The church is a wonder inside," Sophie said. She looked across the piazza to the far side. "And that is the Grand Hotel de la Minerve. Quite old, very nice."

"Are you suggesting that I go and get us a room for the night?" Max said. His interest in the potential outcome of the evening grew.

"No. While a pleasant thought, we wait here. It should not be long."

They both shared another cigarette. Fifteen minutes later, a black Mercedes sedan pulled in front of the hotel.

"That car looks familiar," Max said.

"It should."

They watched the driver walk quickly up the steps and into the hotel. A moment later he came out; Heinrich Schmidt followed. The driver stood next to the open door; then, when Schmidt had sat, he closed it and took his place in the front seat.

"So, the major is staying here. How did you find out?"

"Through my connections. A friend's maid's sister works here in the hotel and quietly makes it a point to know who is staying there. Schmidt's name popped up about a week ago. I thought you would like to know."

"Great. One down, one to go. How about Cattaneo?"

"Working on it."

* * *

Rome, Stazione Termini
July 10, 1943

At the request of her bosses in London, Sophie's assignment during the next few days was to identify those coming to and going through Rome, especially Luftwaffe, Kriegsmarine officers, as well as Wehrmacht senior ranks; regiments, numbers, and unit types were eventually passed on. Max tagged along. No one paid the six-foot-four-inch Schutzstaffel officer any attention; or, at least, no one acknowledged the man.

During the afternoon of July 10, during a soft rain and posing as an SS major and his mistress, they casually strolled through Stazione Termini. Max gently took hold of Sophie's arm and steered her behind one of the marble columns.

"Now what?" she said. Her feet hurt from the new shoes she wore. She was also trying not to get wet.

"The officer standing on the platform, waiting for the Berlin train," Max said.

"There're ten Nazis standing on the platform. Which one?"

"The second to last, the one with the tailored coat and well-polished boots. The Obersturmbannführer."

"Yes, it's Schmidt. Why?"

"We have never formally met. I'm going to say hello," Max said.

"What? Don't. It's stupid," Sophie answered.

Max smiled, ignored her request, and walked across the platform.

"Schmidt? Is that you, Schmidt?"

At the sound of his name, Schmidt turned and immediately had to look up. Max was four inches taller than Schmidt. Max noted amusingly that he outranked the man.

"Schmidt, it's me, Stoltz. Don't you remember?"

Hidden in the shadow of the column, Sophie stood in awe and complete terror.

"Major, you have mistaken me for someone else," Schmidt said.

"No, my friend, no. We were posted in Spain together, a week in Madrid, and then I had to go to Seville. Don't you remember? What great times! Then again in Berlin, before Poland—ah, such memories, especially the bar at the Hotel Adlon."

Farther down the platform, the squeal of iron wheels on steel rails cut through the wet haze drifting above the platforms, and trains lined up across the station. The rain began to fall in earnest. Those not standing under the awning were instantly drenched. The bill of Schmidt's cap kept his face dry.

"I was never in Madrid," Schmidt said, his expression mildly perturbed.

"Of course you were. I am sure it was Madrid. Must be."

The train slid to a stop, and the doors were thrown open. A conductor appeared and placed a step stool in front of the stair to the car.

"Colonel Stoltz, I apologize, but you're mistaken. I must board my train."

"I'm sorry that you don't remember. We had such good times, but I understand. Until we meet again."

"Yes, sir, until we meet again." Schmidt saluted and stepped up into the car.

"*Auf Wiedersehen, Obersturmbannführer Schmidt,*" Max called out. "Until next time."

Oblivious to the rain, Max paced Schmidt for the length of the platform, watching through the train's windows as the Nazi strode through the car and took his seat in first class. He glanced at Max twice. As the train began to leave the station, Max tipped his cap and walked back to Sophie.

"Next time you're going to do something irresponsible and reckless, please tell me," Sophie said. "That way I can be far away when they arrest you."

Max ignored Sophie's comment. "Yes, that's the same arrogant man I saw in Berlin, callous and brutal. A perfect fit for the SS. Shipping him off to our people will be great."

"You have to catch him first," Sophie added.

* * *

Rome
July 12, 1943
Pietro and his extensive spy network of ten-year-old kids came through a couple of days later.

"My boys, they watch good," Pietro said. "I was there at the university this morning. Those two professors the Germans took away, they returned. Their faces are bruised, and their hands are bandaged. A German truck dumped them on the sidewalk. They looked confused. So, I walk up to them and start asking questions. They told me to fuck off. I still asked about the guy. I tell them I have a message for him."

"Did they know Cattaneo?"

"No, and that's what they told the Germans. I believe them. Those guys are lucky they aren't dead. So, while I was talking, a man walked out of one of the buildings. He crossed the piazza and walked directly past us. I asked if they knew him; they said no. It was your guy, Cattaneo. He looked just like the picture you got—he's our man. Positive, swear to God."

"Where was he headed?"

"How should I know? So, I'm one smart cookie, I follow him. He walked toward the San Lorenzo district. He stopped at a small café in a piazza and had an espresso. He was all friendly with the owner. I hung around awhile, then some kids come by and tell me to beat it, it's their streets. So, I left."

"Can you take us there tomorrow?" Max asked.

"Sure, no problem. A hundred lire."

"You are one tough cookie," Sophie said.

"You better believe it."

14

The San Lorenzo District, Rome
July 15, 1943

As was his habit each morning after caring for his mother—except Sundays when he went to church—Massimo Cattaneo walked the two blocks to the café at the corner of the Piazza dei Sanniti. There, following his usual espresso and *panino dolce*, he quickly read through the paper, said hello to friends, and relaxed. Today, Thursday, was already more than two hours old. He began it by waking his mother, helping her with her toilet (today was a good day—she could make it to the small chair he'd built for her), preparing her breakfast, and then measuring out her medicines. Before the laudanum had its effect, he spent some time talking with her. After she fell asleep, he allowed a few hours for himself. Later, after he returned from his shopping around the neighborhood, he would return to his small study and continue exploring the theorems he was intent on verifying, as well as further develop a novel concept about nuclear degradation and an isotope's half-life.

Someday, in a future he would not think about, he would be free to travel and visit the places that Fermi mentioned in his letters: London, New York City, Columbia University, and Chicago. He had to ask one of the students to help him find a map to locate Chicago. Fermi's letters always asked about his mother, told him about the weather, and how big American cities were. But not once did they include any information about what Fermi was doing. Fermi wrote that he missed his friends and colleagues; Cattaneo had not seen or heard of any paper or contribution to their field by Fermi since the summer of 1941.

Feeling especially comfortable this morning—the temperature was perfect—he waved to Dante, the proprietor, and ordered another espresso. A primary reason he liked this café was, at precisely the correct time—and he planned his visits accordingly—the sun would rise over the buildings across the small piazza and wash the tables and chairs with warmth. He closed his eyes expectantly. All he received was a dark shadow. Perplexed, he opened his eyes and saw a tall, broad-shouldered man standing directly in the path of the impending sunshine. Another silhouette, smaller and shapelier, stood next to the man.

"Good morning," the shapely form said in Italian. "Are you Professor Massimo Cattaneo?"

Cattaneo raised both his hands to his brow, forming a V-shaped tunnel. The sun's brilliance was directly in his face. The two dark forms stood there looking at him.

"Si, I am Cattaneo. Why do you ask? I don't know you." He then waved his right hand back and forth at the shadows. "And please stand to one side; you are blocking the sun."

"May we sit?" the man asked.

"Sure, why not."

The sun returned in full force after the two sat. Cattaneo closed his eyes and absorbed its warmth.

"Professor, we need to talk," the man said.

"About what? I don't know you. Besides, I don't talk about

politics or religion. I study physics and have a particular interest in the weather, this morning it is the sun. So, why would I talk with you?"

"America," the man continued.

"I have heard it is a nice place. I understand that they have invaded Sicily. Are you the first to reach Rome? I have friends that live in America. Other than that, it means little to me. Except that, in a few months, America may replace the Germans as our new masters. As I said, I do not discuss politics." He picked up his cup and sipped; it was cold. He turned to the waiter. "Dante, three espressos. That man there, with the terrible accent, is picking up my tab."

"He looks like a fucking German," Dante said.

"The sun, it's too bright. I can't see him well. I only can admire the woman. Bring the espressos anyway."

The woman turned to the big man and smiled. Very pretty, Cattaneo thought. *Ah, if I were freer.*

"Excuse me for being so rude," Cattaneo said. "It seems I am doing all the talking—probably because you are the first people, other than my mother and Dante, I've had a conversation with in two weeks. So, why do you want to talk to me about America?"

"Actually, we want you to go with us to America. Your friends miss you, especially Enrico," the man continued.

"Fermi does, does he? He's the one who ran out on us; he is an opportunist. He had everything he needed to continue his studies here." Cattaneo leaned in toward the two. "Personally, I think the prize went to his head—we all contributed to the work. He received all the glory—so I think his missing me is, how you say . . . bullshit."

The espressos arrived. Dante glared at the visitors and turned back to the café's entry.

"Dante does not like Germans. His son was rounded up in one of Il Duce's sweeps through the district, he was sent to

Germany. The last he heard of Tomas was three months ago. He was grinding steel cylinders somewhere in Germany for the Nazis." Cattaneo opened a package of cigarettes and lit one. He did not offer any to his guests. A moment later, two unopened packs of cigarettes slid across the table.

"A bribe?" Cattaneo asked. "I do not think two packs of cigarettes, no matter how tempting, will get me to agree to go to America. Who are you two? You have balls to come here." He looked again at his watch. "You have five minutes, then I have to go and make my mother lunch."

"I am Sophie Conti. My family lives in San Sebastiano. We are friends of your colleagues in America. I am here to help you get there. And I, for one, believe that two years ago you should have won the Nobel Prize."

"It was not awarded. There is a war, they say. I think it was a way to keep the money out of German hands."

"Such a shame not to be acknowledged."

"Sophie, a pretty name for a pretty face, and smart. For you I might just go to America. But this German, him, I do not think so. So, German, who the fuck are you?"

"First of all, I'm not German. My family fled Germany, but I'm from Chicago."

"I know where Chicago is."

"Good for you; you can read maps. My name is Max Adler. I can offer you a substantial reward if you go."

"Aren't we snippy. And not German? I don't entirely believe you. So, you must be American. You think money can buy anything. Well, American, when are you going to save my long-suffering country? Every day gets worse. Flour is almost gone, precious coffee is almost gone, sugar is so expensive no one can get fat; it is as if we are all on a forced diet. The only thing we have too much of are Germans, fascists, and flies." To emphasize the point, Cattaneo slapped two green and black bottle flies with the folded newspaper. "It's the fucking donkeys."

"We can arrange to have your mother go with you," Sophie said.

"My mother is too sick; the trip will kill her. She has told me a hundred times that she will die in her bed." He again leaned toward the intruders and put his index finger to the side of his head, tapping it against his temple. "I am a good and thoughtful son. I will respect her needs. And I know why Fermi wants me. It is the bomb, isn't it? The concept has haunted the man for twenty years; he and that crazy German Jew, Einstein believe it can be done. It scares the shit out of them, but they think it can be done. And, to be honest, it scares the shit out of me; it's too dangerous. It will only bring Armageddon, the end of the world. They say the fourth horseman is war. I say it is the atomic bomb."

"What's this bomb he's talking about?" Sophie said, turning to Max. "Is this real?"

"I have no idea," Max answered.

"They send naïve children to collect souls; I get it," Cattaneo said. "Fucking governments. Sophie, such a pretty name. Are you part English? You have that look. I once dated an English girl. She drank too much, and her parents did not want her marrying a Dago."

"I'm sorry to hear that. My mother married an Englishman."

"My condolences—a stiff lot they are—probably for money. Anyway, it is simple, really: the bomb I am talking about is called a nuclear bomb. It has the theoretical power of a million conventional bombs exploding at the same time. Some say it will set the atmosphere on fire and kill everyone on earth. Others say it is impossible to build, and still others say it cannot be permitted. I assure you that the Germans are trying to build this abomination. Have you ever tried to tell a child not to do something? It is the surest way to get them to do it. So, Fermi is trying to build his bomb. God forgive us."

"Professor, my orders are simple," Max said. "You are important to Dr. Fermi. As such, you are important to the future of civilization. I ask you to join us."

"The future of civilization? Really? A ten-cent bullet in the head of Herr Hitler would have solved the problem years ago and saved the lives of millions of men and women. Look around. My country is on the verge of civil war between the fascists and the communists, with the Germans in the middle. You have landed in Sicily; I assume the mainland is next. Two men caused all this; in time, retribution will be ours. Until then, I must take care of my mother. That is my responsibility." Cattaneo stood and looked into the open door of the coffee shop. "Dante, he will pay the bill."

* * *

Max and Sophie were speechless by the candid responses and comments by the physicist. They expected a mild-mannered, almost meek, man. They got a sharp-thinking realist devoted to his family and tradition, and someone who would not be going to America—at least not easily.

"He will be hard to move," Sophie said, sipping the espresso. "Family is tough to break through, especially here in Italy. Can we take his mother?"

"I have no idea, but we need him in America," Max said watching the man walk away. Then, twenty feet later, Cattaneo stopped, lit a cigarette from one of the new packages, took a deep breath, smiled, turned back, and walked up to the pair.

It was his shadow that spread over them.

"There may come a time when I can do what you ask, God only knows when. I owe Fermi a lot and he owes me. He knows that. There are unpaid obligations and debts. He is brilliant, and when he came to the university, I was his first mentor—even he will admit to that. But every child needs a parent, and parent a child, so be patient with me. I will meet you here in four days, in the afternoon—it is my mother's nap time. Let me think about what you are asking. And be careful—I assure you, these days one is never alone."

15

Rome, Villa San Sebastiano
July 19, 1943

Sophie stood at the front window of the villa's living room, her mind wandered a moment. A hummingbird flitted aggressively through the garden reasserting its territory. Her grandmother and grandfather sat on a brocade couch that faced General Ambrosia. He sat on a matching couch and held a cup of coffee in his hand.

"The coward couldn't come this morning?" Sophie said not looking at the man. "The attack in Sicily has him scared shitless? Not only is he a fool, but a poltroon."

"Matters of state, Signorina. The prime minister apologizes."

"The Italian army in Sicily has effectively surrendered," Sophie said. "And the Germans are being pushed northward; it is a matter of time, probably just days, before the Allies take the island. They will move swiftly to the mainland, you know that. It is too late for Mussolini; you can tell him that. The offer is withdrawn."

"He is a proud a man," Ambrosia said.

"Pride goeth before destruction, and a haughty spirit before the fall," Countess Conti said. "It was written for the man."

"I fear there are others involved now," Ambrosia continued. "It will not take much to turn the government toward . . ."

". . . what, self-immolation?" Sophie said.

"Most probably. I wanted to tell you in person—his *Eccellenza* will remain here in Rome," Ambrosia said as he sat his coffee down and stood. "I must return to the king."

"Like a dog to its master," the count said.

"Do not judge me so harshly, my old friend. Our world is over. I fear the next one, somedays even more than this one."

The butler, Luciano, led the general to the door and handed him his hat as he left the villa. Sophie went back to the window and watched the car disappear down the drive.

"Rome expects to be liberated soon," Countess Conti said. "They believe that the Allies will sweep up from Sicily and take Rome before winter."

"This war makes us believe a lot of things that will not come true," Count Conti said.

"Yes, truth is the first casualty of war; a Greek said that," Sophie said. "And the Greeks knew a lot about war and lying. I am going to see Uncle Guido."

"Be careful, Sophie. I fear that the direction of the war is about to change for Rome and for us," Count Conti said.

* * *

San Lorenzo, Rome,
July 19, 1943

Massimo Cattaneo stood at the edge of the parapet surrounding the rooftop garden that sprawled above the five floors of apartments. Pots full of vegetables, herbs and even a few lemons were spaced willy-nilly across the tarpaper. His view, from halfway up the hill of the San Lorenzo district, took in the Colosseum, the rail yards, and the monumental white marble building dedicated to Italy's first king, Victor Emmanuel.

Winding all through this part of the city were the excavated ruins of Caesar's ancient Rome. He never tired of the view, especially now as the summer days made his lunchtime visits even more relaxing. He removed the half-empty bottle of red wine, a piece of hard cheese, bread, and a three-inch chunk of salami. A simple lunch for a citizen of Rome—a tired and exhausted citizen.

Two floors below, his mother was finally asleep; the new powders that the doctor had given him to ease both her pain and anxiety seemed to be working. With the less-than-surprise Allied landing in Sicily, the war was now advancing toward the mainland of Italy itself. Cattaneo wasn't sure how long he would be able to continue to procure the opioids, he was trying to stockpile as much as he could afford. For his mother's sake and the cancer that was slowly devouring her, he hoped the war would stay away long enough. He'd come to this rooftop a thousand times in his life. He grew up in this building; his childhood friends were now spread halfway around Europe. His best friend, Dino, was dead and buried somewhere in Libya. Cosmos was last seen somewhere near Stalingrad; and his oldest friend, Julio, was in Sicily. He was sure he would never see them again. His old associates from the university were in America, and other than Fermi's quarterly letters, he never heard from them.

Because Italy believed he was worth more as an old man teaching physics at the university than dying in some foreign desert, he hadn't been drafted yet. And today he felt his age. He poured the rest of the wine into the heavy glass tumbler and finished the last of the bread. How many evenings he's spent here with his mother and brother as they grew up. Especially the hot August and September nights, when it was unbearable in the apartment. They slept on the roof countless times with their neighbors. It was on those nights, when it was so hot, that the rooms became ovens. What would he do with his mother then? When he was young it was like camping, or at least that's what he believed since he'd never been camping in his forty-nine years. In fact, he'd only been out of Italy once, and that's when he traveled with his friends and fellow professors to Stockholm. They joined Enrico when he received the Nobel Prize in physics five years earlier. The trip confused Massimo. He enjoyed the attention and the chance to support his friend, but the pomp and circumstance were beyond him. When he learned that Enrico decided to remain in America soon after receiving the award, he was saddened. Why would anyone want to leave Italy? Everything was here. When a colleague mentioned that it was because Enrico's wife was Jewish, he still didn't quite understand. Why would that make a difference? After others from the university quietly slipped away for England and America, he grew lonely. Was it him? Was it because he hadn't a wife? Was it because he had to stay and take care of his mother? All questions he couldn't resolve, and when he asked other professors, they shrugged and said it was the government. Again, he hadn't understood, yet now was beginning to—it was the Americans. Mussolini seemed like a nice enough leader. In fact, the day ten years earlier when Mussolini and his second in command, Italo Balbo, stopped by the physics lab, Fermi gave them a grand tour. Il Duce seemed impressed, asked questions, posed for pictures, shook hands. Yes, Cattaneo did not understand why Fermi never returned. He'd received letters from Fermi asking him to join him in America. Massimo replied that he must stay with his mother and with the university. Since the spring of 1942, he'd not received one letter from America or any of his expatriate friends. He felt alone and isolated.

It was the evenings that were his most productive. In the small bedroom that was once his brother's, he had set up his library. On large chalkboards he would work for hours on problems and equations. When he found something interesting, he would transfer the lines of text and symbols to his notebooks, which were then stacked neatly on the shelves. There were dozens. If Cattaneo had a vice, it was cigarettes and pipe tobacco. He had become a chain-smoker. Tobacco was inexpensive, and he took advantage of his sin. As he scribbled away with his chalk, he smoked both the pipe to relax and premade cigarettes to energize him. Only a few in the outside world, and none in the apartment building located in the heart of the San Lorenzo district, knew that Massimo Cattaneo was one of the top nuclear physicists in the entire world. In his head were equations that would change the world, he just needed time to move them from his brain to the chalkboard,

His brother, Augusto, had fled to Buenos Aries ten years earlier. He now had an Italian import-export business with a warehouse near the port of Genova. Augusto had returned home to see their mother only once during the past ten years. And when he eventually answered Massimo's letters (or letters he wrote for his mother), his brother would find dozens of excuses not to visit. By the start of the war, Cattaneo had given up on the man. All he knew was that he had married an Argentine woman, had three children, and was directly involved in the fascist politics of Argentina. Massimo did not understand any of it. More than once, he had to lie to his mother when she asked about his brother, her son.

Cattaneo finished the wine and lit another cigarette. He had a tutoring session at three o'clock with a promising young man. It was at the university—that was why he was taking an early lunch. As he stood at the parapet, he looked to the south. A sudden explosion obliterated the horizon. It was instantly followed by another, and another, and then dozens of explosions marched, unstopped, directly at him and the San Lorenzo district. It was a swath of blasts and detonations more than a half-mile wide.

Bombs!

In the clear sky he saw dozens, maybe hundreds, of bombers in formation approaching Rome. The Germans were bombing Rome? Why would they do that? It couldn't be the Americans; they wouldn't destroy Rome—they wouldn't. He turned to run back to the stairwell and was suddenly and violently thrown into the air; his ears exploded from the concussion; his clothes were ripped from his body. He was knocked senseless as bombs tore through the roof of the apartment building, penetrated two floors, and exploded.

The entire building was blown outward into the street. The blasts, one after the other, devastated the floors below. The upper floors then collapsed into the shattered remains of stone, timbers, and stucco. Furniture, exposed and thrown about, hung from the blasted openings of the building. A child's hand and arm lay on the pavement. Halfway up the facade of the building, a woman lay half in and out of the debris. Dust whirled and enveloped everything. Farther up the block, more buildings, one after the other, exploded into the street. Romans out for lunch were hit and killed by the flying debris, stones, and shrapnel. Hundreds of buildings were hit and destroyed, thousands were killed, even more injured and maimed. The Allies' target, the rail yards that surrounded the district, were also hit, but the destruction and death were greatest in the nearby neighborhoods.

For Cattaneo, the world had ended—at least the world that he knew. As he regained his senses, all he heard was a buzzing; his lips and mouth were filled with dust and bits of wood. His arms and legs seem paralyzed—he couldn't move. There was no ground below him. He looked around and found he was high in a tree, and somewhere in the back of his head he thought of the great sycamores that lined Via dei Sabelli. He must be jammed in between the branches; one of his legs was wedged in the crouch of the tree, his back remarkably laid out along a massive branch, and his left arm was stuck in the crook of another limb and branch. Craning his neck, he looked down—he was twenty or thirty feet from the street. He still heard nothing, only a buzzing like a million bees swarming in his head. People ran up and down the street, some carrying bundles of clothes; his mind could not grasp what was happening—then, they were bodies. He closed his eyes and took inventory. Shockingly, nothing screamed at him, and other than his leg and ankle caught in the V of the tree crotch, he could move, and thankfully there was no pain. Nothing alerted him to a broken bone. With his free hand, he patted himself—there was no blood. He figured he had a concussion. All and all, Massimo Cattaneo believed he was a lucky son of a bitch.

Dislodging his ankle, he slowly pulled himself forward on his branch. Sounds were coming back to him; the most annoying was the singsong wail of ambulances and firetrucks. He surveyed the branches below him; the explosion had shredded or blown away most of the foliage, and some of the limbs had been sheared off. He slowly and methodically climbed down the tree; it was almost like a ladder made of mismatched rungs. The last was the ten-foot drop to the sidewalk. Landing, his ankle almost gave way. He tested it and decided that it wasn't broken, just hurt. One of the few fortunate events of the last twenty minutes.

It was then that he saw the entire block of buildings that held shops and businesses, and hundreds of apartments, was gone, all turned into a twisted pile of destruction. A woman kneeled on the sidewalk, a small bundle of cloth at her knees. A man walked toward him, trance-like, his hands bloody; he was in his underwear. Massimo looked at himself and realized that all he was wearing were shredded slacks, his undershirt, socks, and one shoe. To the right, three men were pulling debris from the pile that was once his apartment building. He saw a hand extending out from a pile of stones. Other than the sirens it was quiet, like a cemetery. Then his ears popped.

Shrieks and screams reigned.

"You there, I need help. I think she's still alive," a man yelled at him. "For the love of God, help me."

And Cattaneo did help. For the rest of the afternoon, he pulled stones and timbers from the buildings of his home. His hands were bloody and torn. He wore the shoes of a dead man. They found twenty survivors, some with horrendous injuries. They also located more than forty dead, some killed by the explosions, others by the collapsed buildings. The bombs were democratic—they killed young and old, men and women. Because it was a Monday, many were at work. He hated to think how many would have died if the attack were on a Sunday.

"It was the fucking Americans," a man declared, shaking his hand at the clear sky. "I saw the planes—they were B-17s. I seen 'em in Africa. Death from the air. There's no place to hide from the fucking things. God damn them all."

In the early evening, as Cattaneo's strength was almost gone, he found his mother. She was dead. She was found under the collapsed ceiling of her room. She died from the shock of the explosion. It was instantaneous, a man said, who helped him move her to the sidewalk. "She didn't know what hit her; it was a blessing."

He agreed. Now her pain was gone, and she was with Renaldo, her husband and his father. He kissed her cheek as they loaded her body into one of the carts. *Now my life is done,* he thought. *There is nothing for me now.*

16

Rome, San Lorenzo District
July 19, 1943

Rome was in shock. They had believed, erroneously, that the city would be spared. There would be no bombs, no destruction, no loss of life. Considering the chances of hitting any of the most sacred buildings and monuments built by man for the glory of God—no one would think of bombing Rome. Yet the Allies did bomb Rome. It was to be a surgical strike, yet instead of a scalpel, they used a machete. They attacked the San Lorenzo freight yards, a central location for switching trains, rail lines that the Germans used to transport tanks, equipment, and men south—south to where it was expected the Allies would invade. The Allies had landed on Sicily's southern coast just ten days earlier. During those ten days, enough time had passed for the German command to understand the scale of the attack and begin to develop an appropriate response, and that response required men and materials to be sent south. Time would reveal that more than 500 American bombers participated in the attack, and almost 1,200 tons of bombs were dropped on what turned out to be marginal targets of insignificant value. It was not insignificant to the residents of the San Lorenzo district; over 3,000 were killed and as many wounded.

The bombing brought Pope Pius XII to the San Lorenzo district later that day. It was the first time, since the beginning of the war, that the pontiff had left the Vatican. He prayed for the dead and injured, offered aid to the district, and brought food from the stores of the Vatican. He had earlier implored President Roosevelt "to spare Rome from pain and devastation." Roosevelt replied that he would try, yet also left some room for an attack, "if it were found necessary." Since it was the Italians and the Germans that determined this level of necessity, Roosevelt left it to the pope to keep the bombers away from Rome.

For the next few days, Massimo Cattaneo wandered through the devastated district. He slept in a pew in the rear portion of the heavily damaged Basilica of Saint Lawrence Outside the Walls. It was there he witnessed the pope bless the people and pray for the dead. The pope was just feet away from him. He saw a man torn by the destruction and death; his heart went out to the man, born and raised in Rome, and his burdens. Cattaneo shrunk back from the pope, feeling that his concerns were far less than those of the most holy man in Christendom. Cattaneo needed a place to live, he needed to get back to his work, and he needed the safety of the university. He walked to Sapienza University; it had barely missed being destroyed by the Allies' bombs. The campus was closed for the summer. He found the small office that he shared with a colleague—the man was now at Princeton University in New Jersey, America. If asked, Cattaneo had no idea where Princeton University was. He remembered some cots and blankets in the storeroom down the hall. He moved them into his office, and over the next few days he found clothing and food and made Room 227 his new unofficial residence. The only person who knew where he was in the entire city of Rome, or the world, was the Sicilian janitor, Tony. He brought the professor wine, cigarettes, and food. What was even more important, he brought news. Tony reported that on July 25, six days after the San Lorenzo bombing, Benito Mussolini, prime minister of Italy, was unceremoniously fired by the king, Victor Emmanuel III. He was arrested and taken away from Rome. Marshal Pietro Badoglio, the old man and the butcher of Ethiopia, was named as his successor. Cattaneo hated all of them. While it was American bombs that killed his mother, it was Victor Emmanuel, Mussolini, and the fascists that had started this war.

For the next two weeks, it was only he and the Sicilian who wandered the halls of the physics laboratories. During that time, he further developed his concepts on latent nuclear decay. He missed his mother, but as can happen to a man of his mental strength and lack of personal focus, he began, also, to lose her. Mostly it was her face. He tried to remember every crease and wrinkle, her sharp eyes, her thick silver hair, her smile. But that was the face of his mother of his youth; how she looked in the weeks before her death was something that he never wanted to remember, and soon he succeeded.

As the days moved into early August, he settled into a routine. On the morning of August 9, a Monday, he brewed himself a cup of coffee and began to pick apart the loaf of four-day-old bread that the Sicilian had brought the previous Friday. It was a miracle; it was made from real flour. There was also a hard-boiled egg that the Sicilian's wife had included in the food basket. The coffee was the last of the small bag of beans he'd found in a bottom drawer of another professor's desk. Sequestered there were also tins of sardines, sausages, and boiled potatoes. Cattaneo took it upon himself to rescue these provisions; he also found a grinder in the drawer next to the coffee. After three attempts he managed to finally make a decent cup of coffee using a Bunsen burner he'd liberated from a science lab. He hoped the canister of gas would last as long as the small can of coffee. As he finished pouring, there was a knock on the open door to his office. Seeing who stood there, his heart dropped through his stomach, and if it weren't for the fact he'd been sitting, he was certain he would have fainted.

"Professor Cattaneo?" the Nazi officer asked. "Are you Professor Massimo Cattaneo, physicist, author of numerous scientific papers, and tenured professor here at Sapienza University?"

Stunned by the appearance of this German, he had a hard time understanding the man's mangled Italian. Nonetheless, Cattaneo stuttered a "Si."

"Excellent, you will come with me." The officer entered the small room. Two soldiers followed the man into the room.

"Where are you taking me?"

"We are here to protect you; your life is in danger." While the officer talked, he walked around looking at the certificates and photos on the walls, the shelves filled with books, and the knickknacks on the desk. "Please pack up what you need. If there are other things you require, I will send someone to retrieve them."

"Am I being arrested?"

"No, you are not being arrested. As I said, this is for your protection." The Nazi walked back to the center of the room. "You have five minutes."

"May I finish my coffee?" he asked.

Seeing the cup, the officer asked, "Is there enough to share?"

Cattaneo poured the last of the coffee into a cup and slid it across the desk to the Nazi.

"Danke."

The man said something in German to the doorway; Cattaneo did not understand. Two more soldiers walked into the office, each carrying a box. "These men will help you; please begin. We will leave in . . . ten minutes."

Still dazed, Cattaneo began to put books and binders in the boxes. Then a few things from the desk. Lastly, he removed two diplomas from the wall and a photo.

The German asked that he hold up the photo. The officer then removed a photo from a pocket. It was a duplicate to the one Cattaneo held in a frame. The photo was of the group at the Nobel Prize ceremony.

"Excellent. As I said, if you have forgotten anything, I will send someone to retrieve it. We will go now."

"Where?"

"I assure you, to a safe place."

* * *

Sapienza University
August 9, 1943

Sophie parked her grandfather's Berlinetta Fiat against the curb; the plaza fronting the physics building was directly across the street.

"I am impressed. This is a beautiful automobile," Max said.

"And that is why I'm driving. My grandfather would never forgive you or me if you damaged it. And leave the window open if you must smoke."

"I can drive."

"I have no evidence to support that statement," Sophie said. "When I was here in 1939, I drove this car to Milan and back. My grandmother screamed part of the way—she said I drove like my mother. That's who taught me. Now, you said that Cattaneo is living here?"

"Yes. Pietro spotted the man as he walked through the plaza. He was alone. That building, according to my Michelin Guide, is the physics building, which makes sense. His apartment was about a thousand yards from here. The bombs just missed this place."

"Are we going to wait?"

"For a few minutes. The boy also said that the fascists patrolled the grounds. After my meeting with some of the professors, I'm not surprised. Probably prime hunting grounds for bagging communists."

"Cute."

A black Mercedes sedan pulled up to the opposite curb; a German army truck stopped behind it. Six SS soldiers jumped from the back and immediately lined up on the sidewalk. An SS officer exited the rear seat of the sedan, crossed in front of the truck to the soldiers. The drivers from both vehicles joined the troop. All carried Schmeisser machine pistols.

"Well, this is too convenient," Max said, sliding down in the seat a little. "What the hell is Schmidt doing here? He must be after Cattaneo. We can grab them both at the same time."

"Yes, great, a brilliant idea. All we have to do is go through those soldiers—and here I forgot my own squad of commandos. Shit."

They waited. Two guards remained with the sedan and truck. One pointed to their Fiat, the other gave the universal sign of money with his fingers. The first guard laughed. Max and Sophie did not move. The windows were closed, and while the glare gave them a little protection from being seen, the heat was building in the car.

"Shall I move?" Sophie asked.

"Only if you want to be shot. We wait."

"Shot or cooked—decisions, decisions. I guess we wait."

Fifteen minutes after Schmidt went into the building, he returned. Massimo Cattaneo walked next to him, no shackles or restraints of any kind. Two of the soldiers carried boxes—Max could see the edges of frames sticking out the open top. The other soldiers casually walked behind the two men.

"This is not good," Sophie said.

"When they reach the end of the street, we will follow them. I want to know where they are taking him. What we do after that, I haven't a fucking clue."

17

The German Embassy, Rome
 August 9, 1943

Max and Sophie tailed the Mercedes and the truck. The route was short. They drove down the hill past Cattaneo's collapsed apartment, then to the Via dello Scalo San Lorenzo, through the Parati Caesar gate, then the Piazza di Porta Maggiore, and then three blocks that weaved through the residential neighborhood that enclosed the German embassy. The truck pulled to the side of the entry near the sandbag bunkers with their machine guns. The sedan entered through the gates of the German embassy. The bronze sign on the right, in Italian, read: L'AMBASCIATA TEDESCA, then in German, DIE DEUTSCHE BOTSCHAFT.

"That's the German embassy," Sophie said as they slowly passed the gates.

"That lucky son of a bitch," Max said. "I thought they were going to Regina Coeli prison. Any ideas?"

"None, but I suggest that we watch the entry from up the street. We stand out if we hang around here. If they don't leave during the next few hours, my guess is this is where they will keep him. I have to get this car back to my grandparents before dark."

"I'm certain they aren't going anywhere. Do you think your grandmother will ground you if you stay out past curfew?"

"No. I just don't want them wondering what I am doing out so late. I lie enough to them."

After Sophie dropped Max off near his apartment, he found a phone and called Father Conti.

"My niece—is she all right?" the priest asked in English.

"Yes, she's with your parents. We need to talk, and not over this line."

"Come to the rectory in the morning; wait for me. I have early Mass. I'll join you as soon as I can."

"Yes, Father."

* * *

Chapel of the Holy Family, Prati District, Rome
August 10, 1943

Max stood in the vestibule of the rectory. The nun who took care of the priest offered him coffee and a small oat cake.

"Signor, I'm sorry, but that is all we have," she said.

"Quite all right. I ate something before I left my apartment," he answered with a fib. He was famished.

"Father Conti will be here shortly."

"Thank you, Sister."

The nun left him. This early the vestibule was dark. There were two paintings of religious scenes—one of a man tied to a tree and shot full of arrows, the other of Christ holding up his right hand in a blessing.

"Some conflicting messages going on here," Max said out loud.

"Such is the nature of the Catholic Church," Father Conti said, walking into the room. "I heard from my mother last night—Sophie arrived safely."

"Good—we found Cattaneo. Unfortunately, we were an

hour late. The Nazis have him."

"Do you know where they took him?"

"The German embassy—it will be difficult," Max said.

"You are going to get him out?" Conti asked. "The embassy is the old Villa Wolkonsky, a fine estate with extensive gardens. I attended functions there before the war. The Germans have had a long time to make it very secure."

"Yes, walls, guards, and dogs. I must get into the villa to get him out."

"Impossible and suicidal."

Max walked in a circle around the priest, thinking. "Can your people find out if there is an event scheduled during the next week at the embassy?" Max said. "Maybe I can slip in, look around, and find Cattaneo. Then get him out."

"Really? Just waltz in, ask where the scientist is, and take him out? You'd be dead, or worse."

"Just find out if there is an event. I'll take it from there," Max said.

"With the Allies in Sicily, I would guess that everything is crazy at the embassy. I will ask. Maybe in this confusion we can find a way."

By the end of the day, two sources confirmed a political function. It was a welcome gathering, for the new ambassador to Rome. It would be at the embassy in three days.

Pietro was sitting outside the apartment on the front step.

"I need you to go to Signorina Norcross's villa and tell her something. Can you do that?" Max said.

"Sure, no problem."

"I want her to meet me at the bench near the obelisk with the elephant tomorrow at noon. Can you do that?"

"A hundred lire."

"You are a bandit, Pietro."

"Si, a very good bandit."

* * *

The Piazza Minerve was littered with debris. Max was smoking a cigarette when Sophie sat down next to him. She leaned in and kissed him on the cheek.

"How are your grandparents taking the news about Mussolini?" Max asked.

"Not well. They liked and respected the fool, but he dug his own grave," Sophie said. "We gave him options, and he turned away. And they don't trust Badoglio at all. For the past two weeks, fascists have reacted by wandering the streets and bashing in heads. This is far from over. What's happening in Sicily?"

"Radio talk says it's almost over," Max answered. "The Germans are being pushed north; the Italians are giving up as soon as they can find an American to surrender to. Unfortunately, all this does is reinforce the Germans' hold on Italy. We need to get Cattaneo out of the embassy."

"And how will you do that? Do you have a magic wand or something?"

"The word is that the current ambassador, von Mackensen, has been recalled to Berlin—sounds more like he's been canned. The reports, through your uncle, say that the new ambassador, Rudolf Rahn, will be given a welcoming party. People in the Vatican say that formal invitations have been delivered that request attendance by an assembly of high-ranking Church representatives. My plan is that I will attend, search through the villa, find the man, and walk him out."

"You are crazy," Sophie declared.

"Probably, but this is the best I came up with," Max said.

"Then I'll be there. As the granddaughter of one of Rome's leading citizens, it would seem appropriate."

"Can you get an invitation?"

"The real question is—why would they not invite my grandparents and me?"

Max found out the next day from Father Conti that the response was even more than he could have hoped for, and the priest was not happy.

"They invited my parents, Max," the priest said. "What the hell were you two thinking? They are too old to be a part of this charade. They might get hurt."

"I intend that no one get hurt, Father," Max said.

"The road to hell is paved with good intentions," Conti answered.

"I will be in and out before they even know he's missing. Does your man have the floor plans for the villa?"

"It is a woman; she is a chambermaid. She has worked at the embassy for more than ten years. I will get you the diagrams."

"Thank you," Max said. "I will make sure your parents are not anywhere near where I will be. In fact, they will not even recognize me."

"You make sure of that. I may be a priest, but in Italy, family comes before God."

* * *

August 12, 1943

Two days later, Max and Sophie were parked near the front gates of the Villa Wolkonsky. Max had commandeered an Italian ambulance and they were using it as a lookout. A German staff car pulled to a stop at the gate and three men stepped out.

"That's Schmidt. Is that Kesselring?" asked Max.

"Yes. The other man is General Kurt Student, Luftwaffe. Why he's here, I haven't a clue."

They watched the three men walk through the gate and disappear inside the villa grounds. The staff car idled in the street. Instead of the usual two guards at the gate, there were now six, and a bunker of sandbags had been expanded to both sides of the gates. The muzzles of well-placed and manned machine guns peeked over the wall of bags.

"Generalfeldmarschall Kesselring—this isn't good," Sophie said. "He's good, very good, a respected professional soldier, even by Hitler. He's been with Rommel in North Africa, and now he's here."

Twenty minutes later, the three officers returned to the waiting car and departed.

The invitation for the reception at the embassy was for Count Franco Conti and his wife; it also included Sophie. It was delivered direct to the villa from the embassy. Obviously, the Germans still wanted to keep relationships with the local fascist industrialists, even if Mussolini was under house arrest.

Max's invitation was through the Vatican. He would attend disguised as a monsignor who was working with another important Irish priest in the Vatican, Monsignor O'Flaherty. O'Flaherty was well known for his work hiding and then helping Jews and escaped prisoners of war flee Italy. He also had a decidedly Irish nationalistic stance when it came to Great Britain.

"I have nothing to wear," Sophie said as if telling Max would make a difference.

"That is when you are in your best light," Max said.

"Shut up. I mean it. I need a dress. This will be important, and since this time you will not be going as a German officer, you will have to find a tuxedo."

"I'm going as a monsignor."

"Not a chance. You? A Berlin-born American Jew dressed as a priest? God will punish all of us for your . . . deception."

"So be it. Cattaneo has been in the embassy for three days," Max said. "They will move him soon; we need to get him now. And this is the best and maybe our only chance."

18

Rome, The German Embassy
August 13, 1943

Max arrived at the embassy with three other priests from the Vatican and Monsignor O'Flaherty. They shook hands with the welcoming committee, all German officers, in the foyer of the villa. Then, joining a hundred other guests, they moved into the ballroom. Max, standing off to one side, watched as Sophie and her grandparents were announced and entered the room. They were shown to an area of other older couples in tuxedos and gowns. Sophie wore a black dress with dark sequins. Max was impressed.

"She is pretty, Max," Monsignor O'Flaherty said. "I met her once a few years ago. On some levels, Rome is a small town."

"How do you know I know her?"

"I know everything I can about what happens in this city, and right now it is not good. Father Conti has added to this knowledge. I suggest that when the time is right, and that will be during the speeches, that you proceed with your work. May God protect you." With that the monsignor turned and walked directly to Kesselring. He extended his hand as he approached.

"He is such a nice man," Sophie said, approaching Max. "A mystery to be sure, but important to those who need his help in Rome. Why didn't you tell me about the beard? You look funny."

"Camouflage—anything will help," Max answered.

"Don't wear it again. Are you ready?"

"As ready as I can be. I will go out the far door; the rear stairway is that way. Up one floor, then see what I can find."

A waiter wandering through the guests offered champagne. Max and Sophie walked casually around the grand salon, smiling, and briefly talking with the guests. It was a babel of languages and uniforms. Italian officers, along with some French and even Spanish officers, mixed socially with the dark German uniforms of the army, the navy, and even a few wearing the black of the *Schutzstaffel*. The Vatican was represented by a bright ecclesiastical mixture of priests, monsignors, and bishops in their red and black vestments. Two cardinals—from the political wing of the Church—dressed in their red cassocks, stood off to one side, talking with three pretty women, all guests of Italian officers. The rich sounds of a grand piano, played by a beautiful child dressed in a black dress, underscored the many conversations filling the room.

Sophie smiled. It was a perfect smile, enhanced by the deep red lipstick she had recently freshened.

"What are you grinning at?" Max asked.

"If the Allies were to drop a bomb on this building right now, they would take out much of the Mediterranean general staff of both the German and Italian armies."

They surveyed the key individuals in the room. SS-Major Kappler and the recently promoted General Karl Wolff were deep in conversation—"two very not-so-nice guys," Sophie said quietly. Field Marshal Kesselring was speaking with Pope Pius XII's senior counsel, while various officials with the Italian government hovered on the periphery. The newly appointed

German ambassador and plenipotentiary Rudolf Rahn were in conversation with the Swiss ambassador and the mayor of Rome.

Max turned his eyes toward the tall, striking Irishman in a black cassock with red trim. "How do you know the monsignor?"

"Monsignor Hugh O'Flaherty?" Sophie whispered. "An opiniated Irishman known for his decidedly strong views on the recent Irish independence from the British. He is frequently called on to be an unofficial Vatican ambassador when there are important visitors. He also has connections to the British government. I understand his chief of staff is a British major."

A commotion began down the hallway, sparking light applause that increased in volume until everyone, including Max and Sophie, were applauding the newly appointed prime minister of Italy, Pietro Badoglio. He marched into the room, hands on hips, his crisp Italian uniform impeccable with high-gloss black boots and cropped riding pants. He marched straight to Kesselring, snapped his heels, and extended his hand. Kesselring smiled and took it.

"Now I've seen it all," Max said, as the tension in the room visibly increased. "The balls of the man to walk into this lion's den. No fear, I guess."

"The Germans do not work with anyone," Sophie said, taking another glass of champagne from a passing waiter. "In time, the Nazis will run Italy. I'm guessing that Badoglio is sizing up the opposition."

"How are your grandparents?"

"I wish they hadn't come; they are a little bewildered by all this. You have ten minutes when I signal you. Find the man. I am leaving with my grandparents at ten thirty."

"Got it. You ready?" Max asked.

"Ready."

Keeping to the edges of the gathering, Max and Sophie

talked with two bishops from near Salerno. Max avoided saying anything about his supposed position at the Vatican, and the priests did not ask. He was certain, based on their outward friendliness and attention, that they were aware of his situation. Max understood how lines of allegiance were continually crossed and recrossed in this semi-occupied country.

When it was announced that the prime minister wished to make a few remarks to the new ambassador, Max smiled at Sophie, and walked to the back of the ballroom. There he followed two of the staff as they left the room with empty champagne glasses. A minute later, he was walking down the second-floor hallway.

Max had checked three rooms when a gloved hand took hold of his arm as he exited the next room.

"Monsignor. Don't I know you?"

Max turned and looked down into the eyes of Heinrich Schmidt. The German's expression was stern and unyielding, but he gradually released his grip as Max stared back at him, and then at his hand.

"I don't believe we have had the pleasure of meeting. My name is Monsignor Dominic Fallace, Senior Accounts Manager for his Holiness," he offered in Italian. "And you are?"

"SS-Obersturmbannführer Heinrich Schmidt."

"A pleasure."

"I never forget a face. I know you," Schmidt said, glaring at the bearded priest where his gaze held for a second longer than required. "Why are you up here? Whom do you work with?" he demanded.

"As I said, I am the senior accountant with the Vatican and have been there for five years. I am looking for the bathroom. The one downstairs was occupied—a little too much champagne," Max replied smoothly. "This is an excellent reception. I thank you, and please extend our thanks to the ambassador and Field Marshal Kesselring. Good night. I'm sorry, but I forgot your name."

"Schmidt, SS-Obersturmbannführer Heinrich Schmidt."

"Of course you are. Sorry about that. Again, thank you."

"I suggest that you return to the reception. I will escort you."

Schmidt turned and began to walk away from Max. Max watched and with his free hand opened the door next to him. At the click of the lock, Schmidt turned around and reached for his pistol.

"It's you. I saw you at the train station. What the hell are you—"

Before he could finish, Max slammed his fist into the man's jaw, instantly knocking him out. Max caught the Nazi before he hit the floor. He dragged the man into the open bedroom and dropped him in a chair. Looking around, he spotted long silk tassels hanging from the window curtains. With his penknife he cut cords and bound the hands and feet of Schmidt to the chair. He also gagged and blindfolded the man. When done, he locked the door behind him and began to search the rest of the bedrooms. The last bedroom was locked—it was the first secured door on the floor. A good push with his shoulder broke it open. Massimo Cattaneo sat at a desk. Piles of papers filled the surface. He looked at Max, confusion etched on his face.

"Who the hell are you? What are you doing here?"

19

Rome, the German Embassy
August 13, 1943

Max said, "Here to rescue you," as he crossed the room. "Get your things; we must go."

"You, you are the American, and a priest? What are you doing here?"

"Certainly not to hear your confession," Max said as he stripped out of the black cassock. "Put this on." He handed the robes to the physicist.

"You—you are a Nazi!" Cattaneo said, looking at Max.

Max, stripping off the beard, walked across the room in his colonel's SS uniform. He'd attached his hat to a spot on his belt; the fullness of the black cassock had helped to cover the uniform and hat.

"Lots of surprises, Massimo. But if we don't get out of here right now, both of us will be dead by morning." Max went to the window, which looked down on the front portico. Cars were arriving. He saw the Berlinetta Fiat; a valet stood next to it. Sophie was helping her grandparents cross the gravel of the parking court.

"We must go," Max said. "It's now or I will leave you here

and the Germans can figure out what to do with your body."

"You wouldn't."

"Do not test me."

Max looked out the door. Schmidt was maybe a hundred feet and four rooms away. Max hoped that he stayed knocked out for another five minutes. There was a stairway next to the bedroom—the sign read *AUSGANG*.

"Down, now, go."

He pushed Cattaneo through the door and down the stairs; they passed no one as they went down the two floors. The door, he had been told, opened into a short corridor. One direction led to the kitchens, the other to the front parking area. For all Max knew, when he opened the door it could be into one of the sandbag bunkers full of guys named Fritz and Adolf. He looked at Cattaneo.

"I could use your blessing, Father," Max said with a grin.

"Che cosa? Non capisco?"

Max pushed the door open; he was immediately hit by low branches from a large shrub, not a Nazi in sight.

"Go, that way. There's a Fiat sitting next to the curb about fifty feet away. Walk natural. Go straight for the car. I will be right behind you."

"Is that gun loaded?" Cattaneo asked, seeing the pistol in Max's hand.

"Yes. Go."

They crossed the lawn and reached the car at the same time Sophie arrived with her grandparents. Two soldiers were helping the Contis.

"Thank you, gentlemen. My grandparents are fine now," Sophie said. "And thank you, Father, for the evening. I will drop you at the church on the way."

The soldiers noticed Max and immediately went to attention.

"Thank you, men," Max said. "Father, please take the front

seat. Please help the count into the back, men. Signorina Conti . . ." Max held the rear door open.

"Thank you, Colonel Stoltz," she said to Max. Then, in a whisper, "I will get you for this. If you hurt this car."

"Thank you, Signorina." Max was last into the car. He followed a large Mercedes out the gates, past the machine guns, and into the summer night of Rome. One block from the embassy, he accelerated until he was weaving in amongst the light traffic. He had one eye on the road and the other on the rearview mirror, fully expecting to see the lights of German police following them. They passed the Basilica di San Giovanni in Laterano, down the Via Dell'ambia Aradam to the Piazza di Porta Metronia and the Via Drusso. They entered through the Porta San Sebastiano and drove the narrow road to the villa's entry. Max exhaled; he hadn't taken a breath for five minutes.

Max parked the Fiat in front of the stairway.

"It is good to see you again, Colonel Stoltz," Count Conti said as he helped his wife from the car. "We missed you at the reception."

"I was involved with some work with the Generalfeldmarschall—never a moment's peace. You look divine, Countess."

"Thank you, young man," the countess said. "And the monsignor, we have not met."

"Grandmother, this is Monsignor Mazzetti," Sophie said. "He is a friend of Uncle Guido. I promised him a nightcap before he returns to the university."

"And what university is that?" the countess asked as they climbed the steps.

"Sapienza," Cattaneo said before Sophie could stop him. "I teach ancient religious texts and scrolls. I also dabble in the sciences a little." He gave Sophie a smile and a wink.

At the top of the stairs, an older man met them. When he saw Max and Cattaneo, he gave a sour frown to the pair.

"Colonel, this is our butler, Signor Luciano," Sophie said.

"He has been with the family for more than thirty years."

"Signor Luciano," Max said as he passed the butler.

"Signor Luciano, these are friends." Sophie went into the villa; everyone followed.

In the living room, the Contis said goodnight and their goodbyes to Cattaneo and the colonel. Then, with the assistance of Luciano, the count and countess proceeded to the grand staircase and their bedrooms on the second floor.

Sophie went to the bar and poured the three of them a drink.

Max told them about Schmidt and how he left him at the embassy.

"Drink it fast. We do not have much time," she said. "Once Schmidt's found, he will begin to chase down every lead. My guess—we will be first."

"The car, ma'am?" Luciano asked when he returned to the living room.

"Yes, the car. Wake one of the boys and have them take the car and park it in the garage at the factory. If nothing happens, then we can bring it back in a few days. I do not want it here. Please make sure my grandparents stay upstairs. We are going to the cellar; I will return shortly."

"Yes, madam. Will there be anything else?"

"If the authorities arrive, please buzz. I will come up through the library stairs. Keep them here in the entry if you can. Do not get in their way. They will be very upset."

"Yes, ma'am."

"It will be only be a matter of time until this whole thing blows up," Max said. "Schmidt will question the guards; they will connect the dots and put us in the car with you. We need to get out of here."

"Luciano, please clean these glasses and remove them. Max and Massimo, follow me," Sophie said and walked back through the villa to the kitchen. There, a hallway went to the rear of the villa. Off to one side, a door. When opened, it led to a stairway. "Down here."

The stairs were stone and narrow. At two places, they turned sharply forming a bottleneck.

"Kill zone?" Max said.

"I hope it does not come to that," Sophie said.

"Kill zone?" Cattaneo repeated. "What's that?"

"Keep moving," Sophie said.

At the base of the stairs, she led the two men through a labyrinth of shelves stacked with wine, old cheeses, barrels of what smelled like pickles, and household goods that spanned more than a hundred years. Reaching the back of the room, they faced a stone wall. She grabbed one of the light stanchions mounted on the wall and pulled it. A rough piece of the wall, about one meter by two meters, swung silently out.

"In there."

Beyond was a large room, with tables and chairs, shelves filled with canned goods, bags of rice, flour, and sugar. Again, there was the odor of pickles and vinegar.

"Emergency food stores and someone must love pickles," Max said.

"The vinegar defeats the noses of the dogs, makes them almost worthless down here."

"And what is 'here'?" Cattaneo asked.

"The underworld. It is from here that the Romans will take back their city."

On the far wall a door opened, and three men walked out. Each carried a German Schmeisser machine pistol.

"Luca, Marco, and Angelo, I would like to introduce you to Max Adler, and regardless of his evil uniform, he is an American; and the priest is Massimo Cattaneo, an Italian scientist. They are my friends."

"An SS officer and a priest—there has to be some kind of fucking joke here," Luca said as he raised his weapon. "Tie them up."

"No, they will not be tied up," Sophie said. The three noticed that she now held a large-caliber Beretta. It was pointed at Luca. "They are my friends. We just left Kesselring and his senior officers at the embassy. Max just kidnapped this guy from under their noses. We will be receiving unwanted German guests within the hour. I want these two out of here. We've kept this place secret for half a century. I do not want it compromised tonight; it is too valuable to the resistance."

20

Heinrich Schmidt stood in front of the two soldiers. Behind Schmidt sat Generals Kesselring and Student, and the new ambassador, Rahn. The officer of the guard stood at attention behind his two men.

"Let me get this straight," Schmidt said looking at the men. "You helped the two elderly Italians, Count and Countess Conti, to their car. With them was another woman, who we believe, according to the guest list, is their granddaughter, Sophie Norcross. When the valet brought up their car, two others, a Schutzstaffel colonel and a priest, joined them. They proceeded to get in the car and leave. And nothing about this seemed strange?"

The men, obviously shaken by being called on this seemingly innocuous issue, said in unison, "No, sir."

"What do you mean no?"

"It did not seem strange," the corporal on the right answered. "We had assisted a number of priests and other senior officers from the Italian army and even Spain in acquiring their automobiles and assisting them into their vehicles. In fact, the automobile that left just before the Fiat was a Mercedes filled with a bishop, two priests, and two young women who we assumed were hitching a ride."

A snicker rose from one of the generals behind Schmidt. He failed to see the humor.

An hour before, after successfully knocking over a large table and lamp that made a horrific noise, the bound and gagged Heinrich Schmidt had been discovered. It was thirty minutes after the reception had ended. When they searched the embassy, they discovered that Cattaneo was missing. Furious, he wanted to find who had taken the scientist, and even more to the point, he wanted to know how they knew where he was and why they wanted him. But mostly he wanted this officer who the woman, in the parking court, called Colonel Stoltz.

"Why did you detain the man, this scientist, Major?" Kesselring asked.

"I am not a liberty to say. The request came directly from Berlin," Schmidt answered.

"I understand that he is a professor from the Sapienza University—a physicist?"

"I cannot confirm that."

"The detail officer you employed for the man's apprehension has told me about the operation. Are you saying that the professor is not who he is?"

"Again, I am not a liberty to confirm the man's identity."

"You are conducting an operation in my house," the new ambassador said, standing up, "in a manner that has put the security of the Reich at risk. This priest you saw, who you now claim is an SS colonel, or whatever he is, had the run of our embassy for God knows how long. You have no idea who he was, what he's seen, or possibly compromised. You said you recognized this priest from an incident at the Stazione Termini a few weeks back. Then he was an SS officer, now a priest. Damnit man, what have you done?"

"I am following my orders, Ambassador. You will have to talk to Berlin to find out specifically why they want the professor."

Kesselring stood and walked across the room to Schmidt. "Schmidt, I have too much to deal with right now. We have lost Sicily, the Allies are about to strike the mainland, the king and his idiots have Mussolini, the Führer's friend, in prison, and General Student has his orders to proceed with an operation to try and rescue the fool. And now I must deal with this bullshit of yours. Go, get out of my sight. Do what you must do, but do not cause me any more problems. If you do, I will make sure that you are on the next plane to Berlin, or worse. Then you can explain your failures to Reichsführer Himmler in person. You are excused."

Schmidt saluted the Generalfeldmarschall and the other officers and left the office. He had not wanted this assignment, this Cattaneo affair. He had his orders, orders that came directly from the Reichsführer. This operation about the physicist was an annoyance and had now turned into a disaster. But it also pointed to something else, something that he did not want to discuss with Kesselring or any of the others in the room. The Americans and the Allies wanted this man, and the leaders in Berlin knew this and anticipated it. And even more unsettling, the Americans had people in Rome capable of infiltrating the German ranks at the highest levels. How else did they get passes, invitations, and access to senior fascist industrialists, the Church, and maybe even politicians? He knew where to start—at the villa of Count and Countess Conti. A little pressure there might put him on the trail of this scientist.

* * *

At the Sebastiano Villa, midnight
August 13, 1943
"Secret passageways and catacombs under Rome," Max said.

"What else have you been hiding?"

"For more than ten years," Sophie said, "there have been groups opposed to the government of Mussolini. He destroyed or murdered most of the opposition after he took power. Even after the collapse of the most violent socialist and communist factions twenty years ago, there have remained those that believed that the future of Italy was not communist or fascist. These men have waited a long time for this—they are what's left of the centrist Italian People's Party. They have the support from the Catholic Church. They are called the Christian Democrats."

"Yes, loyalty to Moscow and Stalin—that's not going to go well with the Americans," Max replied. "But the Catholic Church? Really? I thought it has tried to stay out of politics."

"Three and a half weeks ago, the day the bombs that destroyed San Lorenzo and killed my mother, the only leader to appear and comfort us was the pope," Cattaneo said, inserting himself into the conversation. "His Holiness stood not five feet from me. So yes, I believe that Italy needs the Church, especially when this war is over. It's obvious from the riots of last week when over eighty were killed during the demonstrations celebrating Mussolini's arrest. There will be civil war, like what nearly destroyed Spain. God save us from ourselves."

"I need to get this man out of Italy," Max said to the three men standing in the room. "He is critical to the Allies' effort to end this war. Will you help me?"

From somewhere in the room, a series of short buzzes filled the air.

"What's that?" Max asked.

"The alarm; we have guests," Sophie said. "They got here quicker than I thought. That's Luciano's signal if there is trouble upstairs. I need to go. Luca, get them out of here, someplace safe. I will find you later."

Sophie disappeared through the short tunnel they'd just

entered. Max heard the stone door slide back into place.

"First you will change and get out of that evil uniform," Luca said. "There are clothes on the shelf there. There are also boots."

"Do not lose this uniform. I may need it," Max said.

"Yes, and I will make sure you are buried in it. We will leave as soon as you are changed."

"And where are we going?"

"Signorina Conti says you need to get to the coast. I will make that happen."

"How?"

"This tunnel is an old buried aqueduct," Luca said. "It extends for thousands of meters in two directions. The closest exit is in a church across from the old Roman baths. The other direction leads to a dry cistern that fed the system."

"Where's that?" Max said.

"Out beyond the San Callixtus catacombs. It currently bypasses the German encampments."

"How far?"

"Two thousand meters, all underground. There are secondary exits, but they are unsecured. Callixtus is at least secured and hidden inside the entry to the catacombs. The Germans do not know about this. There we can move you to a safe house. Then, to the coast if that is where you need to go."

"Jesus," Cattaneo said. "You said the other direction is the baths?"

"Yes, the Termini di Caracalla. It opens into the cellar of Saint Nereo church. That is where we came from."

"I know that place; it is in the middle of the city."

"How far?" Max asked.

"Maybe six hundred meters," Luca answered.

"We go that way. I'm claustrophobic," Cattaneo said.

"Yes, Father," Angelo said.

"I am not a priest," Cattaneo answered.

Max studied the young man called Angelo in the dim light of the room.

"How old are you?" Max asked as he changed. He moved the Luger he carried from the SS holster to his pocket.

"Sixteen," Angelo said.

Max then turned to Luca. "Awfully young for this work."

"Maybe, but he has killed a dozen Germans since they murdered his parents. The Germans say ten Italians will die for every German soldier killed. Angelo vows to kill twenty Germans in return for his parents. We go, now."

* * *

Midnight, the Villa, August 13, 1943

Sophie walked down the hallway and crossed the entry to the ornate and intricately carved front doors of the villa. Luciano stood off to one side, carefully straightening the piece of tapestry that hid the button to the alarm buzzer.

"I told them to be patient, Signorina," Luciano said. "But the Germans have been insistent. They will break down the door."

"Open the door. It will be fine," she said.

As soon as it opened, Major Schmidt stormed into the vestibule followed by six of his soldiers. All wore the sharp-edged SS on their right lapels.

"I apologize for the intrusion, Signora Conti," Schmidt said with a slight nod.

"It's Signorina, Major. Why the hell have you broken into our home at this hour?"

Schmidt pointed to three of the men. "Check this floor. Leave no room uninspected. Find them. You three upstairs, the same."

"This is unacceptable. I will talk with the Generalfeldmarschall. I just left him and the ambassador not an hour ago. I'll see that you—"

"Shut up. An hour ago, you were seen with two men leaving the ambassador's residence. Where are they?"

"Yes, one was SS-Standartenführer Stoltz, the other was Monsignor Mazzetti. They were guests of the Reich at the reception, like my grandparents."

With the mention of her grandparents, a scream came from upstairs.

"If your men have harmed my grandparents . . ." Sophie said and ran toward the stairway. Coming down the stairs were two soldiers; the count and countess were ahead of them. Countess Conti was in her bedclothes and was crying. She held dearly to the railing, taking one step at a time.

"You are devils, all of you," Count Conti said as he held his wife's arm.

"Take them into that room, sit them down," Schmidt said, and, glaring at Sophie, added, "And you with them."

When they were settled, the third soldier from upstairs reported that they found no one else. They even checked the attic. Moments later, the three searching the main floor reported the same.

"The cellar?" Schmidt asked.

"We are headed there now," the sergeant answered.

Schmidt turned back to Sophie and asked, "A colonel in the Schutzstaffel—you said he was a Colonel Stoltz?"

"Yes. I met him in Madrid. He has just arrived here in Rome; he was a Reich liaison or something to Generalissimo Franco."

"A very pleasant and handsome man," the countess added, a quiver to her voice. "He is one of you, but nicer."

"He is not one of us; he is an imposter. And the priest?"

"His name is Mazzetti. He teaches at the Sapienza University—old manuscripts and scrolls," Sophie said. "We do not know him. He arrived with your comrade Stoltz. All I know is what he told us during the drive here to the villa."

"Where are they?" Schmidt yelled.

"I don't know," Sophie answered in return. "I let them take the Fiat. Colonel Stoltz said he would have it returned in the morning."

"And you trust him?"

"Yes, why not?" Sophie said. "He is, after all, a loyal member of the SS and a pleasant fellow at that. Why wouldn't I? Is there something about him that you are not telling us? Did I mistakenly put my grandparents at risk?"

Another soldier came into the room.

"There is no car here, sir. None matching the description we were given at the embassy. Shall we continue looking?"

Before Schmidt could answer, the six other SS soldiers returned.

"Nothing, sir. The basement is empty. There were resent steps and obvious disturbances in the dust, but nothing there now."

"Major, we had a celebration a few weeks ago. It was for the return of my granddaughter. People were in and out of the basement all evening. My granddaughter had—" Count Conti began to say.

Interrupting and cutting him off, Sophie said, "—just returned from Spain. I was there for a week." She looked at her grandfather, who stopped and did not add anything more.

"It is a difficult time to travel, is it not?" Schmidt said.

"Other than a bandit attack in Spain and having to travel at night, it wasn't too unpleasant. Mussolini has made the trains arrive on schedule, you know."

Ignoring the snide remark about Mussolini, Schmidt continued, "Do you know where this Colonel Stoltz is staying?"

"How would I know that?" Sophie said, but had an idea. "I find his company enjoyable, which is more than I can say for this invasion. However, he did mention the bar at the Grand Hotel de la Minerva—maybe he is staying there. Has this man done something wrong? Why are you after him? He is, after all, one of your own."

Ignoring the woman, Schmidt looked at the count and countess. "You are warned. If you had anything to do with these men escaping from the embassy, I will see that all of you are thrown into Regina Coeli prison, or worse. Harboring enemies of the Reich is punishable by a firing squad."

Sophie's grandmother gave an audible scream.

"Escaping from the embassy, these men? How would we know?" Sophie said. "Your soldiers did nothing to stop them. Maybe you should talk to them."

Sophie watched the color rise in the Nazi's face. Then he turned to his troop.

"*Raus, schnell, jetzt!*" Schmidt ordered. The men went back out the entry doors and down the steps to the waiting truck. He turned back to Sophie. "Remember what I said. I do not care who your grandparents are, and I will find out everything about you. Even the least amount of suspicion will require me to again interview your grandparents, and it will not be here, but at the prison. You look fit, but they, your grandparents, I am not so sure. So be very careful about this charade. I am leaving two men here to watch the villa; it is for your safety. Since Prime Minister Mussolini's unfortunate removal, Rome has become very dangerous. They are here for your protection."

Sophie watched the truck and sedan disappear down the dark road toward the Porta San Sebastiano. She knew she had dodged a bullet. She hoped that she could duck the next one.

21

After climbing up the stairs from the aqueduct and the catacomb, the church's interior was dark. If it weren't for the hundreds of votive candles offering their feeble light, it would have been impossible to see. They moved quickly to the front vestibule.

"Wait here," Marco said and slipped out the door. He returned a minute later.

"It is prepared. Signorina Conti did make the call. The truck is there too. We go."

"Go where?" Max asked.

"Here is what's happening, *idiota*! I have other things to do, like kill Germans and fascists, but I owe a debt to Signorina Conti. So, there's a truck out there—in its back are coffins. Some are empty, some not so much, so be careful which one you choose. You two will climb into your own little box, then I will drive to Ostia where you will be buried and never heard from again."

Max slipped his hand around the Luger in his pocket. Angel began to laugh.

"Americano! Don't you think Luca would make a great comedian?" Marco said. "He makes me laugh. Look. I have tears in my eyes; he is so funny."

"Yes, he's a real Jerry Colonna," Max said.

"Colonna, I love that guy," Luca said.

"I take it we are not going to be buried," Cattaneo said.

"Sadly, no," Luca said. "But you wouldn't be the first. When we reach the port, and God help us make sure it's still dark, you will be taken to a fishing boat. Then if the proper signals are received, the boat will meet an American destroyer thirty kilometers out in the sea. Our part is done when you are put on that boat."

The stench of death hung around the back of the truck as the two climbed into the rough caskets laid out in the back.

"Those aren't empty," Cattaneo said.

"No," Luca said. "They are unfortunates found in the rubble of San Lorenzo who will be making their last trip. They will be buried in Ostia. I have made this sad trip at least twenty times in the last few weeks. I'm an undertaker by trade. There will be guard posts, but the guards change. Be quiet—play dead." Angelo snickered. "I will tap on the box three times; then you can get out. When we get to the port, move quickly. The boat must leave with the outgoing tide. It is not much of a tide, but with the flow of the river, they will drift until they can start the engine. Be quiet the whole time."

The road was the Via Cristoforo Colombo, the same road on which the bus had brought Max to Rome just five weeks earlier. Max tried to get comfortable with his six-foot-four-inch frame stuffed into a box built to house a smaller guest. Every bounce and pothole was like a punch to his kidneys. He knew he should have put Cattaneo in one of the boxes, wished him good luck, and walked away. But he owed the physicist. The man was here because he believed in what Max told him. Blind faith. *Hell*, he thought, *I'm not sure I believe in what I'm do-*

ing either. An hour later, the truck came to a sudden stop. He heard another motor, then muted, inaudible conversation, then the increased noise from the new motor and the clashing of gears. In moments, it faded. Then there were three taps on the coffin's lid. Max pushed the top upward and sat up. He heard Cattaneo doing the same thing from his coffin.

"The driver of that truck, an old friend, told me there's a new roadblock ahead," Luca said. "It's SS. Never been SS, usually Italians. We had some fascist bandits, but never SS. You must get out here—we are about a mile from the port. Walk parallel to the road. Watch me as I move down the road, and stay in the shadows. After we pass the roadblock, look for my flashlight, then get back onboard."

They did as they were told. The roadblock was two armored vehicles, and by Max's guess, six soldiers. Max and Cattaneo hid fifty feet off the road. Behind him he imagined farm fields, but adjacent to the road were pine trees and oleanders. If it were daylight, there was nothing to hide behind; they would be found. The guards had gas lanterns suspended over the road. The vehicles were pinched in at the front making an attempt to drive through difficult, if not suicidal. The shadows of deep drainage ditches flanked both sides of the road. It was a perfect location to trap an oncoming vehicle from either direction.

"*Fermatevi*," a loud and commanding voice yelled. A lamp swung back and forth across the gap between the vehicles. Max watched as Luca slowed to a stop.

A conversation in Italian began; it became heated.

"What's Luca saying?" Max whispered.

"They want their papers; Luca is giving them to him. They want to know what's in the boxes, and where is he going. Luca told him bodies for the cemetery at Ostia. The officer wanted to know why they weren't buried in Rome. Luca said he's just the driver, he takes them where he's told. He wants them to open the coffins. Luca said they were sick, died from disease; you sure you want that?"

"*Erschiefs die Särge*," the officer yelled in German to one of the soldiers.

Three bursts of automatic gunfire shattered the still, moist air.

Cattaneo silently laughed, then continued. "Luca asked if he felt better now that he's killed the dead. Then Luca asked if he wants to check to see if they really are dead. The guard then said something about Luca's parentage. They are getting back onboard."

Three hundred meters farther down the road, the truck slid to a stop. Max saw the flashlight click on and off. They came out of the blackness.

"Bastards. Good thing you got out," Luca said, "or I *would* be burying you in Ostia."

Max and Cattaneo rode in the back of the truck; the foul smell of the dead never left them.

The aroma of the river and ocean filled his nose before he saw it in the dim light. At the end of a wooden pier, a fishing boat was tied. A man sat on the gunnel smoking a cigarette. Max, Cattaneo, and the three resistance fighters walked down the steep dirt slope that rose up along the river. Marco slipped and landed on his butt; Angelo snickered again. Max was positive that there was a screw lose in the kid's brain.

"Two? I was told there was one," the man with the cigarette said.

"Change in plans," Max said.

"Twice the money? I want it now," the man said.

"Do you honestly think that I'd carry money with me?" Max said. "Luca knows where it is and who has it. You will get it from them. I'm going to the American destroyer with the passenger, then you will bring me back. If I don't make it back, Luca will make sure you don't get a penny. In fact, he might make sure you never smuggle another refugee or pilot. If we all don't make it back, who the fuck cares. *Capisci?*"

"Just take him to the American ship, Aldo," Luca said. "I know you have four others onboard—with them that's six. A good day's work. I will get the money before the next trip."

"Who are the others?" Cattaneo asked.

"An American pilot shot down over Aranova and a family of Jews from Rome—the husband and wife and their daughter." The captain shined a flashlight on his watch. "It will be light in an hour; we go now. I want to be a dozen kilometers off the beach when the sun rises. I don't want a howitzer shell up my ass for target practice."

"You don't have to go. I'll be fine," Cattaneo said to Max.

"My job was to make sure you get into American hands. I don't trust these people an inch. I'm going—they think this is all a game. We know it's not."

"You, Max Adler, are full of surprises," Cattaneo said.

The scientist and OSS captain climbed onboard and took seats at the stern. Another man came out of the shadows of the companionway from the bow. When he got close enough, Max waved his own flashlight in the man's face. He was really a boy, maybe Pietro's age. The boy pulled the lines in. Then quietly said, "Okay." In minutes the boat slowly drifted away from the riverbank and out into the main flow of the river. The truck, the stench of the dead, and the shore quickly disappeared into the night.

22

Ostia, the Tiber River
August 14, 1943

The fishing boat was the *Santa Maria*—she was about fifteen meters long, an open deck in the stern, and a small cabin amidships. The three Jews sat in the open area of the foredeck, forward of the cabin. The American pilot sat near the cabin smoking a cigarette. The engine, a two-cylinder diesel, pounded away at a top speed that Max guessed to be six or seven miles an hour. If the destroyer was where he was told it would be, they had a trip of at least six or seven hours. He checked his pockets: pistol, flashlight, and one pack of cigarettes. He hoped it would be enough.

As the light rose to the east, the pilot stood and walked back to Max and Cattaneo. He wore a fleece-lined leather flyers jacket; he was probably the warmest person on the boat.

"Captain Ralph Bowen, US Army Air Corps. What's your gig?" he asked, putting his hand out.

Max took his hand. "Max Adler, captain, US Army Intelligence," he said, telling a half-truth. "This guy is Jules Verne, an important scientist. I'm escorting him to the ship. Doesn't speak English."

"Scientist? Interesting. I fly bombers—was shot down last week over some town north of Rome. Lucky, I guess. Parachuted into a monastery. They got me to some guys connected to the Catholic Church, and here I am. Ocean cruise. Don't know where my crew got to."

"Luck? No shit. I've met a few pilots who've been hiding for months, just waiting for the chance to get out. Most don't want to end up in an Italian prison camp."

"Or German, I get that."

A tall, gaunt man walked toward the two Americans. In halting English, he said, "I'm Julian Panaro—my wife, Susan, and my daughter, Freida. I was a banker in Rome."

"Making a run for it?" Bowen said.

Panaro looked around. "Run? Where?"

"That's okay, Signor Panaro, no problem," Max added.

The captain came out of the small cabin and addressed the group in English. "Welcome to my *Santa Maria*. There's an inconvenient pot to piss in up front, no *bagno*—you tell the ladies how to use it. Sorry. You guys can piss over the rail or in the pot. There's wine and water inside the cabin. Also, some bread and cheese, not much more. I'm a taxi service not the *Conte di Savoia*. If we are lucky, and the seas don't get rough, or the German or Italian fighter planes don't blow us out of the fucking water, and the Americans are where I was told they are, we should be good. My biggest concern is the German patrol boat that works the coast here; sometimes she's out here, and sometimes she's not. The captain is an asshole. He might take a shot to scare us; he has never hit a damn thing that I know about. But he can do thirty knots—chances of outrunning him are zero. So, we pray." He crossed himself.

"What do we call you, Captain?" Panaro asked.

"I'm Demetri. The boy is my son Sextus. The sixth of my kids, but the smartest. He's working for me."

Past the cabin and down the rail, Max watched the girl,

maybe ten or eleven, go to the side of the boat and vomit. He wondered if this were the fate of all the passengers.

The sea was glass with a soft swell; luckily, the child was the only one to get sick. Sextus stretched a red canvas canopy over the foredeck on supports for shade. Even though it became hot as the day grew older, the breeze of their forward progress kept it comfortable. About noon, the captain tapped Max on the shoulder. He'd been dozing.

"To the starboard, maybe five miles, is the destroyer. Let's pray she is the one I've done business with—she's the USS *Rowan*. If not, well, nice knowing you."

They closed in on the destroyer; it was the *Rowan*. The transfer was quick. A small boat was lowered from the destroyer. It motored across the hundred meters that the *Santa Maria* maintained.

"If I get too close, they will think me a *bomba*, maybe blow me out of the water. So, we stay here," the captain said.

The tender maneuvered next to the fishing boat. Two armed sailors jumped into the boat. In seconds, the Panaros were loaded, then the pilot. Max shook Cattaneo's hand.

"If you get to Chicago, go to Pompeii's Grotto—it is a restaurant owned by some good friends. Tell them I sent you."

To Max's surprise, Cattaneo gave him a hug. "*Buona fortuna*, Max Adler. And maybe someday you should marry that girl. I think she likes you."

They did not wait for the tender to reach the destroyer before Demetri turned the *Santa Maria* back toward the coast. Max stood at the stern, watched the tender pull alongside and onload its passengers. He wondered if he'd ever see the physicist again.

A bottle was handed to him. He took a long drink of the wine.

"That was easy," Demetri said. "Too easy. We will be cautious going back. I want to arrive at night, so the trip back will be slower. Maybe fewer questions when we reach the river. Go get some sleep, American."

Max found an uncomfortable pile of canvas sails. The boat used sails when it could; fuel was hard and costly. What seemed like a minute later, he was kicked on the soles of his boots. It was evening and getting dark.

"*Abbiamo visitatori*," Sextus said.

"*Chi? Dove?*" Max answered.

The boy pointed over the port gunnel. Max saw the shape of a fast-approaching boat.

"The patrol boat," Demetri said in English. "Maybe he won't see us, or even better, ignore us."

Neither happened. The boat turned and headed directly at them.

"Now what?" Max said.

"You and Sextus are crew. We were out looking for fish."

"Wasn't very good," Max said.

"Such is the luck of a fisherman."

An explosion and a fountain of water detonated a hundred feet ahead of them; then another, even closer.

"I think he wants you to stop," Max said.

The fishing boat began to slow. Another volley of shells exploded near the sides of the boat. It continued to slow.

"Shit. I'm stopping, fuckers," Demetri yelled.

Two more shells hit the water near the stern, then another ripped a portion of the stern away.

"God damn it, for the love of God . . ."

Machine gun bullets ripped through the hull of the boat; splintered wood exploded from each impact. Then the cabin was hit, shredding the panels. The roof was torn open. When Max crawled across the deck to the cabin, he saw that Demetri had been nearly severed in two—his head was half gone. Sextus came in from behind Max.

"Don't look. Your father is dead. We have to get off the

boat."

More slugs smashed into the hull.

"Now, over the side."

"I can't swim."

"No matter. Put on the life vest—we go now. I'll take care of you."

They slipped over the side. Max took one of the lines from the kid's life vest and hooked it over his shoulder. He pulled hard with his arms, opening a distance between them and the burning boat. Behind them, more shells from the larger gun blasted the hull. One shell found the fuel tank. The diesel didn't explode, but the burning fuel rapidly began to consume the *Santa Maria*.

Max kept swimming. The darkness now hid them. The attacking craft slowly maneuvered itself past the burning boat.

Sextus, his head above the warm water, looked back and said, "It's not the usual Italian patrol boat—it's a German E-boat. Only seen one of those. Damn those men."

The sleek boat was twice the length of the burning *Santa Maria*. It fired another volley of shells into the fishing boat. It began to sink. Max kept swimming away from the two boats. From high over the E-boat's cabin, a spotlight swept the water. Only luck would save them from either being captured or just shot where they floated.

After five minutes, the *Santa Maria* was awash and almost gone. The E-boat, now acting disinterested, slowly passed between the two swimmers and the sinking hull. The roar of its engines filled the night as it accelerated away from the crime. A small fire, where the ship disappeared, still burned on the surface.

"How far off the coast do you think we are?" Max asked.

"Papa said maybe two miles; too far to swim."

"Don't worry about that. We swim; I'll tow you. Maybe somebody saw the fire, and maybe they will send out a boat."

"Maybe."

Max used every skill to keep moving to the east. He kept the north star to his left; he'd sweep his hands out and pull them back, sweep and pull, slow and steady. He remembered his hours in the pool and the breaststroke. The boy began to mumble. Max continued to sweep and pull. He had no idea of the time, but he never lost sight of the star. Slow and steady.

Ahead he thought he saw a flash, a flicker. He put it off to his imagination, then another flash, too low for a star. Slow and steady. Then the light became steady itself. It was a lantern, and it continued directly toward him.

He yelled. "Here, over here!"

The boy woke from his silence. "*Qui, qui, aiuto, aiutaci!*"

There was no sound when the sharp bow of a rowboat appeared. It almost passed over them. Max yelled again. Hands, huge hands, reached over and grabbed the boy, and pulled him into the boat. Then they reached for and pulled Max over the gunnel. A bottle was put into his mouth, and fresh, clean water filled his mouth. He coughed and spat it out. Then he tried again; this time it went down.

"*Sei dannatamente fortunato*," a voice said. A lamp was held high. Max could see Sextus. The boy was looking at him and smiling.

Yes, they were lucky, damn lucky.

* * *

The two men in the rowboat pulled hard and fast. Max just laid in the bottom of the hull and looked up at the stars. It was all surreal, so strange, so bizarre. Their rescuers asked a few questions. Sextus talked to them. He knew them. They had seen the fire, heard the gunfire, and they went out to see if there were survivors. He knew they were lucky. Then he thought of Demetri and how totally unnecessary the attack by the Germans was. At least Cattaneo and the rest had made it to safety—one small favor.

The boat slid onto the fine gravel of the beach. Max climbed out and walked across the narrow shingle to the road. One of the men followed them.

"Ostia?" Max asked in English.

"There," the man said, also in English. He was pointing across the narrow mouth of the Tiber River. "Ostia."

"Thank you."

The boy also said thank you, then turned to Max. "I must go home now; I must tell my mother. This will break her heart."

"I understand," Max said. He hugged the boy, who then walked away.

"Americano?" one of the rowers asked.

"Yes."

"You friend of Luca, the undertaker?"

"Yes, the undertaker," Max said.

"Si, si. We all know Luca. I will call him. He will come and get you."

"How can I repay you?"

"This is what we do—we fishermen. Someday I will need help, and there will be someone to rescue me. Signor Americano, all you need to do to make us even is to throw the fucking Germans out. Simple, yes?"

In the early light of the sunrise, Max could see a smile that warmed his cold wet body. Yes, it was a debt he would try his damnedest to repay.

23

Rome, the Campo Marzio District
August 15, 1943

Luca slowed the truck at the intersection. Max shook the man's hand and climbed out. His exhaustion was thick; he felt like he was still swimming through an ocean of molasses. Each step was beyond his effort.

He knocked on the door of the apartment hoping that Kent or even Pietro was there. He had no defense; his Luger was on the bottom of the Tyrrhenian Sea. When the door opened, Sophie grabbed him by the shoulders as he stumbled through the doorway.

"We thought you were dead," Sophie said. Kent stood directly behind her. He took an arm and slid Max over his shoulder. The three stumbled down the hallway.

"Cattaneo made it. I got him on the destroyer. I almost died on the way back," Max said. "The boat was sunk, shot out from under us, the captain killed. Shit—the whole thing is so fucked. I'm exhausted."

Kent slid a glass of wine in front of Max. He slowly drank it all.

"But you, you are okay? What happened at the villa?"

Sophie told him; Max could barely keep his eyes open. He nodded, especially when he heard that her parents were okay.

"Good. I'm glad that bastard didn't blow the villa up. Give me an hour. I'll be good."

Max found the couch and lay down. Even in the August heat, Sophie spread a blanket over the man. In a moment, he was asleep.

It was dark outside the window when Max slowly opened his eyes. The sound of muffled voices carried up the hallway. Sophie walked into the room. Max swung his legs out and stood unsteadily.

"I don't think a canon going off would have woken you," she said.

"What time is it? Seems my watch has stopped." He looked again and saw the water sloshing around inside the crystal.

"It's 9:30 p.m. You got about six hours of sleep."

"Good to go then," Max said. "Who was at the door?"

"One of Pietro's friends. He says that the Germans picked the boy up."

Stunned, Max looked at Kent who had followed Sophie into the room. "When did they pick him up?"

"This morning. They think one of the other kids ratted him out. They caught him a block from the Spanish Steps. He was just walking the street."

"Fuck. We have to get out of here, and that means right now," Max said.

"He won't say anything," Sophie said.

"He's fifteen—they will tear him apart. And once they make the connection to us, they will be merciless. Get together what you can; we need to go."

Kent stood at the window. Three cars turned the corner and began to slowly make their way along the street. A truck then blocked the end of the street.

"They are here—we go now," Kent said. "Up, across the

roof. It will take them time to roust the apartments looking for us."

"Pistol?"

Kent pulled open a drawer and removed a Colt automatic, tossing it to Max along with an extra magazine.

"You?" Max said, looking at Sophie. She already had out her Beretta.

"Now," Kent said.

Kent looked down the hallway. From below he heard screams and the sound of doors shattering. Then heavy boots pounded on the stairs, each moment growing louder. The three went down the hall to a door. Next to it was a small sign that read, TETTO.

"Up," Kent said. "The roof is open here. The parapets between us and the next roofs are low, easily jumped. Three buildings over is another small building—it is the entry to a stairway that goes all the way down to the street. You two go that way. I have a spot a hundred feet from here where I can cover you. If you hear shooting, just keep going. Do not worry about me. I will get away. I will meet you at the Piazza Navona safe house."

Max pulled open the door. A cool breeze blew down the wooden stairway. At the same moment, a bullet slammed into the doorframe six inches above his head. Kent returned fire. They heard a man's scream from down the hall.

"Climb, go," Kent yelled.

On the dark roof, Kent said, "See that small building? That's the top of the stairway in that apartment. Down four floors are two doors. One leads to the street, the other to the cellar and the underground tunnels and drains in this part of the city. Go to the street, stay hidden, don't run. I will meet you later—Piazza Navona."

Pounding could be heard through the open door of the stairwell they'd just climbed. Kent reached into his pocket and then held up a hand grenade, pulled the fuse, and flicked it down the stairway.

"Go, run," he yelled.

Max and Sophie hadn't run fifty feet when the grenade exploded with a whoomp. The roof of the stairwell blew off. Kent was fifty feet in the other direction and heading to another stairwell. The pair had crossed two of the adjacent rooftops when the first gunfire opened up behind them. Bullets hit the walls and ricocheted off the tiles. More gunfire; a pistol responded. Max knew it was Kent and his big Webley. They dodged another collection of fireplace chimneys. The stairway that Albert had pointed out was fifty feet away. Max heard a volley of rifles, bullets buzzing by. Sophie, running next to him, fell, and tumbled across the roof.

He grabbed her and started to pull her up.

"I can't. A fucking bullet in the thigh—burns like hell. You go, get out. If you stay here, we are both dead. Go."

"I can carry you."

"Down the stairway? Then what? I'll bleed to death before we can reach the river. Take this scarf, wrap it tight, then get the hell out of here."

Kent was shooting into the soldiers that had made the roof. Max hoped he had another hand grenade. He tied the scarf tight.

"Go. Find me," she said.

He leaned in and kissed her. Leaving her was almost next to impossible. He started to say something.

"Do not do that. Go. Find me."

* * *

An hour later, having managed to dodge patrols and policemen, Max reached the safe house a block from the Piazza Navona. The grounds included a chapel and rectory. He knocked on the door of the rectory and waited, then knocked again. At last a tiny door at eye level opened. A metal grate hid the face of the man peering out.

"*Si?*"

"*Sono qui per vedere il prete, ho bisogno di confessarmi,*" Max said.

"The priest doesn't hear confessions until the evening," came the answer.

"There is a great need to hear mine," Max insisted.

"Wait."

Max stood outside the rectory door. He heard scraping sounds and then silence. The cold kiss of a pistol's muzzle pressed against his neck didn't surprise him; he had expected it.

"Not a sound."

"Wouldn't think of it," Max answered.

The guard reached inside Max's coat and removed his pistol, then a hand went past him and tapped four times on the door; it abruptly opened. In the light of the entryway stood a man dressed in a black cassock. He held a Luger in his right hand. He smiled and gestured with his gun hand for the two men to enter.

"Hi, Max."

Max stared at the priest and the gun he held.

"Sometimes God needs a little more help than a prayer," Father Conti said with a grin.

Max was directed down a narrow corridor. At the end of the hallway, the priest opened another door. Inside, two men sat at the end of a heavy wooden table. Max recognized Albert Kent, then slumped into a chair.

"You made it," Max said.

"Barely. Sophie?" Kent asked.

"She was shot in the leg; she stayed behind. They must have her," Max said.

Father Conti grabbed Max and jerked the bigger man to his feet. He then slammed a fist into his jaw. "You let them capture my niece? You son of a bitch. As the Lord is my witness, I will take you right now and throw you into the street and leave you for the Krauts. Hell, I'll even call them."

Max, stunned by the reaction, said nothing. He almost wished that the priest would do exactly that.

Then, a few moments later, Father Conti cooled down. "What happened?" the priest said. He offered Max a glass of brandy.

Max swallowed the liquor in one gulp. He slowly explained what happened on the rooftop. "I'm going to find her."

"She might be dead," Kent said.

"Kent, tell your people to stay away from that building—it's blown. We have to find her." He started to rise. "Got to go."

"It was the boy, Pietro. They tortured him," Father Conti said. "The Germans then killed him and left his body on the street as a warning to the other kids. It's just not right. The word is they have photos of you and Sophie at the embassy."

Max nodded. It was starting to make sad sense now. He swore that he would avenge Pietro, and soon.

"I will ask about Sophie, but it has only been three hours," the priest said. "Hopefully, we will have news before morning. If she's still alive, they will probably move her in Regina Coeli prison until they can question her."

Four agonizing hours later, the word came down that a woman had been brought to Regina Coeli. The name was not released, but the description fit Sophie.

"Can we get her out?"

"You know how this goes, Max," Kent said. "We can't afford to lose the people we have now. With the Germans pouring agents into Rome, it's getting hard to even scratch your ass in public. Besides, how the hell can we get her out of *that* prison?"

Max asked for a cigarette and took a few long drags to calm his nerves. His heart told him to find a hundred men and batter down the walls of the prison, but that would be suicide.

They couldn't outgun the Nazis. If he had any chance of saving Sophie, he needed to outsmart them. This was now a job that required finesse and cunning. When you wish to charm a bear, you use honey.

"Maybe we can make them give her to us," he said thoughtfully. "Father, when is the next must-attend Nazi event at the Villa Wolkonsky, or anywhere else in Rome?"

"I will make a call." The priest left the room.

"Your men still have those German field uniforms?" Max asked.

"Yes, but what do you have in mind?" Kent said.

Max explained his idea. Kent nodded and said it was suicidal. Max agreed. "I need my SS uniform. It is in the basement of the Conti villa. There's an undertaker named Luca."

"I know him."

"Tell him to get the uniform to me. Father Conti knows the man too."

Father Conti returned. "The undertaker? Luca—yes, I will call him," he said. "Good news. According to the Vatican calendar for the archbishops still here in Rome, there is a reception tomorrow night. Again, like the reception four days ago, to celebrate the new ambassador. A senior official is coming in from Berlin, and the Church has been asked to provide suitable emissaries from the Vatican to legitimize the reception. Why?"

"My guess, with this bigwig coming to town, all the senior Nazi officers will be there. No one will want to miss the chance to be seen. And since they no longer trust the Italians, it will be nothing but Germans. This may leave a limited complement of officers at the prison."

The other men nodded, catching the drift of Max's proposal.

"Germans love to follow orders," Max told them.

24

S ophie, stripped to her bra and underwear, sat on a steel chair in the center of a windowless prison cell. A blood-ied bandage wrapped her right thigh. Her hair, once wet from a bucket of cold water, had now dried and stuck to her forehead. She couldn't brush the hair away from her swollen face because her arms and legs were bound to the chair with wire. A knotted rag was stuffed in her mouth, and a thick streak of congealed blood ran from her right ear and down her jaw. She threw a fiery glare at the young man standing in front of her.

"That was just a kiss," the soldier said in German.

He held a long stick with exposed wires secured to its tip. An electrical cord secured to the stick's end led away to a box on a table.

"A touch to help you understand."

"Once more, Corporal," Schmidt said.

The officer stood just outside the ring of overhead light that illuminated the woman.

The soldier touched the tip of the rod to a spot just above

her right breast. She gagged on her muffled screams. Urine dripped onto the stone floor.

"Again," he demanded.

Schmidt marveled at the strength of the woman. He knew she was British; a British spy no less, his first English catch. There would soon be others—the pressure he'd put on his people was paying off. The woman would be an excellent source of information. He would squeeze her for every bit of knowledge she had about the Roman resistance and maybe Florence and Milan too. Her information would be invaluable. Tonight, his orders were simple: torture the woman until she was dry—or dead.

That morning he'd received news of the death of his family in Schwabach. He took it as only a stoic Nazi SS officer could, quietly and internally. The American bombers had overshot their targets. Thousands of tons of explosives had leveled the unimportant village of Schwabach. Hundreds were killed. Schmidt's wife, son, daughter, and father were among the dead. He also remembered the death of his younger sister and her children—their train two years earlier destroyed by bombers near Frankfurt. Schmidt was now alone. His vengeance would be his duty to the fatherland. His thoroughness would not be questioned, his resolve unquestioned, and his success would honor his family.

And now I want your partner—you will give him to me or die.

"Again. This time, strip her."

The corporal, with a flick of his knife, deftly removed her bra.

Muffled screams filled the room as the tip of the prod grazed a nipple.

"Again. Pull the gag."

The interrogator looked at Schmidt.

"Again, to the count of five."

"I don't think the pig can count that high," the woman spit

in perfect German. Blood sprayed from her split lip.

"Oh, I assure you he can count; but he must do it slowly," Schmidt answered.

Again, the prod touched her skin, and again she cursed and shook. Sweat flooded her pale skin.

"*Eins, zwei, drei, vier, fünf*," the soldier deliberately counted.

She tried to muffle her own screams, but the easiest release was to scream louder.

"Good. You see—he can count."

She tilted her head back, trying to see him. "Is that you, Schmidt? Is that the nasal whine of the Nazi butcher of children and women?" she hissed. "Is it you—you miserable shit?"

"You are well informed, *Fräulein Norcross*. Until now, you have done well keeping hidden from our spies and agents. But I knew. I knew you were a spy."

"Spy? Soon I will be out of here and I'll shove that rod up your ass," Sophie said.

With that, Schmidt slammed a long cane across the bandage on her thigh. She fought to retain consciousness.

He looked at his watch. The rest of the interrogation could wait until morning. There was a reception planned for the ambassador in one hour, and he would not be late.

"Cover her with a blanket. We are not barbarians," he said to the soldier. "Feed her something. We will continue with the questioning in the morning."

"Shall I return her to her cell, sir?"

"No, leave her here. It is easier to clean up one mess," Schmidt said, glancing at the floor before looking at the woman's drooping, swollen eyes. He lifted her chin with the end of the rod. "You are strong, but we are stronger. You will tell me everything, I can assure you of that, *Fräulein*. How long your misery will last is up to you. We will continue in the morning. Sleep well."

A pail full of water sat just inside the doorway. Schmidt

pointed to it and said, "Throw it on her. She stinks."

* * *

Max stood in the shadows of a copse of lindens outside the ancient prison where Sophie was being held. The Tiber River was fifty feet below him. His black SS major uniform melded into the darkness. A loyal Italian guard had confirmed Sophie's confinement. She was being tortured, but she was still alive. Max watched Schmidt walk out the door of the prison, salute the two guards, and climb into his staff car. It quickly accelerated, rounded the corner, and disappeared. Max lit a cigarette and walked toward the prison; the cigarette lighter signaled a German truck to follow him. As it caught up, he swung into the passenger seat. The truck pulled to a stop in front of the prison's entrance. The truck hid the two German sentries should anyone pass by on the street. Albert Kent, dressed in a German sergeant's uniform, jumped from the driver's seat. Three more men, also in German field uniforms, jumped from the rear and came to attention alongside the truck. They faced the stone wall of the prison.

Max dismounted and casually walked up to the sergeant on guard and spoke in German.

"Please tell your commanding officer that I am here for the woman prisoner. She is to be transferred to Gestapo offices at the embassy on SS- Obersturmbannführer Schmidt's orders. It is the same English bitch he is interrogating."

The two guards glanced at each other and then at Max's men.

"Obersturmbannführer Schmidt just left. He left no order with us," one of the guards said.

"Yes, I watched him leave in his car. Do you think he tells every puke soldier his plans?" Max barked.

The two men hesitated.

"Well, do you? No, he does not. I received the orders not

more than an hour ago, and I am assigned to move the woman. Put the officer in charge on the phone," Max said, pointing to the wall where a metal box hung. "I will not be late! Tonight after the reception he wishes to continue the interrogation at the embassy. Now would not be soon enough."

The soldier picked up the phone and after a brief call turned back to Max.

"The officer of the watch is coming," the guard said.

The steel door opened, and a portly German officer stood silhouetted in the glare from the interior lights.

"What the fuck's going on? I need some identification and your papers." He held his meaty hand out.

Max coldly stared at the man, and then slapped him across the face, reddening his plump cheek.

"You swine, is this how the officer of the watch dresses? Clean yourself up. Now, where is the woman? Bring her out, now."

He waited as the man rearranged his uniform. Then, he slapped a collection of documents into the man's hand—all written on official Gestapo stationery. In the dim light, the officer studied the paperwork.

"Swine, what is your problem? Major Schmidt wants the girl at the embassy when he returns from the reception. A delay, your delay, is not acceptable! I will tell your feeble brain something important, listen closely: he is with the field marshal and the ambassador tonight. You know he does not tolerate problems that become fuckups, and right now you are becoming a serious problem. Do I have to send someone to the embassy and bring him here to verify this?"

Max turned to the Englishman.

"Take three men to the villa. I'll wait here with the others for SS-Obersturmbannführer Schmidt's return. Be sure to mention this idiot to him." Max pointed his finger at the officer.

The German officer hastily returned the papers to Adler and turned to the guards.

"Have the woman brought out," he said to the guards. "With her gone, I'm less concerned about the communists or partisans trying to take her. Let the Gestapo deal with her."

The guards disappeared and were gone fewer than five minutes—minutes that felt like an eternity to the men standing by the truck, but none moved. Max asked Alfred for a cigarette; he also offered one to the watch officer.

"American cigarettes—I took them off a dead American near Naples," the Englishman said in German. "The fool had a carton in his pack that he wasn't going to need after I shot him."

The Nazi officer laughed cautiously at the joke. He eyed the SS death's head on Max's steel lighter as he lit his cigarette.

"Handsome lighter," the officer said, trying to ingratiate himself.

"Given to me by Himmler for helping clear the Warsaw ghetto."

The door to the prison rattled as the locks were released, then opened, and two soldiers held a body between them. It was wrapped in a blanket, and obviously little else. The three stumbled through the doorway and to the officer. Seeing Sophie's bruised and damaged body, Max shuddered. He didn't say a word; her eyes, seeing him, gave away only the slightest hint of recognition. She staggered forward, then fainted into his arms. He wanted nothing more than to sweep her up and take her away from this horrific place. He also wanted to shoot every German standing here.

"Get this bitch off me; God damn, she smells," Max yelled back to his men; two grabbed Sophie. "Throw her in the back; secure her hands and feet. I don't want her jumping out."

He spun back to the officer and saluted.

"I appreciate your help. She is such a prize, I believe Obersturmbannführer Schmidt wants to personally break her, if you know what I mean."

He poked the officer in his round belly. The man responded with a grin.

"Mount up," Max ordered.

Max still wanted to shoot the officer and every man at the gate but wasted no further time.

* * *

Ten blocks from the prison, Schmidt realized that, in his haste, he had forgotten his overcoat. It would be improper to attend the reception without a coat. He ordered his driver back to the prison.

The sedan made a U-turn in the street. As they crossed the Ponte Mazzini, a German truck passed traveling in the opposite direction. The glare of the car's headlights caught the faces of the driver and the passenger—for a moment, nothing registered. As his car stopped in front of the prison, Schmidt remembered the man, the officer. It was the same face as the photos taken at the embassy, the priest, the train station. His interrogator stood in the glare of the streetlight, yelling at the fat watch officer.

"Was that truck here? Who was in it?" Schmidt demanded, already guessing the worst.

The watch officer responded, "The woman prisoner, as you ordered." He waved the handful of papers. "She is being delivered to Gestapo headquarters at the embassy."

"You goddamn fool. I did not make such an order. Are you part of this?" Schmidt demanded, wheeling on the torturer.

"No, it was this fucking idiot. It was the partisans, I'm sure. You passed them as you came down the boulevard."

"I know. I recognized their leader in the truck. It's her goddamn partner."

The watch officer, still smoking the cigarette given to him

by Alfred, winced as Schmidt turned back to him. With his bare hands, Schmidt drove the man back against the stone wall of the prison. The back of his head hit the stones hard. Schmidt plucked the cigarette from the man's mouth and crushed it out against his cheek.

"Where did they take her?" he demanded.

"I don't know. He had the proper orders and papers. It's not my fault."

Schmidt smashed the man's head against the wall again. The officer collapsed, unconscious, to the ground.

"You are all idiots. Put out the alarm, find that truck before it disappears. Do you understand me?"

Without waiting for a response, Schmidt climbed back into the staff car and ordered his driver to find the truck.

"Ponte Umberto. They may head through the city and cross the river there. Then they would head north along the river. Stay on this side; go past the Vatican. We will catch them at the bridge."

"Yes, sir," the driver responded.

"Weapons?"

"Two, sir. A Mauser and a Schmeisser."

"Excellent. As soon as we reach the bridge, we'll arm ourselves. I will not let that man dupe me again."

They passed the Vatican and continued weaving through the thin evening traffic, all military. There were no roadblocks near the Vatican due to political agreements that Schmidt thought insane. They passed the massive circular Castel Sant'Angelo, and ahead, he saw the Ponte Umberto and the faint outline of three trucks backed up on the bridge.

"Sir, I have to swing around the plaza ahead of us. We may lose sight of them," his driver said.

"Drive through it. I will not lose them."

Schmidt watched the stationary trucks on the bridge. They were now halfway across the bridge.

His driver hit the gas, and the car jumped the curb and sped down the length of the plaza, wheels whirring on the pavement as the driver swerved to avoid the few pedestrians out. He expertly piloted the vehicle back onto the Via Triboniano and stopped just as the first truck tried to leave the bridge. Schmidt retrieved the Schmeisser from the trunk. He ran to the bridge, waving the machine pistol. He pointed it at the cab of the first truck.

"Stop," he ordered.

Three shocked soldiers glared at him through the windshield. They weren't the people he was looking for.

Turning to his driver, he yelled, "Hold these trucks here. I don't want anyone to pass."

Running along the bridge, he went to the second truck. Again, three soldiers—nothing. He steadied himself as he approached the third truck—more soldiers. He looked in the truck's back. A dozen men looked back at him; men with the dark stare of combat and death. The stench of war palpable.

"We missed them," he said angrily, as he climbed back into the car. "Someone will pay for that imbecile's decision. I will have them shot."

25

Rome, Villa San Sebastiano, Night
August 16, 1943

As Max and his gang of Nazi impersonators roared past the returning staff car, their headlights lit up the driver.

"That was Schmidt," Max said. "We need to get Sophie to safety and hide this truck. They'll have alarms out all over the city."

"We have the garage. It will be safe there, but she needs medical help," Kent said.

"They will be watching the garage, now," Max replied.

He pointed toward the next intersection ahead.

"I have an idea. Turn here, double back across the Tiber at the Ponte Mazzini, then back past the prison. They won't be looking that way."

"Bloody hell, you say. Don't forget, Adler, right now we're dressed like Germans. If we are caught, we won't make it ten feet before they line us up against a wall."

"I know." Max looked out across the river toward the hills to the east. "When we pass the prison, keep going south, along the river. Then, at the Palatino Bridge, cross over. Then head south into San Sebastiano Park—I'm taking Sophie home."

"Home?" Kent said. "That will be one of the first places they will look."

"I'll hide her in the catacombs. She can get care there. Stop. I'm going into the back."

The Englishman pulled the truck to the side of the road. Max climbed into the rear. One of Kent's guards was holding Sophie. Max took his place and cradled her head on his lap. With a jerk, the truck accelerated; he held her tight as the truck swerved and bounced on the cobblestones. She moaned with every lurch of the truck's bed.

"Give me a clean blanket," he asked one of the men. Under the dim light of flashlights, he wrapped the cuts and gunshot wound to her leg with rough clean bandages; he tucked the blanket around her. She was beginning to shake from the cold and shock. Max fought back tears. Sophie's eyes quivered, then opened.

"I knew you would find me—I knew you would. Where are we going?"

"Home," Max said.

She slowly closed her eyes.

Deep in the enclave of estates and villas that made up Parco San Sebastiano, Kent slowed the truck. The road was enclosed on both sides by ancient stone and brick walls; ivy clung to most of the façades. Pines planted on the grounds of the estates overhung the cobblestone road. Max banged on the back of the truck cab; Kent stopped.

Max came around to the driver's window. "I'll open the gate, then take us to the front of the villa. I will carry her in."

Max went to the Conti gate built into the enclosing wall and used the phone mounted in a box. A moment later, the gate opened, Max reboarded, and Kent drove up the narrow lane to the front of the villa. Two men stood at the steps waiting. One was the butler, Signore Luciano. The other was Franco Conti.

With the help of Kent's men, they lowered Sophie into Max's arms.

"Get the hell out of here, Albert," Max said. "These people are fascists."

"You may need some help," Albert said.

"I can't chance it; Franco believes I'm an SS colonel. He will be shocked to learn otherwise. Your guys are valuable—get them out of here. I'll meet you at the safe house across from the Villa Medici. Give me a couple of days."

"What the hell are you doing here?" Signor Conti demanded. "Who is that?"

Max glared at the count as he gently adjusted Sophie in his arms. "This is your granddaughter. This is what the Germans do to those that challenge them. We need a doctor. If not, she will die."

Conti looked at the bundle in Max's arms. He slowly removed the blanket that covered Sophie's face. He let out a gasp when he saw the open wounds and blood.

"Bring her in. Luciano, call my doctor," he said.

Max, with Sophie in his arms, climbed the steps.

"*Colonnello Stoltz, portala da sua nonna.*"

Max did as directed and carried Sophie up the stairs and into the villa. Max heard the noisy grinding of gears as Kent drove the truck out of the estate.

The countess stoically stood in the foyer as the men entered, her hands clasped across her breasts. Next to her, a maid and housekeeper. Sophie opened her eyes, looked at her grandmother, and whispered, "*Nonna, aiutami. Non lasciarmi morire.*"

At those words, Ester Conti pointed to the staff and said something that Max didn't completely understand, but the intent was clear. He followed them up the stairs to a bedroom and laid Sophie gently on the bed. In the light he saw the damage Schmidt had inflicted; it ripped his soul. The women took over; towels and a first aid kit appeared. Ester took Max by the shoulders, then pushed him out of the bedroom.

Franco Conti met Max in the hall. "The doctor is coming," he said in German. "What happened?"

"Can he be trusted?" Max answered.

"Why? Is this a problem?"

"Signor Conti, yes, it can be a problem."

"The doctor is an old friend."

"Signor Conti, this is the work of the Germans. They tortured your granddaughter—they wanted information. They want me."

"Why would they want you, one of their own?" Conti said, passing Max a sniffer of Cognac.

"Signor, this has all been a charade. I apologize. I am not a Nazis or an SS colonel. I am a captain in the United States Army. I am here to rescue an Italian the Americans need to end this war. He was the man you met, the priest. Our mission—your granddaughter is involved as well—was a success. But now the Germans want us captured or dead."

Stunned, Conti took a step back. "You are a spy?"

"Yes, and so is your granddaughter. Your daughter is aware of all this and so is your son-in-law. They are important to the war effort in England and the Allies. And your son Guido—I am working closely with him."

Max spent the next fifteen minutes explaining to the count what had happened. He saw the man become angry; Conti's fists clinched and his body tensed.

"I've been such a fool. Ester guessed almost the same thing after Mussolini was arrested. This whole country has been living a lie. But why did she come back here? She was safe in England."

"Because she loves you. And after what has happened during the past year, I believe that you no longer believe in the fascists. Am I right?"

"They bought me; I admit it. Twenty years ago, my company was struggling, airplanes were new. I proposed exciting changes. But no one believed in them, then Italo Balbo came to the plant—he saw the possibilities. And his being so close to Mussolini, he helped me expand and grow the company. I was blinded by the money and the success—it drove our daughter from us. And our granddaughter as well. But the war has changed everything. The unnecessary deaths in Ethiopia, Greece, and North Africa. And recently the Italian soldiers sent into Hitler's war machine. Men taken from the streets to work in Hitler's factories. This all must stop. When Sophie came to convince Mussolini to surrender Italy, I supported her. It was a way to try and stop the madness and killing."

"So, that's why she was here?"

"Yes. It was all in secret; it was hoped that something could be negotiated with Mussolini to save Italy from the coming invasion. When Sophie said she was coming home, Ester was so excited—she came to us with that hope. Can you tell me more?"

"I can't, but please know that she loves you. As soon as we can, we will be going back to London. This fight is not over."

"Thank you, Captain, and I speak for Signora Conti as well. This is a lot to understand. We knew that Mussolini was corrupt and was taking the country the wrong way. And this alliance with Hitler has turned our country into a hell only the great Dante could have imagined. We are prisoners in our own land."

"That hell is about to get worse, believe me."

"Yes, the Allies are coming, I know that. Can I do anything for you?"

"Another glass of Cognac."

Max stayed late into the night. He expected Schmidt and his men to arrive any moment. His Nazi disguise, while helpful in rescuing Sophie, put him in a disadvantage if he were to try and cross Rome in daylight.

"Signor Conti, a small favor. My uniform, I was wondering . . ."

"Say no more. We are both large men—one of the reasons I like you. I think I have slacks and a jacket that will fit you. The pants might be a bit short, but I think they will suffice."

"Thank you. I must get back to my people. I will call to-morrow to ask about Sophie."

As Max dressed, Franco Conti asked, "What are your in-tentions regarding my granddaughter, Captain?"

Max paused. It was not a question he'd expected, or at this moment wanted. "Signor Conti, with what we are facing here in Italy, I do not think it is appropriate or prudent to make plans. I like your granddaughter very much, but circumstances make it difficult and even dangerous to link her to me. When this is over, and if we survive, we can have this conversation again. Until then, I am a loyal American doing his duty."

"An honorable and honest answer, thank you."

His SS disguise wrapped in a paper bag, Max went out the back entry of the villa, and walked to the trolley. Over the next few hours, he slowly traveled through the streets of Rome to what he hoped was still a safe house across the river from the Vatican.

26

The terror of the last weeks of August darkened the already desolate hearts of the Romans. Through the rest of the month, the Allied bombs continued to fall. The day Max delivered Cattaneo to the destroyer, the areas around the rail stations below the San Lorenzo district were bombed again. During the next week, air raid sirens interrupted life almost daily. The tension in the city was profound, and food was scarce. Rome had been declared an open city by the Germans. Yet, when people tried to flee, go to the countryside, they were turned around or arrested. Men who were caught were arrested and shipped to Germany's industrial machine. Others fled beyond the city's boundary and set up camps that surrounded Rome to the north and south. Open city or not, the streets were filled with German military, their trucks, their armored vehicles.

Sophie told her grandparents about the cellar and the secret tunnels. The count felt the fool for not knowing. Luca and Marco, initially skeptical, gave him a tour. As an engineer, he offered suggestions about strengthening the tunnels.

"A bomb or an earthquake could knock this whole section down," he said as they walked to the ancient baths. "We will need to reinforce it."

"And when should we do that, Count?" Luca said.

"When the bombs stop falling, of course."

The Contis believed that it was only a matter of time before the Germans would return and raid the villa. Sophie was moved from the upper floor to the cellar and continued to heal. After a week and no raid, Ester Conti insisted that she be moved back to an upstairs bedroom.

Max visited Sophie when he could. The surge in Germans in Rome made his trips across the city difficult, and the fascist police had become more emboldened. Twice his papers were pushed back in his face by Italian authorities claiming he was a German. *"Bugiardo, sappiamo chi sei, Tedesco!"*

He looked so much like a German that often the police didn't believe he was a laborer from Cortina. He was Gestapo, or worse; they gave him room. Even he knew that it was a cover that could get him killed; the resistance would also see him as a German.

On one visit he brought her a bouquet of summer flowers.

"Where did you find those?" she asked.

"There's that flower shop near the Porta San Paulo," Max said. "They had tubs of them. Even in war flowers grow. The people are getting used to the air raids, and many are now moving about the city. A little color in this room is nice."

"How's Albert?"

"Grumpy, but good. There's a lot of chatter over the radio, more than during the past few weeks. Like it was before Sicily. So, something is coming."

As if to emphasize the comment, a dull concussive of far-off thunder came through the open window.

"Where?"

"Maybe Ciampino Airport, again. There can't be much

left—it has been bombed so many times."

"Any word from London or Tunis?" Sophie asked as she placed her feet on the floor.

"None, but maybe soon. When will you be able to travel?"

"Maybe a week. I can stumble along. But to get to the coast, I need a few more days."

"I'll see what I can do."

That evening they had a simple dinner in Sophie's room. Count Conti carried the tray, the countess the wine. The staff, other than Luciano, had gone home.

"Sophie said that you have friends in Amalfi," the countess said. "I love that village. Sometimes, when it's hot here, we would go and enjoy the cooler weather. But that was a different time and after a different war."

"She means the First World War," Sophie said with a laugh.

"And that was not so long ago, young lady," Franco said. "Thirty years can go by in a flash. And right now, time seems to be speeding up. So much is changing, yet the politics stays the same. Maybe after this war, the world will find a better way."

"Count and Countess, when Sophie is well and can travel . . ." Max began.

"You will be leaving. We know," Ester said. "We have selfishly kept you here too long. Your injury was a gift to us. But you are needed elsewhere. When you are ready, we will be too. I hate long goodbyes. When you see Donna Marie, tell your mother that we love her and hope she can return soon to her home."

"And tell your father I understand now why he does what he does," the count said. "The world needs more peacemakers."

Sophie took Max's hand and squeezed it. "I will."

* * *

Rome
August 30, 1943

The last days of August were hot as only Italy can be in mid-summer. The days stifled the brain, and the citizens of Rome took to the rooftops in the evenings. With a nighttime curfew strictly enforced, the nearly deserted streets were left to the callous impulses of the fascist police and local bandits. To walk the streets at night risked an encounter with either, and the Romans were not sure who was worse.

Schmidt stood at attention in front of the desk of Kesselring; the field marshal annoyingly tapped the edge of a file on the desk.

"I have been informed that the physicist found a way out of Rome and Italy," Kesselring said. "He was seen in Tunisia, at the airport. That was a week ago. By now he's in the United States."

"And that is my fault?" Schmidt replied. "I hope that he is a failure for the Americans. I found the man to be obtuse, almost naïve. What Berlin saw in the man, I haven't a clue."

"It is not our jobs to understand Berlin," Kesselring said. "It is a soldier's job to follow orders."

"And those are," Schmidt said, trying to change the direction of the conversation.

Kesselring tossed the folder across the table to Schmidt. "It's the Jews. We expect that this country is about to collapse. All the signs are here. Throughout Italy there's internal political squabbling, a weak king, and the Italian army is in total disarray. When the Allies invade, the whole country will fold. We must be prepared to continue with the Reich's mandates regarding the Jews, political adversaries, and other undesirables. You did well in Poland and France. Your orders are to prepare for their removal from Italy with the same thoroughness."

Dismissed, Schmidt walked out to the front of the German headquarters, climbed into his motorcar, and directed the driver to head down the deserted street toward the German embassy at Villa Wolkonsky. No one in the car paid attention to the battered ambulance that pulled out onto the street and followed a block behind.

The ambulance parked at the side street that intersected with the entry to the German embassy.

Schmidt saluted the guards and crossed the entry to the Villa Wolkonsky. An army officer greeted him and directed him to an office off to the side of the entry hall.

"The photos. I do not have much time," Schmidt said.

As the officer laid out the photos on the table, Ambassador Rahn walked into the small office. "You could have, at least, had the courtesy to stop at my office."

"Time, Ambassador. We are short of time. And what happened at the embassy a few weeks ago was an embarrassment."

"I would suggest that the loss of an important prisoner is an even greater embarrassment, especially when the prisoner is under your control," Rahn added.

Schmidt ignored the remark, even though he was still fuming over the loss of the Norcross woman. The SS officer who led the recovery of the prisoner fit the description of this Colonel Stoltz who also fit the description of the priest who had tied him up at the embassy.

"That is for me to determine. Are these photos recent?" Schmidt asked.

"These two are from yesterday," SS Captain Priebke replied, pointing to the photos. "I thought you would be interested."

Schmidt nodded.

"As you can see," the captain continued, "these on the left were taken at the embassy reception. We do that secretly, so the guests are not disturbed. The others were taken by one of my agents—we are sure it is the same man."

"Who is he talking to?" Schmidt said, tapping his finger on the face of one of the men in the photo. The photos were of the sidewalk tables outside one of Rome's more popular restaurants.

"He is a partisan who has connections to the Vatican, the Jews, and the communists. He is on our list for liquidation, when the time is right. He has already led my men to two others, whom we have quietly arrested. He is incompetent, but we watch him since he has been such a rich source of what you might call captures."

"Pick him up. I want him off the streets—do it quietly."

"Yes, sir."

"This man, do you have his real name? I want him, Priebke."

"We have determined that the name he gave at the reception at the embassy was obviously false. There is no record of a Monsignor Fallace in the Vatican."

"He is the same man I saw at the train station. He called himself Stoltz then. There is no record of the officer?"

"None. We have checked with Berlin—nothing. And to think he was within reach of our leaders and senior officers. I have kept this quiet. There may be others involved, maybe even here on the embassy staff. That's why I have brought them to you."

"It's in your purview as Gestapo captain here in Rome," Schmidt said. "If there are fools and traitors among us, they must be cut out, along with this one." Schmidt gestured at one of the other photos of the man. "He was seen that night with the family of Count Conti, and that physicist. I know. I went to the Conti villa that night looking for them. Have you found any connection?"

"Possibly. The Contis are prominent fascists in political and industrial circles," Priebke added. "They had close ties to Mussolini. However, their daughter, Donna Marie, married the

British ambassador Norcross thirty years ago—she now lives in England. There was a scandal earlier this summer involving their daughter Sophie Norcross—she's the one you caught on that roof. She is the woman who escaped from the prison. When she was in England, she professed allegiance to her grandparents and support for the fascist government here in Italy and even made positive remarks about Spain and Germany. She was effectively thrown out of England. She went to Spain, spent a few weeks in Madrid, before coming here to Rome."

"Interesting."

"Yes. She is at the Conti villa you inspected the night of the disappearance of Cattaneo."

"We found nothing at the villa," Schmidt said.

"Those villas can hide things. I would suggest a more thorough search," Priebke added.

"I have other orders now. Why would I waste our time on these people?"

"Fear. Soon we will be required to control this city; it's obvious. The Romans must learn that we will never let them get away with anything, especially those that make fools of us."

"Be careful, Priebke."

"Yes, sir. Just let me know when to start."

Schmidt looked at the photos again. "I know that man's face," he said, thumping his finger on the enlarged photos. "I saw him in America when I was there, and Berlin maybe seven years ago. I couldn't place him, but now, now I remember—I want his head. Find him—no one walks into our house and steals from us, ever."

"And where should I start?"

"Start with the woman, Priebke. Find her."

27

Rome
September 7, 1943

During the late hours of September 6, Kent handed Max a piece of paper. It was scribbled over with notes and codes. Max saw the unmistakably obtuse intent of Zebadiah Jones all over it.

Proceed to Gaeta. Pick up two injured tourists and take them to Rome for a blessing. More information soon.

"This ought to be interesting," Sophie, fully recovered except for a slight limp, said. "Any clue?"

"None. We wait."

The follow-up was a short phone call that gave an address in the Trastevere district and the time, noon. Nothing more. Crossing the city in daylight on crowded trolleys, they found an Italian ambulance parked at the curb and an Italian soldier standing in the open door, smoking a cigarette. Another lounged at the back, his feet dangling over the sill of the rear door.

"Are you here to retrieve the injured tourists?" Max asked in English. He was dressed in a white medical coat.

"*Si, si*—are you the doctor?" was the answer, also in English.

Max nodded, gave Sophie a kiss, and then climbed into the back of the ambulance.

"She's beautiful. She your girlfriend?" asked the lounging soldier.

"No," Max said and reconsidered the man's question, then looked at Sophie. She smiled. "Maybe."

They watched Sophie walk away.

"If I had a girl that gorgeous, I sure as hell would know whether she was my girlfriend or not," the other soldier said as he threw his cigarette to the cobblestones.

Ten minutes and one roadblock later, they were headed eighty miles south to the coastal village of Gaeta.

Pushing aside the curtain behind the driver, Max looked through the grimy windshield and saw German military trucks filling the road ahead of them. Germans now controlled the major highway intersections and the flow of civilian traffic. Their pace was measured, yet steady. The ambulance driver gave way to the German columns whenever demanded. For most of the trip, the Italian sitting in the back with Max took quick, passing glances at him. Max had not met an Italian who could be this quiet. The back of the ambulance was stifling, and at midafternoon they pulled to the side of a remote and empty road north of Gaeta. Max climbed out, glad to stretch out the kinks in his back from the three-and-one-half-hour ride. Not a German was in sight.

"I don't know you, do I?" Max eventually asked the driver.

"And for me, that's a good thing, Doctor. The less you and I know about each other, the better," the man said, with a laugh.

For twenty minutes, they waited. The view from their hillside location was across the broad Tyrrhenian Sea toward the haze-obscured tops of the Pontine Islands. At least the Italians had cigarettes—Max bummed two.

At four o'clock, a black Fiat limousine turned onto the road, Italian naval flags fluttering from mounts on its hood. The car slowly approached and then stopped ten paces from the rear of the ambulance. The three men waited, each gauging if they would have time to reach the ditch paralleling the road if a machine pistol appeared through a window. The rear door swung open and, to Max's shock, two uniformed American officers climbed out, one a brigadier general and the other a colonel. An Italian admiral, also in full uniform, followed. The Americans looked disheveled and dirty. Max's initial assumption was that they were prisoners.

"Great, we come to Italy, and the first non-Eyetie we meet is a German," the brigadier general said, as he and his companions approached the ambulance.

"I doubt that, sir," Max said. "Welcome to Italy. I assume you are the two injured tourists that require assistance to Rome."

"I can tell a Midwesterner from a mile away, son," the general said. "I'm Brigadier General Maxwell Taylor. This here is Colonel William Gardiner. He's a politician, but don't hold that against him. And this is Admiral Franco Maugeri. He's with the Italian naval intelligence. I suggest we get on our way. We had to drive through a lot of the German army to get here. It would not be wise to get caught."

"Sir, there are a hell of a lot more of the bastards ahead of us," Max offered.

"Then let's get off this hillside before someone shoots us," Taylor said.

The admiral signaled to his car. The driver slowly backed away and turned around. Before they were loaded into the ambulance, the admiral's car had disappeared over the rise of the hill.

For the next three hours, they paralleled the same troops they'd passed on the way to Gaeta from Rome. Taylor and Gardiner said little as they all sat on the floor of the ambulance. The Italian admiral often winced as the truck bounced along the uneven highway.

To take their minds off the road and what might happen if they were caught, Gardiner asked, "How did you get this job, son? General Taylor and I volunteered. Are you military or something else?"

Max smiled at the man and his political paternalisms. He guessed Gardiner to be about fifty years old; Taylor looked to be in his early forties. Both wore American officer's field uniforms, their ranks clearly displayed: Gardiner's Army Air Corps and Taylor's regular army. They even had their combat ribbons pinned to their jackets. They also carried a two-way radio in a leather case.

"Captain, US Army, OSS, sir. I've been helping the cause by being what you might call a reporter. I see something and I send the information home," Max told them. Then with a questioning expression on his face, he tilted his head at the Italian admiral.

"The admiral is okay—he's on our side," Taylor said. "They tell me you are the one who passed on the information about the Italians and their potential flip-flop."

"Yes, sir. I assume you're here to change their minds."

"We hope so. Too much is riding on this trip—too much is going to happen. And we don't have weeks or days, just hours."

They headed north through the coastal village of Terracina, then on the shoulder of the crowded Via Appia. Through the curtains, Max counted down the stone markers, kilometer after kilometer. The other men in the ambulance, blind to what went on around them, kept their thoughts to themselves. If caught, the American officers would spend the rest of the war in a German prisoner-of-war stalag. The other four, including the admiral and Max, would be dead with a bullet to the back of the head. They were stopped once, and their papers examined. The "prisoners" remained quiet. After a few excruciatingly long moments, the ambulance was waved through.

At eight o'clock, they reached Rome and wound their way through the streets to the Palazzo Caprara, a four-story residence across the Via Firenze from the Italian war office.

"This is where I leave you," Max told the two officers. "I'll pick you up when your meetings are over. While I would love to sit in, my place is out here. But if you do need anything, let me know. I would suggest that you remember that these are proud men, and they are in way over their heads. Anything they can do to delay the invasion they believe would be to their benefit."

"And definitely not to ours," General Taylor said.

Max waited near the ambulance, smoking cigarettes, and talking with the driver and his partner. Both had been conscripted into the army, had fought in France, and, to Max's surprise, had family members living in New Jersey. As soon as the war was over, the driver said he would leave Italy and join his cousins in Asbury Park. The other planned to go back to his family's farm in Umbria, find a wife and grow old. Neither said anything about the war that was about to sweep through the Italian countryside. They, like most of their countrymen, prayed to God that it would not happen.

At midnight, Taylor, Gardiner, and Maugeri exited the door to the palazzo. With them were General Carboni and two of his aides. Taylor waved Max over.

"These sons of bitches are wavering, just like you said. We're going to Badoglio's to get that asshole to hold up his end of the bargain. This whole thing is screwed up. You follow—we're going in Carboni's car."

The limousine, with its flags and banners, passed through the dark streets and climbed to Badoglio's villa on Rome's outskirts. They passed a few German tanks that commanded key intersections but were not stopped. Max sensed Rome's pensive, almost expectant, mood. Usually, there were people about, even late at night. The weather had been warm and rainless for weeks, yet moisture still found its way up the Tiber River from the sea. The warm, damp, brooding fog, hovering over its narrow banks, was thicker than usual.

Arriving at Badoglio's villa, the two officers with their naval escort were shown immediately through the huge bronze doors.

"Ever been here before?" Max asked the ambulance driver.

"No, and I'm scared shitless! I go where I was ordered, nothing more. Quite a day. If my mother could see me, she would be proud. I hope I can tell her before I'm shot."

"If this will help to get the *Tedeschi* out of Italy, I'm all for it," the man said to Max. "This bambino has had enough of this fascist war. First, we finally get rid of that clown Mussolini, then the Germans start moving in. My whole country is fucked up."

For an hour, they waited. The quiet city below was blacked out by the time Taylor and Gardiner emerged from the villa. The admiral remained behind.

"Back to the Palazzo Caprara," Gardiner said. They reversed their route, and once back at the palazzo, the American officers again entered the building. Max and the two Italians slept off and on in the back of the ambulance. They waited all morning. By noon, all three were famished. From inside the palazzo, a woman came out with sandwiches and a bottle of wine. The men ate and drank, all the time speculating about what was happening.

At midafternoon, Max and his team received a note from the general: *Be ready to go to Centocelle Airport.*

"Now the sticky part, Max," Taylor said, as he and Gardiner climbed into the ambulance. "We are supposed to have a plane waiting at the airport, and we have ten thousand Nazis between us. Can you get us there?"

"Try my damnedest," Max said.

For the next hour, they wound through the streets of Rome to Centocelle Airport. No one stopped them. Max believed that the old gods of Rome were looking over their collective shoulders. It was as if they wanted this to succeed as much as the Italians and the Americans.

"I'll bet you're wondering what this is all about, Max," General Taylor said, as they again sat uncomfortably in semi-darkness in the rear of the ambulance.

"Not my place to know, sir. Today I'm a chauffeur, not a spy."

"And a good one, but you are also an American and a patriot. You should know why you've risked your life. As you know, it seems our Italian friends had cold feet about surrendering. It was our job to make them come to Jesus, and that's what we've done. We now have Badoglio's complete and unconditional support for the surrender they signed a few days ago, even if we had to kick him in his old bony ass to get it. They made a pact with the devil, and now they have to tell the devil to go back to hell. It won't be easy. The Italian army in Rome has few weapons and little ammunition. They won't last five hours. The Germans react in a mean and certain way when they're faced with traitors and cowards, and that's what they will call the Italians. To the Nazis, they are now worthless. When we invade, there will be reprisals and martial law. It's best if you try and find a safe place to hide for a while."

"I'll be okay. I've survived the last three months here. I know a little," Max said.

"Jesus H. Christ, three months? How the hell did you do it?" Gardiner said.

"My excellent variety of Midwestern bullshit, sir."

According to Taylor, concurrent with the invasion, an airborne landing and attack on Rome was planned, with paratroops ready to seize the airport and fight from there.

"That's now gone," Taylor said. "The operation would be suicide. We need to get back and stop it."

The Italian campaign would have to be fought from the south to the north, the general went on to say. It was anyone's guess when Rome would be liberated.

"Soon, I hope. But I'm sure the Nazis and Kesselring will have something to say about it," the general said.

"I met Kesselring," Max said. "He's a Nazi through to his black heart, and he'll be unforgiving and brutal."

"You met him? Damn," was the general's response.

They reached the airport without incident, and as arranged, an Italian trimotor Savoia-Marchetti sat idling on the runway. At the gate, an Italian guard pointed at the plane and then saluted. To Max, it was too bizarre. They pulled up to the plane; a metal ladder was already in place, dangling below an open hatch.

"Max, it has been a pleasure. You have treated these tourists well," Taylor said. "I hope to see you again, son. Keep safe."

"Be safe," Gardiner echoed. "If you can, pray for us and Italy. There is hell and damnation coming."

"Can I ask you a question, sir?"

"Sure. There are no secrets in foxholes, my boy," the general answered.

"Can you tell me when the invasion will be? Is it soon?" Max asked as the two men headed up the iron steps.

General Taylor paused, his hand on the airframe of the door, and studied Max.

"Tomorrow," he said.

"Where?"

"Salerno."

28

Rome, Villa San Sebastiano, Midnight
September 8, 1943

Sophie said to Max, as he threw clothes into a leather bag, "You can't go. It's impossible."

"I have to. They must be told. I can take the ambulance and retrace my steps to the coast and then south to Naples. From there, I can go over the mountain on the back road from Castellammare."

"It is beyond suicide. There are half a million Germans between us and them. You haven't the proper mobilization papers to move through the German advance, and even with your best bullshit, they will shoot you on the spot. You cannot reach Amalfi in time."

Still talking, Sophie pulled out a bag from under the bed and began her own hurried packing.

"We'll be stuck at some bloody crossroads with a thousand goddamn Nazis," she said. "Then the Americans will bomb the hell out of them and us. Then what do you have?"

"You're not going."

"The hell you say. You go, I go. You are not going alone. We have orders, and they do not include a midnight run to the middle of an invasion, no matter what the reason. Besides, what if you do pull off a miracle, and show up in time—pack them up and move them out of harm's way? What do you think you can do then?"

When he ignored her, she planted herself between him and his bag. He made a move to grab it. She picked it up and threw the bag across the room, and his clothes tumbled out.

"Listen to me, Max Alder! This whole damn country will be burning in six hours. You heard the bombings to the south. That was to get the Nazis' attention. Roads and railroads will be targeted at first light—you know that. From Salerno to Rome, every rail line, crossing, and highway is a target. What can you do if you're dead? The dead can't help anyone."

Max placed his hands on her shoulders. His arms shook with emotion and fury.

"This is fucked up. We're all fucked. I know you're right, but I have to do something to save them."

"Try to call them—maybe you can get through. If you want a miracle, call Lucia."

* * *

At half past seven on the evening of the eighth of September 1943, the Roman radio announced and read General Dwight D. Eisenhower's statement that Italy had surrendered to the Allies. This was followed by a short, dignified affirmation by Prime Minister Pietro Badoglio. Cesare Fallace sat in the large chair in the living room; Lucia paused mid-stride in the center of the room. They listened intently, disbelieving what they were hearing. Shortly after the announcement, Lucia opened a bottle of Prosecco.

"I was saving this for something special, and this is as good a time as any," she said, pulling the cork from the sparkling wine. She poured four glasses: two for her husband and herself; one for the cook, Maria; and one for their live-in houseboy, Nicola. The teenager wrinkled his nose when he tasted it.

"Maybe this war is finally heading to an end," Lucia said.

"I pray for it and we've been lucky. Only the larger cities are being bombed. Maybe our fortune will hold. To good fortune," Cesare said, raising his glass.

After Maria left, Nicola said goodnight. The two old lovers sat on the terrace and finished the wine. The night was clear, but a soft haze obscured the view of the sea.

"The children will be all right. Florence is safe for now," Cesare assured his wife. "They will stay in the school. They will be fine."

"I know. Their papers should keep them safe," Lucia answered.

"Our luck will only last for so long. The Allies are in Sicily—who knows what will happen now."

The phone rang. Lucia answered, smiling at the sound of Max's voice. Very quickly, she handed the receiver to Cesare, a worried expression replacing her smile.

"I can hardly hear him," she said.

"Strange that . . . what? Calm down. Yes, we are all right. Took you ten tries to get through? . . . Yes, we're okay . . . What? . . . My God, tonight? Are you sure?"

"What is it?" Lucia said as she listened to Cesare's side of the conversation.

"Yes, we'll go up into the hills," Cesare said. "There's a cave there. You remember it from when we went hiking. It's as good as anything. Yes, we'll leave now . . . you take care, Max. Yes, yes, we will . . . yes. Soon. God bless you and be with you."

Cesare gently took his wife by her shoulders, speaking calmly but rapidly.

"The Allied invasion is tonight. They're attacking Salerno and this whole bay—thousands of ships and guns and soldiers. None of us is safe. We need to go to the cave. Get food and water—only what we can carry."

"I'm going to call Maria. She needs to know."

Lucia picked up the phone and heard nothing. She rattled the receiver cradle. Again, nothing.

"My God, the phone's dead. I have to go tell them."

Cesare put his hand on his wife's arm.

"No, you can't," he said quietly. "It's already too late. Anything that moves is a target. Get clothes and blankets. We are going up into the mountain, now! I'll wake up Nicola and get him ready."

They spent a frantic twenty minutes gathering food into canvas bags—bread, cheese, salami, and bottles of water— anything that didn't need to be kept cool. Lucia handed the shotgun to Cesare, along with a box of shells. He didn't say anything as he slung the old gun over his shoulder on its well-worn leather strap. Nicola, still with sleep in his eyes, shouldered one of the backpacks of food.

How long they would be away, they didn't know. For all their past fears, they had never thought about being a part of the war. Yet now it was coming from the sea as an unstoppable, hell-born firestorm.

The cave was halfway up the narrow valley that rose steeply north behind Amalfi. A mountain ridge at the canyon's end overlooked the small villages of Castello and Oliveto. Beyond that sat the town of Castellammare, Vesuvius, and when clear, the whole of the Bay of Naples. The climb was more than a mile along a narrow stony path. They carried flashlights and no one said a word. Cesare led the way; he had made the hike up this valley countless times, yet tonight the landscape played tricks. He imagined enemies hiding in the undergrowth; his eyes darted into the blackness, then up to the starry sky. He was more nervous than scared, and he was very scared. The moon was halfway to full. Its light helped to define the top of the ridge and the broad shape of the canyon. They marched on and up the tight trail; the cool of the late evening condensed moisture on the stones, making them slippery. Twice Lucia asked to stop and rest. At the second pause, Cesare aimed his flashlight at his watch: twelve thirty. They had been climbing for nearly an hour, and they were becoming exhausted by both the climb and the adrenalin rushing through their bodies.

"Just a few hundred meters more," Cesare assured her. "Then we can rest."

They reached the ledge twenty minutes later. The view south down the V-shaped canyon to the sea and the Gulf of Salerno was open and clear. Behind them a waterfall that oozed and dribbled from the rock face fed a small stream that flowed down through the valley to the sea. No mist or fog drifted up from below. Lights could be seen on the distant shore. The aromas of the dry summer grass and the herbs that grew on the steep slopes perfumed the air. Any other evening, they would have enjoyed the quiet, but tonight Lucia feared for Nicola, her husband, and the morning.

Cesare made a second trip down the mountain to retrieve the remaining sacks. More determined on this return passage, he ignored his fears and concentrated on his family. Later, in the darkness, he stood outside the cave and smoked a cigarette, listening as Lucia settled Nicola in for what remained of the night. What the sunrise would bring, he could not imagine.

29

Amalfi, Early Morning
September 9, 1943

From their vantage point high up the valley above Amalfi, Cesare couldn't see Salerno, but he imagined the familiar coast and farmland far to the south of the city. When Lucia joined him, she looked out to the sea and said, "Those lights should not be there—those and those there. See the blue ones? There should be nothing there."

"They must be signals," Cesare said.

Far-off rumbling, like thunder, rolled across the water and up the canyon, followed by staccato concussions, then a pause, an expectant silence. Then massive explosions ripped the air. On the horizon, bursts of light appeared, like flashbulbs exploding. For over an hour, the sounds of schizophrenic drumming and flashes continued, rolling across the sea. The top of the far ridge behind and above them suddenly illuminated then disappeared, then again it flashed, backlit by fiery explosions beyond the ridge. Seconds later, like the count between lightning and thunder, concussions tumbled over the crest and down into the valley. Lucia and Cesare watched as more bursts of fire flared off the smooth and oily Bay of Salerno.

"Muzzle flashes from the cruisers and battleships. The first explosions on the shore had to be bombers. The next concussions will be from the big guns of the ships," Cesare said.

The reports echoed off the sea and up the valley like hell's thunder. More flashes and detonations extended across miles and miles of water.

"Nicola is sleeping—for how long I don't know," Lucia said. "Our poor families in Salerno and on the farms—all we can do is pray."

"They won't attack and try to land here," Cesare said. "It's too steep for an invasion of any strength, but the roads that climb over the mountains to Naples must be controlled."

The Allies would land at the seaside villages of Maiori, Minori, and maybe Amalfi, Cesare guessed. Their canyon and cave didn't have a road leading to the top. Troops heading their way would most likely first go to the Cava-Nocera Pass and the Chiunzi Pass. From there they could see the whole of Naples' plain from Vesuvius to the bay spread out below.

Lucia said, "From that ridge there, they will be able to direct their guns to kill Germans. Innocent people, our countrymen, will die."

Below came the muffled sounds of voices. Lucia and Cesare stepped out of view and waited. Cesare held the shotgun, unsure what he would do if they were Germans or even Americans. A massive explosion beyond the ridge across the canyon illuminated five people, heads down and carrying bags. Lucia flashed her light at them; they stopped.

"Don't shoot. We are from Amalfi," a woman's voice called out.

"Stay there. One of you come up and tell me who you are," Cesare ordered.

A young woman cautiously approached and put down her bag, squinting as Lucia shone a light on her face.

"I know you. You are the baker's daughter. Julia, right?"

"Yes, and my family. Are you Lucia Fallace?"

"Yes—move everyone into the cave. This is the best and safest we can do for now."

Over the next few hours, nine more people climbed the path from Amalfi. Some carried food, others bedding and clothes. There was a lull in the explosions at about four o'clock, two hours before sunrise. The sky to the southeast continued to show detonations and flares. When the largest bombs on the shore exploded, the flash revealed the silhouettes of hundreds of ships in the bay.

Lucia and the women made the three children comfortable. There were two men in the group; they were tough men. They had lived and seen much of life, but nothing approached this. One had fished the waters of the Tyrrhenian Sea for fifty years.

"All our boats will be destroyed. I'm too old to start over," he said. "When this is done, there will be nothing."

Grayness rose above the eastern ridge. Cesare stood with the men at the ledge, watching and waiting; at least, between them, they had enough cigarettes for a few days. A great flash, as if the furnaces of hell had been opened, rose from the sea. Seconds later, two massive projectiles, fired by a battleship off the harbor of Amalfi, roared up through gray haze and the steep valley as if a great pair of locomotives had been unleashed from their rails. They exploded on the high ridge that overlooked Castello. Fire and death ripped through the olive groves and woodlands that climbed the face of the mountain to the crest. A half-minute later, another salvo tore great fiery slashes higher up the mountainside. The next salvo flew over the top of the ridge and disappeared on the far side where the village of Castellammare lay.

"May God have mercy on their souls," the old fisherman said, crossing himself.

Five more salvos followed before the onslaught stopped.

Cesare's ears rang.

Then, in the growing light, they saw three dots rising over the sea. Caught in the sunrise, the dots flashed and flared, and grew larger as they headed straight toward the Sorrentine and their mountain cave.

"Quick, everyone down," Cesare said, as three British Spitfires climbed over Amalfi and headed right at them. The planes curved up the valley, nearly touching the rooftops. The pilots were level with their perch as they roared past. One pilot caught sight of them on the ledge and waved. A moment later, his machine guns fired along the ridgeline above them—the ridge that separated them from Naples and the German army. A second later, the side of the mountain was ripped open by machine gun fire by the fighters. Then the planes climbed, almost vertically, out of the end of the valley, banked right, and were lost behind the far ridge. Minutes later, the same three planes repeated their flight, and again fired their machine guns. This time, there was return gunfire from the ridge; tracer bullets ripped through the air at the approaching planes and exploded into the mountain above the cave—loose rock tumbled down the stone face.

"Into the cave!" Cesare yelled.

The men and women standing on the overlook turned and ran. German machine gun fire, from high above them, impacted the mountain and found their small world. The old fisherman spun around and fell to the ground. Cesare grabbed the wounded man by the edge of his shirt and dragged him into the cave. A woman ran to the fisherman and pressed the hem of her dress against his side, a valiant effort to stop the bleeding.

"We have been spotted. Most likely by Germans trying to come over from Naples. The planes are attacking them," Cesare said to Lucia.

The children were now awake and crying. The roar of the

planes up the valley was unceasing. Sortie after sortie flew past, dropping bombs, and firing into the stone face of the ridge. Cesare ventured a quick peek outside and saw the far hillside was burning.

"The pines and oaks across the valley are on fire, but we should be okay, for now. There's not much to burn here," he told Lucia. "How's the old man?"

"He's dying," Lucia said simply. "His wife is with him."

Cesare nodded. So, it truly had begun.

"Make sure everyone stays inside," he said quietly.

Morning advanced into the afternoon. Through the thick haze and smell of cordite and burning trees, the sun was dimly visible. The small party in the cave shared bread and cheese. Cesare sipped wine from a metal cup. Six more people, up from Amalfi, joined them as the afternoon explosions and the concussions of shells and artillery echoed back and forth through the valley. The view south, to the bay, was gone; smoke now obscured everything.

"They landed in Maiori and Minori in the middle of the night," a new arrival said. "Americans—they headed inland to Chiunzi Pass. If they control that, then the Germans can't use the road."

"Castellammare, Gragnano?" Cesare asked the man.

"I don't know. As we climbed, we could see the Americans approaching Amalfi from Minori. The road's wide open. They marched silently in two columns on each side of the road. Others rode in open vehicles. My God, they are so young."

More explosions from along the ridgelines began, and then a series of concussions, one immediately after the other, marched up the side of the far mountain.

"Mortars," one of the new men said. "We used them in France and Africa."

"You were in the army?" Cesare asked.

"Yes, until yesterday. I was on leave. When Badoglio and

Eisenhower announced Italy's surrender, I was one of the first to unofficially resign." This brought a smile to his sunburned face. "Now we Italians will fight the Nazis together with the Americans," he said.

He carried the only other weapons among the twenty people now in the cave—an Italian Carcano rifle with about a dozen rounds and a Beretta pistol with two full magazines. With Cesare's shotgun, they would lose any fight within minutes.

"If the Germans come through this valley, they will have to come through us. There is no other route," Cesare said, stating the obvious as the others looked up at the mountain.

The old trail wound up the side of the mountain to Gragnano and Castellammare, a hard day's hike but not more than five miles as the crows fly. But today, even the crows would be shot down. More planes, these much higher, flew in tight formations from the west.

"Bombers heading to Salerno," the ex-soldier said. "Jesus Christ, I remember those from Africa. They would destroy everything for a thousand meters in every direction if you weren't underground. I'm lucky to be alive." He crossed himself. "I pity those who are about to receive them."

Lucia walked up to Cesare.

"The old man is dead," she said quietly.

"You know what to do," he said, keeping his voice low as well.

He kissed her on the cheek.

"We will put his body behind the rocks, there," he said, pointing.

Turning to the men, he asked, "Can you help?"

They gently moved the old fisherman to a spot off the trail. His wife, after a kiss, laid a handmade quilt over him. She sobbed into a white handkerchief. Then, as the explosions began again, Lucia walked her back into the cave.

Sharply and without warning, the valley face directly below

them exploded and immediately was followed by concussions that climbed, one after the other, up the face of the canyon. Everyone again ran into the cave as the German mortars found their range and began to detonate above them and below. Ears painfully popped as each shell exploded on the mountain. The woman and children screamed. Cesare saw terror in Lucia's and Nicola's eyes; he held his family close. Dust and rock debris rained down from the cracks and fissures in the mountain above them. Three of the women were on their knees, praying.

For long minutes, the mortars continued, and then they heard the roar of the fighter planes. The ground shook from fresh bombs impacting the mountain. Three more mortar shells landed, then silence. Cesare worked his way to the cave entry and watched as the same fighters they'd seen earlier roared past their ledge, dipped their wings, and disappeared through a cleft in the ridgeline. The mountainside, where the German mortars had been placed, was a ragged scar. Smoke from the concussions and fires covered the hillside.

"We have protectors," Lucia said, joining her husband at the cave's mouth.

"This isn't over. The Germans will fight—you've seen them. They will continue to try and find a way through here."

Late in the afternoon, one of the men tapped Cesare on the shoulder.

"We have company," he said. "I can't understand them. You need to come out."

Cesare went out and faced five armed American soldiers. Their uniforms were dirty, and their faces were still covered in camouflage soot applied before their landing over twelve hours earlier.

"You the boss?" the tallest American said, in a mangled form of Italian.

"And you are Americans, thank God," Cesare answered in English, his New Jersey accent obvious, to the surprise of the soldiers. "Yes, I lived in Newark, New Jersey, for ten years. Where you boys from?"

"We're with the Fourth Battalion Rangers, landed at Minori. Been up and down these damn mountains like goats the last few hours. We're heading to Castellammare. Do you know where the hell it is?"

For the next fifteen minutes the soldiers, now joined by ten more men, quizzed Cesare and Lucia about the terrain and the trails that led to Castellammare. Three of the soldiers watched the ridge for signs of Germans. They offered some of their rations to the families and chocolate bars to the children.

"Nothing but Americans behind us, ma'am," the officer said to Lucia, as he pointed back toward Amalfi.

"And the whole country is full of Germans that way," Cesare said, pointing north. "I'm Cesare Fallace, and this is my wife, Lucia; and the boy is Nicola. Who are you, sir?"

"Darby. Lieutenant Colonel Bill Darby with the US Rangers. I want to use this position as an observer post. We can watch above and below as we work our way up to the top. There we will set up a better position. It's now safe to take your folks down the trail to the village—just be careful."

Darby pointed to three of his men and ordered them to remain on the ledge. He shook the Amalfi men's hands, and then he and his squad headed up to the ridge top. One of the men volunteered to lead them to Gragnano. Cesare watched them disappear around the face of the mountain. The three Spitfires again buzzed the canyon and shredded the far side of the mountain with their machine guns and disappeared over the ridge.

30

Rome, Villa San Sebastiano
September 10, 1943

Midday, the day before the Allies invaded Salerno, 140 miles south of Rome, the ancient village of Frascati, southeast of Rome, was attacked by hundreds of American Flying Fortress bombers. Word had somehow gotten to Allied bomber command that Field Marshal Kesselring and other high-ranking Germans were in the village. When the bombers finished, the town was in ruins, a thousand of its citizens were dead, along with one hundred fifty Germans. Somehow, Kesselring managed to crawl out of his collapsed villa and return to his duties as German commander.

The concussions and the rolling thunder of the bombing in the east could be heard, and the smoke could be seen, from the upper floors of the Conti villa.

The evening of September 8, Rome radio announced the armistice. Italy had surrendered to the Allies. The population of Rome was stunned—was the war over? Were the Americans about to enter Rome? From where? Which direction? Were they still in Sicily, hundreds of miles away? While the citizens of the villages and hill towns surrounding Rome celebrated,

Rome remained calm and pensive. The curfew and martial law were still in effect; the streets were quiet.

News of the invasion at Salerno was slow to reach Rome. The city prepared for its own response to the Germans who had announced that they would not tolerate any Italian opposition. The Germans called the Italians traitors, and worse; Rome knew that the Germans would march on their city. Prior to the announcement of the invasion, the Germans disarmed the Italian army. There was a fear that the citizens of Rome and the surrounding regions would revolt against the occupiers, even though they had few guns, little ammunition, and certainly nothing that could destroy a German tank, let alone armored vehicles. Worst of all, they lacked organization and leadership. Many Italian soldiers shed their uniforms and disappeared into the population. Others joined the resistance, but they, too, were short of ammunition. Chaos ensued. The Germans, always organized, had penetrated the communications of the Italian army. The Italians could not hide their intentions.

Max stayed at the villa with the Contis after the call to the Fallaces miraculously made it through. Since that initial call, he tried twice to reach them—nothing.

"They will be okay," Sophie said. "From what you've told me, they are tough."

"They are that," Max answered. "How are you this morning?"

"Better. I even made it to the bathroom. The leg is stiff, but I can walk."

"Good. If I ever get my hands on that son of a bitch . . ."

"Don't think about it. We have our own war now. The Germans will occupy Rome; they have to," Sophie said.

"Signorina," Luciano said, tapping on the door. "There is a phone call for Signor Max."

Max followed the butler down the stairs. *At least the local phone lines still work—but for how long?*

It was Albert Kent. "The story from the south of the city is that the Germans are moving north to the gates at San Pablo, San Sebastiano, Porta Ardeatina, and the Aurelian Wall. Resistance groups are forming to meet them."

"It's suicide."

"Yeah, probably. But there's no way to stop them. I'll find you later." Kent hung up.

Luciano said something to Sophie. She stood at the base of the stairway.

"There are dozens of fighters coming through the cellar and out to the wall," Sophie said. "They are going to the gates."

"As if we could stop them," Max said.

To counterpoint Sophie's comment, explosions from beyond the wall shattered the silence. More concussions followed the first volley. The phone line again was dead. Max looked up the stairs. The count and countess stood at the landing.

"There's fighting at the San Pablo Gate," Max said.

"Signor, there are Germans coming up the driveway," Luciano said, panic in his voice.

From the villa's windows, Max could see that a black sedan and an armored truck had pulled into the opening just before the gravel parking area. They sat there like two beasts watching their prey. He pulled the Colt from his waistband.

"Sophie, get the staff and your grandparents into the tunnels. I'll try and delay them."

"That's suicide. And the only staff in the house is Luciano. I told everyone else to stay home."

"Good. Now get your family downstairs."

"Young man, I will not be thrown out of my own home," Signor Conti said as he led his wife down the stairs.

"If you don't, you will die here. Think of your wife and granddaughter. Go, go."

Max looked back out the window. Two explosions engulfed the truck. Soldiers were tossed in the air. The other SS soldiers took cover and returned gunfire into the woods beyond the lawn of the villa. From behind him, he heard the hard footsteps of boots on the marble floor. Three men and a woman appeared. Max recognized Luca and Marco. Luca tossed Max a German machine pistol. Max slipped the Colt into his waistband. They ran past Max and broke the windows on either side of the double doors and immediately began firing their weapons at the Germans.

The vehicles reversed and backed down the driveway out of sight. The resistance gunfire continued.

Max went to Sophie. "Get them downstairs. I'm right behind you."

More gunfire raked the villa. Mere wood, stucco, and glass couldn't stop the bullets fired from the high-caliber machine gun mounted on the armored vehicle. Slugs ravaged the downstairs. Everyone dove to the floor.

Max took a position behind the thick stone façade, looked out, and saw Schmidt standing near the armored vehicle directing his soldiers. Using the machine pistol, he fired half a clip at the Nazi, missing high and right. More gunfire from the woods clipped tree branches and kicked up dirt around the Germans. The machine gun swung away from the villa and fired into the shrubs and undergrowth. Max could see damage was being done. A man slid across the villa floor behind him to the open window—on his shoulder was a stolen German *Faustpatrone*. He fired it as soon as he had the vehicle in its sight. It hit the truck broadside, the upper area of the carrier exploded, the machine gun flew out, and the gunner was thrown over the side. The fighter looked up at Max and in Italian said, "Just like North Africa."

The grinding noise of a tank cut through the smoke.

"We must go now," Luca said. "They are bringing up tanks and heavier weapons. The Germans are massing south of here in support of the advance units at Porta San Pablo and the other gates. We are being massacred. The Germans said that Rome was an open city—bullshit. They want it and will take it. Right now, I need to protect as many of my men as possible. Max, you and Sophie do what you must. Get the Contis out of here."

"Thanks, Luca. We'll go north. Same route as before. God be with you!"

"And you."

Max ran through the entry toward the central part of the villa. Everything was ripped, torn, and bullet ridden. Glass and wood splinters covered the floor, and plaster dust made breathing difficult. Then he saw the blood. Sophie was next to her grandfather—he was on a lounge, his upper body crimson. Ester Conti stood behind them, holding her husband's hand.

"How bad?" Max said.

"Very bad," Sophie answered.

"We must go. I'll carry him. We go down and through the tunnel to the church near the spa. From there we go into Rome. Kent has a place."

"He can't be moved," Sophie pleaded.

"If we don't go now, we will all be dead. No arguments—we go now."

Max passed Sophie the machine pistol, slipped his arms under the man, and lifted him. Moments later, they were taking the stairs to the cellar. They passed three more men coming out of the tunnels.

"Luca, Marco?" they asked, not stopping.

"Upstairs," Max answered.

Max laid Franco Conti on the table. The man's eyes fluttered, then looked at his wife and Sophie.

"*I miei amori*," he said in a whisper.

"*Ti amo*," Ester Conti answered. Sophie squeezed her grandfather's hand.

"We go."

A massive explosion shook the house; dust and debris fell from the ceiling.

"Tanks. Now."

Max picked up the count, Sophie grabbed a canvas bag from a shelf, and they climbed through the opening to the tunnels. They went north. Remarkably, the electric lights were still on. They stumbled forward. Twice, fighters passed them heading south. Fifteen minutes later, they reached the stairs to the church.

"I'll go up and see if it's safe," Sophie said.

She swung the machine pistol off her shoulder and took the steps two at a time. A minute later, she returned.

"It's clear. We'll go into the church. We can dress Grandfather's wounds there."

In the front pew of the St. Nereo church, Max gently laid the man out. His breathing was shallow, raspy. Max saw the hole in his chest where the bullet had entered. He didn't want to think about the internal damage. He was shocked that the man was still alive. He looked at Sophie and slightly shook his head.

Sophie opened his shirt, and immediately placed a heavy gauze pad from the bag she carried. There was little blood—Franco had lost so much. She looked at her grandmother and took a deep breath.

"I don't believe he'll survive, *Nonna*. He's lost too much blood and there's nothing we can do here."

Ester slid along the pew next to her husband and put his head on her lap, caressing his cheek.

Franco looked at his wife and the breath from his lungs slowly escaped. She then kissed his forehead.

"We must go. The priests will take care of *Nonno*," Sophie said.

"I am staying. We have been together for more than fifty years. I will not leave him now. You go—be with Max. Stop these evil men. I will stay here with Franco and God."

Max heard pounding from below. The Germans had made it into the tunnels. Pistol shots rang out.

"Sophie, now," Max said.

"Give me your pistol. I will hold them off," Ester said. "Give you some time. Go."

Sophie removed a Beretta from the bag and handed to her.

"Can she shoot?" Max asked.

"She taught me." Sophie kissed her grandmother.

"Tell your mother I love her."

"Yes, *Nonna*, I will."

Max and Sophie ran down the aisle to the front door. They opened it slowly and saw no trouble immediately in front of them. The sounds of explosions and gunshots filled the air.

They crossed the road and ran into the first battered walls of the ruins of the old Caracalla bathhouse. "We go through the ruins, then north past the Circus Maximus, then to the river. If our luck holds—"

A pistol shot came from the church, then a burst of machine gun fire. Max never wanted to see that look on Sophie's face again. It was unmeasurable pain.

"You can't go back."

"I know, but at least they are together."

31

Field Marshal Kesselring's notice was posted and broadcast throughout the city. "*After midnight, September 15, anyone found in possession of arms will be shot.*" Quiet had returned to Rome. For how long, no one knew or would even try to guess. The Germans and fascists were taking what they wanted from the city and doing what they wanted. It was announced that the king, his family, and Badoglio and his family had fled Rome. There was also a story circulated that Mussolini had been rescued from the prison he'd been locked in. German paratroopers had landed near his mountain jail and flew him off to Berlin—there he met with Hitler. A new fascist government was announced with Mussolini as its head—no one in Rome cared. In the south, the Germans managed to stop the advance of the Allies as they moved to take Naples. There were rumors that the invasion was failing; Romans hoped the Allies would be in Rome in a week. Now they weren't sure when Rome would be freed.

Max and Sophie made it through the chaos and street fighting to the safe house near the Piazza Navona. At night, standing on the roof, they could hear the occasional pistol shot or far-off boom or thunder of canons. The city was incredibly hot, and food was almost impossible to find.

Kent handed Max a short note.

Get to Ostia. I want you two out of Rome. Z.J.

"And how does he propose that?" Sophie said. "Swim down the Tiber?"

"Not a bad idea—at least it's cooler than this thick, hot air," Max answered.

"They pulled a dozen bodies out of the river. No fucking way I'm swimming to the sea. I'm no Olympic champion like you."

"Boat?"

"We'd be target practice."

Word reached them that the villa, though damaged, had survived. Luca and Marco had also made it out and had fled the city, to the south. They were in the hills with other resistance fighters. The phone would work intermittently, but you could never be certain who was listening, and, under edict, only Italian could be spoken.

* * *

Schmidt limped around the office of SS Major Kappler, favoring his right leg. His left arm was suspended in a black cloth sling. The Beretta used by the woman in the church surprised him. Intent on the two suspected agents, he'd been caught off guard. That would never happen again. The defense of the villa also surprised him. If he'd had any suspicion that Franco Conti had been an anti-fascist, he would have come to the villa more heavily armed. The chaos generated by the resistance, combined with his hasty action to apprehend the Norcross woman, contributed to the fiasco. He knew better. He'd been rash, stupid, and the result was the loss of five good men.

"Your arm, is it better?" Kappler asked.

"Yes. Stiff, but I can still shoot," Schmidt answered.

"Now, my friend, back to work. I have requisitioned rail cars and locomotives; they will be at your service. You will also have the soldiers you need, both SS and Heer."

"I prefer my own SS personnel; they know their jobs and I will not have to deal with the scruples of the army. There may be some Italian fascists that might also be of assistance. I will also need them for language issues."

"Understood. We have already seized Jews near Lake Maggiore, Milan, and Cuneo. Those that survived are being transported."

"Congratulations on your recovery of Prime Minister Mussolini," Schmidt offered. "It was, I understand, quite an operation—brilliant, in fact. I believe that the Führer was pleased."

"Just doing my duty. And your duty will be to remove the twelve thousand Jews in this city and ensure their transport to Poland. The Jewish leaders do not believe that this will happen; they are fools. We will use it to our advantage. Begin the planning. You are dismissed."

Schmidt left the newly established headquarters of the SS and SD in Rome, the converted German Cultural Office on Via Tasso. He had his driver take him to the Hotel Minerve. There were few vehicles in the city, and all of these were German armored trucks, staff cars, and other military vehicles. German tanks commanded many of the intersections, and manned bunkers provided additional security. It had not taken long for the German army to take command of the "open city."

He had two reasons for returning to the hotel. The first was that he desperately needed a bath—it had been four days. His uniform and his own body reminded him of the days leading up to the attacks on Poland. Days and nights living in basements. The other was that today was his birthday, September 15. A small party had been hastily planned at one of the few German restaurants in Rome. The owner was a supporter of the Reich and somehow found ample supplies of veal, sauerkraut, German cheeses and sausages, and, more importantly, wines. He would turn it into both a birthday and victory celebration.

Regarding himself in the full-length mirror in his suite at the hotel, Schmidt saw nothing that he couldn't admire, especially for someone whose forty-third birthday party was this evening. His uniform was impeccable, each button polished, and the patent leather facing gleamed. His new boots, made by one of Rome's finest shoemakers, were as exquisite as that of any general in Rome. He had hoped not to wear the sling for his arm, but the pain was more than the damage to his ego. Besides, he might gain a little respect knowing it was his first wound—the Wound Badge was pinned to his left uniform pocket.

His friend Karl Hass, from Berlin and assisting in the conversion of the Via Tasso office building into SS headquarters, was sponsoring the event. The two had attended school together, and both joined the army from their positions as policemen in Nuremberg. Other friends and comrades would also join them at the restaurant.

As Schmidt walked through the lobby of the hotel, voices lowered, and conversations stopped. Pretending not to take notice, he stopped for a moment and lit a cigarette. He sensed both respect and fear; he welcomed both. His driver, a sergeant and decorated veteran of Poland and France, stood at attention near the door. Together they had, during the previous months, traveled the length of Italy, inspecting the ports and weak points along the Italian coasts. Like his travels in the United States, Schmidt's goals were clear: to assess and report his findings. However, after his meeting with Kappler, he was pleased to be back doing what he knew best—transporting the criminal Jews.

As he approached his driver, the sergeant gave a rigid right-armed salute, his heels clicking smartly. Heads throughout the lobby jerked toward the sound. The pose was held long enough to be marked indelibly in the minds of those watching. Schmidt wanted these people in this hotel and Rome to fear Germany's power.

* * *

Max, seated in the lobby of the Minerve Hotel, was carefully positioned behind a newspaper that concealed most of his upper body and yet still afforded a good view. Schmidt acknowledged the salute of his driver. The sergeant held the door as the doorman stood to one side. Max then leisurely stood, folded his paper, placed it under his arm, and casually followed a group of well-dressed men and women heading out to dinner. Schmidt climbed into his car parked alongside the ornate chain and bollards cordoning off the cobblestoned Minerva Square. As Schmidt's car pulled away, an ambulance left the curb up the street and stopped in front of the hotel. As Schmidt's sedan turned the corner, Max climbed into the front seat of the ambulance.

"Quick. When we see him, slow down. I don't want him to know he's being followed," Max said.

"For Christ's sake, this isn't our first tail," Sophie said. "Besides, you have a good idea where he's going."

"He may change his mind."

"I doubt it. Our people tell us that particular German restaurant has been his base of operations since he arrived. I'm beginning to think the man does not appreciate Italian food."

"He's the worse for it. I've had enough schnitzel and sausages to last a lifetime."

They tracked the car's dim rear running lights as it wove through the narrow streets of Rome, over the Tiber River, and into the Trastevere quarter. Once sure that their quarry was headed to the restaurant, Sophie turned onto a parallel street and parked. They walked in the early evening gloom to a restaurant one block over. Only three people sat in the room. Even with the doors open, the September air was stifling.

"We only have lentil soup and old bread. The supplier was murdered by the SS two days ago," the owner said.

"That will do. We haven't eaten since yesterday," Sophie answered.

Schmidt's restaurant was a block north near the church of San Pietro in Montorio, an area known for its eateries and other evening entertainments. Even after the chaos of the occupation, two of the neighborhood's working girls strolled by Max and Sophie as they left the restaurant and walked up the Via Garibaldi.

"Two for one," one girl said in Italian. "If she stays, we can make a special offer."

"Go look for a donkey," Sophie answered, in perfect Italian.

"Bitch," was the reply.

"That wasn't very nice. They have to make a living," Max said.

"We have other business tonight. Besides, if they interest you, I must be slipping."

"No, you aren't, and they didn't."

"Pay attention. My God, how your mind wanders. But then again, you are a man."

Since their escape and the death of her grandparents, they had moved every day from house to house. It was difficult to stay free of Italian spies and German attention. With his height, he stood well above the normal Italian male, but at least his Aryan features would allow for some to dismiss him as a German in civilian clothes. Sophie, on the other hand, could pass for Italian, English, or even French. Her French was excellent and favored a well-educated Parisian accent. Once, when pressed by a German soldier the previous morning, they passed as a German businessman with his French mistress. The roles suited their characters.

"Four staff cars, three limos, and Schmidt's car. Quite a celebration," Max commented as they hid in the shadows across from the restaurant. The curfew was about to go into effect.

"It's his birthday," Sophie reminded him. "MI6's dossier is helpful. That's why Jones wants him. When he comes out, I'd just as soon shoot the son of a bitch."

"His birthday? Today?" Max said.

"No, actually tomorrow. He was born in 1900."

"As Nazis go, he's a bit long in the tooth at forty-three."

Sophie agreed. Most Schutzstaffel were younger. It hadn't been too difficult to find Nazi followers after Germany's economic collapse in the 1920s.

"Are we going in?" she asked Max.

"Not a chance. Small room, and the alley behind may have one of those officer's cars blocking it," Max said. "If there is one thing I've learned, it's how efficient these bastards can be. Security comes to them as naturally as goose-stepping."

"I'll move and park the ambulance across the street."

Max hugged Sophie a little closer with his right arm; he felt her hip against the pistol in his pocket.

"Pay attention," she ordered.

* * *

Schmidt was pleased to see the other cars in front of the restaurant. He recognized each of them. Yes, the evening would be enjoyable.

"Yes, there is work to be done, Schmidt," a friend said. "Live a little. Besides, the food and the wine in Rome, not to mention the women, are a lot better than in Warsaw, or even Paris. Please, tell me that you will find some time to get involved with this city. She has beguiled men for two thousand years."

Schmidt smiled, only slightly.

"I'm not easily beguiled. Besides, Rome today is not the Rome I want to live in; Julius Caesar's Rome is my Rome."

He directed his friends to the feast of sausages, schnitzels, potatoes, sauerkraut, and other delicacies.

"Eat up, my friends," Schmidt said. "For as the ancient Romans said, 'eat, drink, and be merry, for tomorrow we die.'"

"Happy birthday!" twenty voices shouted.

Schmidt raised his beer and smiled. "*Prosten!*"

"*Prost!*" was the reply.

The diners stayed past midnight, and then in groups of twos and threes they began to return to their hotels or other prearranged accommodations or assignations. While most were his friends, Schmidt also knew where most were going. His carefully guarded dossiers included army staff and other attachés posted to Italy and Rome. Three were going to see their mistresses; one was a bachelor and was never seen in public with anyone, although there were unproven rumors about his attention given to young men under his command. The others were returning home, four having brought their wives and families with them to their posts in Rome. They were a good group of friends if one thought of them that way. To Schmidt the reality was simpler; they were associates, comrades in arms, and he would fight and die for them. He wanted to be sure *they* would fight and die for Germany.

* * *

In the front seat of the ambulance, Sophie and Max sat in darkness, sharing what was left of the bottle of Barolo left over from dinner. The owner of the restaurant had offered them a good price—he preferred that they drink it rather than the Germans. At half past midnight, staff cars pulled to the curb. Their drivers stood at the doors. In groups, the officers began to leave the restaurant. They shook hands, grasped shoulders, and in a few cases saluted. Some walked to their vehicles, and smoke from cigarettes filled the air. Beyond, in the boulevards and alleys, occasional snaps of what sounded like firecrackers echoed through the thousand-year-old streets. Max knew they were not firecrackers.

Soon after the last vehicle left, a car's headlights approached from their rear and passed them. Schmidt's driver pulled up to the curb, dismounted, and hurriedly disappeared into the restaurant. A moment later, Schmidt followed his driver out, lit a cigarette, and surveyed the street. While the German was visible to them in the dim streetlights, Max felt sure that Schmidt could not see them hidden in the ambulance. There were no streetlights.

"When?" Sophie asked.

"We will pull up to the Mercedes," Max said. "I'll get out the back and grab Schmidt, while you make sure the driver stays in the vehicle. Pull close. Keep him from opening the door; block it."

"He won't go easily."

"I know."

The driver stood near his boss. Schmidt smoked half the length of his cigarette and then blew a final breath of smoke before crushing the cigarette with his heel on the paving stones.

"Start moving toward him," Max said from the back.

"Hold—there's a problem."

"Now what?"

Max climbed back into the front and watched two men bolt from the alley behind Schmidt. They picked him up and slammed him against the fender of his limousine. A third man crossed over from the opposite side of the street, calmly aimed a pistol at the driver, and shot him as he stood next to Schmidt. The sharp pistol report reverberated in the narrow street. The shooter then turned his attention to Schmidt, who was being held tightly by the two men. The German twisted and turned.

The shooter swung the barrel of his pistol across Schmidt's face, slicing across his left cheek. Blood began to pour onto Schmidt's spotless uniform.

The shooter tried to swing the pistol in the opposite direction. Before he could strike again, Max fired his Colt. The bullet whizzed just past the man's nose. Max fired again, just missing the two accomplices.

"You are a much better shot than that," Sophie said through the window of the ambulance.

"I *am* trying to miss them. Please shut up—you are messing up my aim."

Max let off another round. The two men dropped Schmidt to the street and took off running. The shooter glanced toward Max, considered firing back, and then he, too, sprinted away. The three disappeared into the night. Max heard an engine start and the whirr of tires on stones. A second later, the front door of the restaurant opened and the owner ran to Schmidt. He was carrying a machine pistol. He held his apron against the SS major's bloody face.

"Why did you save that piece of shit? They were doing us a favor," Sophie demanded as Max climbed back in the ambulance.

"I don't know why. God damnit—who do you think they were?"

"My guess? Some of Germany's many dissatisfied Italian customers. But why not just shoot him? He's right there," Sophie said. "Fuck this, I'll shoot the son of a bitch right now." She started to open the door.

"Stop, wait. I know it's personal, and now even more so. I want him to know it is us. And I have an idea how we can trap him."

32

Rome, Gestapo Headquarters
September 16, 1943

SS-Obersturmbannführer Schmidt sat motionless as the doctor methodically stitched up his left cheek. The cut from the pistol was ragged; it began just below the eye and extended to the top of his jaw. "No chloroform or morphine," he said. "Just finish."

Schmidt had fought through the war for five years and had not even a scratch to show for it. But today, his ankle was swollen from the incident in the tunnel six days earlier, his shoulder ached from the bullet hole put there by that old woman, and now his torn face. And all of it due to those two fucking spies—a firing squad would not be adequate punishment.

"Do you wish a dressing over the wound?" the doctor asked.

"No. While it is messy, the bleeding has stopped. Leave it as it is."

"Yes, Colonel," the doctor answered and then placed his tools in his bag and left.

"It will give you a rakish look, like Colonel Otto Skorzeny and his scar," Kappler said. "Mine." He pointed to his cheek.

"Gives us character, authority."

"That lucky bastard Skorzeny—talk about the right place and time," Schmidt said, spitting blood on a towel. "Mussolini owes his miserable hide to that man . . . mountaintop rescue, then flown off to Germany. Then again, Otto has always been a glory hound."

"He does get the job done," Kappler added.

"Yes, I'll give him that."

"By the way, happy birthday, Colonel."

"It's all bullshit," Schmidt answered rudely.

"Be careful, Schmidt."

The speaker box on the general's desk buzzed. "Yah," Kappler said, answering the intercom.

"A message for Colonel Schmidt."

"Bring it in."

The adjutant opened the door and handed Schmidt a paper. Schmidt read it.

"That villa in the San Sebastiano district, the one where—"

"—you fucked up," Kappler interjected.

Schmidt glared at his commander. "Yes, that one. Our surveillance has paid off. The Norcross woman, the granddaughter of the dead Contis, was seen sneaking back into the villa."

"Why would she do that? She should know the place was being watched."

"All we know is that she's there—she went in two hours ago," Schmidt said.

"And you want to go and arrest her?"

"Yes."

"It's a waste of resources right now. This rebellion by the Italians has not been completely put down; there's a lull, but we've seen this before—Warsaw, Kiev, even Amsterdam. I will not have you go seeking revenge. There will be a time to deal with them. Right now, your orders come from Berlin. Continue collecting the Jews. They think we don't care about them now;

I want to show them that we do care, and that when we find them, they will be immediately shipped to Poland."

"I will not leave these two here to cause mischief. They are spies, probably part of a larger network. I can catch them, and I can destroy that network."

Kappler studied the older man, then said, "Since today is your birthday, I will give you the two spies. They are yours. But you have just today. If you have not apprehended them by midnight, you will return here to carry out your orders. Do you understand? Is this acceptable?"

Schmidt hesitated, then said, "Yes, thank you." He stood at attention and saluted the head of security in Rome.

An hour later, he was heading across Rome in his open Mercedes. He would not need an army to capture these two.

* * *

"We should have shot him, right there at the restaurant," Sophie said. "And this charade would be over. He deserved it for Dominic, for my grandparents, and for Pietro. It would have been easy, as Cattaneo said, just one ten-cent bullet."

"I'm not an assassin. I can't walk up to a man and put a bullet in his head," Max answered. "Even if he is a murderer. Easy? Easy for who? Somewhere a line must be drawn, even if it's through your own soul."

Two days after the partisan attempt on Schmidt's life at the restaurant, Max and Sophie were going back to the villa. It was early. They hoped too early for the Nazi watchers who they were sure were outside. The German ambulance gave them some cover.

"Turn here," Sophie said as they approached a split in the road. Right went to San Sebastiano, left to the Porte Latina.

"That's not the way to the church at the spa," Max said.

"There are more ways in and out of the villa. This one I used as a child; I'm not sure who else knows about it. It starts in an obscure chapel on the Via Latina and follows a smaller tunnel to the villa."

They parked the ambulance near the Porta Latina, the Latin Gate. It was unguarded. The small church fronted a structure built into the wall behind it. Max forced the lock, and they went down a circular stair more than forty steps. He complained about how cramped it was.

"I was much smaller when I found it," Sophie said as they pushed through a door hidden behind a panel of stone that held the roof of the tunnel. She led them on a short but cramped hike. "The villa is above us. We are in a parallel tunnel to the larger aqueduct. You said you had a plan, what is it?"

"When you go fishing, you need bait; and the prettier the bait, the bigger the fish," Max said as he and Sophie passed through a small door and climbed the steps up into the basement under the villa.

"Bait? I'm bait?" Sophie said.

"No, me. Who could resist me?"

"You are an idiot. Word will pass on to Schmidt. Even after the chaos of the past four days, you are guessing that he will have someone watching the villa—just in case we came back. A dangerous guess."

"It's an educated one, based on human nature. And right now, he wants us. Luca says he saw Schmidt leave the church where your grandparents died; he was wounded. I hope to God it was your grandmother who put that bullet in him."

"At the cost of her own life," Sophie said as they entered the hallway outside the kitchen. "I will shoot the fucker."

Pistols out, they passed the kitchen and entered the main portion of the house.

"So far, so good. At least there's not a platoon of Germans waiting for us," Sophie said. "They must know someone is here; can we go now?"

"We wait a few minutes. Wave your flashlight around, like

we are looking for something."

"I think we are looking for a good way to get killed."

Sophie looked at the damage done by the firefight to the house where she'd spent her childhood summers. It made her ill. She passed the flashlight over the furniture and the walls; the stairway was a devastated mess. The panels had hundreds of holes, plaster dust covered everything, and some of the doors were blown off their hinges. The hundred-year-old chandelier, made with Venetian glass, lay broken in the center of the foyer where it fell.

During the next hour, Sophie recovered some of her grandmother's personal items, things she remembered from her childhood. She placed them in a small bag.

"We were lucky," Sophie said. "All this can be fixed. How are we going to trap this son of a bitch?"

Standing in the foyer, Max waved his flashlight over his watch. "Time to go. Back to the ambulance."

"Stand where you are," a voice demanded in English.

Sophie screamed.

"Place your weapons on the floor and move away from them."

Max and Sophie did as ordered.

"You took your time getting here, Colonel Schmidt," Max said. "I thought that an hour was more than enough time."

"You knew he was coming?" Sophie said.

"Of course. The man lives for revenge. We bested him; he was not satisfied with the previous outcomes. He's a fool."

Standing next to Schmidt was a single soldier; he held a Schmeisser.

"I am sorry about your driver the other night—we had nothing to do with that. It was the partisans, I think—or maybe the communists. Nonetheless, I was not going to let them just kill you on the street, so I intervened."

"It was you who fired at them?" Schmidt said.

"Yes, and Sophie, your guest at Regina Coeli prison, wanted you dead right then," Max said. "I had to stop her. There would be a better time for revenge. You should thank me for your life."

"I told you we should have just shot him then," Sophie said.

"You Americans, so cocky, so full of yourself," Schmidt said.

"Don't I know it," Sophie said.

"Shut up. I'll get to you later. We can finish our conversation back in Regina Coeli. Right now, I want to know who the hell you are."

"We have met many times, Colonel. Berlin, Chicago, train stations, even at the embassy a month ago."

The man glared at him; then a change began.

"You *were* at the Olympics, at the Bund meeting, the priest in the embassy. Who the hell are you?"

"A Berlin Jew who is now an American; you have much to atone for, Schmidt. I am here to collect that debt."

"You are fools, both of you. Turn around. Corporal, secure their hands."

The corporal set the machine pistol on the nearby table and removed two short lengths of rope from his pocket. He took one step, and the muffled pop of a silencer filled the room. The soldier dropped. Schmidt spun around. A flashlight, full in his face, blinded him. A pistol crashed across his arm and wrist, knocking the Luger he was holding to the floor.

"On your knees, NOW!" a voice with a Cockney accent yelled.

Blinded, Schmidt remained standing. Max took a step forward and smashed his fist down onto the man's wounded shoulder. Schmidt yelled, crumpled, and dropped to his knees.

"Thanks, Albert—cutting it a little close," Max said.

"I had to make sure he came alone—just him and his driver. He will have others here soon; we need to go."

"Then we go."

Schmidt, tears in his eyes, looked up at Max and Sophie.

"Who the hell are you?" Schmidt asked.

"Captain Max Adler, American Strategic Services, and this is Sophie Norcross, MI6. This is her villa, and you are so fucked."

Schmidt glared at the two of them. Kent jabbed a hypodermic needle into Schmidt's neck.

* * *

Late the next morning, the ambulance pulled to a stop at the San Lorenzo district's Tiburtina Station. The driver leaned out of the window and demanded information from one of the guards where to take a prisoner he had in the back of the ambulance.

"He was injured in the roundup. The doctors say he's good to transport. Where do I go?"

The SS corporal looked across the rail yard to the twenty-car freight train sitting in the hot sun. "See that sergeant at the end of the train? Be quick—it is leaving in an hour."

Albert Kent, dressed in a sergeant's SS uniform, leaned over to the SS-Standartenführer seated next to him. "You heard?"

"Yes," Max answered. "This is fucked. We need to do something; somebody needs to do something."

"You know it would be suicide, there's a hundred men surrounding the train. If there's any action, they will machine-gun the whole train."

Max leaned back to the small window that opened to the back of the ambulance and said, "Get him ready."

Kent wove his way through the tangle of railroad tracks and crossings. He approached the rear of the train where the SS sergeant stood, a clipboard in his hand.

"Fucking hot, isn't it?" Max said to the soldier as he got

out. "Even for October."

"Colonel, what can I do for you?" the sergeant looked up from his board, stiffened and saluted.

"I have a prisoner; he is to go with this train. He was wounded during the sweep. The doctor says he can go—not that it makes a difference to me. He's heavily sedated. Can your men help me get him onboard?"

"The cars are already full; there's no room."

"There's always room—you know that. And besides, there will be room soon enough. Isn't that the way it works?"

A baby's cry came from the last car; Max's heart began to tear itself in two. "Get the fucking man onboard. He's an escaped prisoner; his tattoo says that he was once an inmate at Auschwitz. It will save time in processing when he gets there." Max handed the soldier a folded pile of documents.

The sergeant grunted at the joke. "Second car down—there's more children, more room. You two, go with the colonel. Help him load the prisoner."

Kent opened the back of the ambulance. A stretcher sat on the deck of the vehicle; a man was strapped to it. He wore a suitcoat, a dirty shirt, slacks, and scuffed shoes. A bandage wrapped the man's face, a bloody red seam ran down his cheek. To anyone looking at the man, he was either unconscious or heavily sedated—his eyes looked to the sky and would not focus. The two soldiers from the ambulance slid the stretcher out and carried it to the second car from the end. The sergeant never moved or looked; he just studied the paperwork. They set the stretcher on the gravel near the rails, and one of the German soldiers threw open the lock and waited. Two German soldiers walked down the train and joined the first two from the ambulance, they took over. An Alsatian walked next to another soldier that approached. When the door was slid open, Max's heart completely tore itself apart. Children and women stood at the opening. The dog began to bark, lunging at its chain lead. The children screamed.

The soldiers lifted the man and tried to slide him into the boxcar. A man's voice yelled from inside, "There's no room. For the love of God . . ."

"Shut up," one of the guards yelled. Max saw that he wasn't German but an Italian in a fascist uniform. "Make room or I'll shoot three of you and make room."

The crowd drew back from the door. They lifted the stretcher to the deck of the boxcar.

"I want my stretcher back," Kent said.

The two guards looked at Kent. One said, "You want it back?"

"Yes. Our men need it more than that bastard."

Not wishing to argue with the logic, they cut the cloth restraints, lifted one side of the stretcher, and rolled the man into the boxcar. One of the soldiers then slammed the door shut and threw over the latch.

Max walked up to the sergeant. "Shitty job, isn't it?"

"I do what I'm told. It was this way in Poland, in Holland, and in France. The bastards get what they deserve as far as I'm concerned. This paperwork looks okay, a little out of the ordinary."

"That prisoner is out of the ordinary. Are you traveling with the train?"

"Yes, through to Vienna, then I'm relieved and then return here."

"Vienna is lovely this time of the year," Max said, trying to close his ears to the noises coming from the train.

"Sachertorte, nothing better. That prisoner, you were going to say something?"

"Yes, Sergeant. A word of warning. He was caught impersonating a German officer, a senior SS officer to be exact. We checked—it's all a lie. He will say anything. We found out who he really is, a Polish Jew, a soldier with money. Bribed his way out of the camp. Just be careful—especially your men. Be careful."

"Thank you, sir. May I have your name for my report?"

"Of course, Sergeant. SS-Standartenführer Max Stoltz."

* * *

Heinrich Schmidt slowly opened his eyes; his mouth was full of dirt and filth. All he felt was pain. His body rolled and bounced on the rough wood; his shoulder burned beyond what a normal man might take. Through the detritus blowing up through the cracks in the wooden floor, all he saw were shoes, children's shoes, canvas shoes, men's polished dress shoes, workmen's shoes, and women's shoes in multiple colors. All were covered with dust. He saw children's bare legs, cuffs of linen slacks and cotton trousers, then the multicolored hems of women's skirts. The stench was unbearable. And between the legs he saw a face. It, too, was flat on the wooden deck; it was a woman's face, pale, gray, the eyes open and lifeless. It stared at him.

In time, he was able to push himself to his feet. The boxcar lurched, and he held tight to the wooden wall. The dust made it impossible to breathe. Coughing and choking provided the background noise to the train's clattering and screeching as it lurched its way through the countryside. They stopped three times, twice the door was opened, and a bag was thrown in. The first time it was full of apples and pears; the second time was raw potatoes. The doors weren't opened at the third stop.

Schmidt screamed at the soldiers when they opened the door the first time. The sergeant from Rome stood there, his clipboard in his hand. "This is a mistake. Let me out; I shouldn't be here," he yelled in German. No one in the car could understand him. "I'm an officer of the Reich!" The sergeant directed the door to be closed after the apples were thrown in.

At one point on the third day, one of the older men in the car confronted him. "Be very careful, my friend. Some here are beginning to believe you. And for a chicken bone, they would strangle you. I would keep quiet."

Through the cracks in the panel boards, he saw the mountains of Austria and then the open fields of Poland. The heat burned into his brain. He counted five dead—three were children. The corner of the boxcar was a putrid septic mess of straw, urine, and feces. The large tank mounted to the wall, once full of water, had never been refilled. On the morning of the fifth day, the train slowed to a stop. The sound of dogs barking, heavy boots, and men's loud and rough voices penetrated the wooden walls.

The doors slid open. A gust of cold rain pushed its way into the car—it was a relief after the past five days.

"*Raus, raus, raus, eine, Linie bilden, raus,*" was screamed by the soldiers. The dogs ripped at the Jews, tearing clothes and flesh. "*Raus, raus.*"

Once on the ground, Schmidt, filthy and stinking, pushed his way to the front. "I am a German; I'm not a Jew. I'm an officer in the Schutzstaffel."

A club came down hard on his back. "I was told about you, Jew. Welcome back to Auschwitz."

On his knees, in the mud, he saw two children, a boy and a girl. The boy was about twelve, the age of his Johannes. The girl was a little younger—she looked like Elsie, his daughter. They looked back at him, then turned to follow their mother and all the others.

33

Naples, Italy
Late November 1943

The fisherman's boat—with Max and Sophie among the weary and storm-battered passengers—slowly motored its way through the dozens of Allied ships that filled Naples' harbor. The bows and sterns of sunken ships, scuttled and destroyed by the Germans just a month earlier, filled the harbor. Besides the massive Allied transports and cargo ships, the tired company passed cruisers and destroyers that lay at anchor. Above them, commanding and menacing the southern horizon, stood Mount Vesuvius.

"Good God," Max said, as they neared the long stone quay that jutted out into the bay. "I don't recognize the city."

Beyond the boulevard that encircled the harbor of the ancient city lay a shattered and flattened ruin initiated by the brutal mixture of German demolition squads and finished by the Allied aerial bombs and artillery shells during the advance from Salerno in September. Little was left standing.

"My family survived," said the fisherman. "But many thousands died in the explosions and collapsed buildings. The Germans escaped north, killing any they found."

After landing, Max and Sophie sought out their counterparts in OSS and MI6. Jones left orders that they were to return to England as soon as possible.

"First available transport to London is in three days," Sophie said. "I found us a jeep. Do you think your friends are all right?"

"If anyone could survive, it would be Lucia and Cesare," Max said, hoping that his own fears would not come true.

They drove the same road over the Sorrentine mountains that Cesare and Lucia had taken Max when he'd arrived from Marseille, four long years earlier. The verdant green he'd remembered was now gray with ash from fires that had burned the steep hillsides. In places, the road had been hastily repaired. The debris of burned-out vehicles and blasted vegetation was still evident.

"Bombs did that," Max said, looking at a small stone building that was a shattered relic. As they climbed to the ridge that overlooked the Bay of Salerno, it was obvious that hell had visited this place. Massive rents and tears had churned the mountainside into rubble; buildings were now piles of scorched stones. Stripped and desolate forests of charred trees climbed the sides of the valley.

"I'm afraid of what we'll find," Max said when they reached the seaside road that connected the village of Amalfi to Salerno to the east. "The sea looks as if nothing happened."

Amalfi, to his shock, remained unharmed.

"They are unbelievably lucky," he said.

His mood brightened as he parked the jeep at the bottom of the wall that supported the Fallace villa. From the bottom of the stairway, there was no sign of destruction or even damage to the buildings. He pulled a canvas bag from the back. Muffled, yet unmistakable, sounds of clinking glass bottles came from the bag.

"Something I owe Cesare," he said quietly.

"What an astonishing view," Sophie said, as they climbed the stair. "I could actually enjoy spending time here when this war is over."

"It's something that a kid from Chicago wouldn't have dreamed of. I'm still struck by it all."

Max bolted up the stairs, only to come to a stop at the top landing. He gently set the bag down on the bare stones.

"Oh, my God," Sophie said. "I'm so sorry."

The Fallace villa was a burnt ruin of tumbled stonewalls and collapsed timbers. The one stone fireplace stood, phallic-like, amidst the devastation.

"This happened months ago," Max said, seeing bits of green sprouting among the collapsed walls. "Everything was burned. This wasn't an explosion or even a result of artillery."

"Signor Max," a voice said from behind them.

Max studied the teenager who appeared over the rise of the stairs, trying to place the face with the body.

"Nicola?" Max finally said, more as a question than a greeting.

"Yes, it's me."

Nicola wasn't the happy child Max remembered. His face was thin, his eyes deep and dark.

"My God, are you okay? What happened? Where are Signora Lucia and Signor Cesare?"

"No one knows. They have been gone now for more than two months. They disappeared after the house burned."

"But you're here now," Max said.

"Yes, I had nowhere else to go. My brother was killed when he tried to plow his field—a German mine killed him, his wife, and the mule. They were planting tobacco."

"I'm so sorry," Sophie said.

Nicola gave the resigned shrug of one who had seen too much.

"We needed the money; now they don't. So, I now live in the cottage."

"And no one knows what happened to the Fallaces?" Max asked.

"Someone might, but I don't. I'm waiting for them to return. I have only been here a few weeks."

For the next hour, they looked through the ruins, making sure that the Fallaces hadn't been caught in the fire. They found no bones, but a few exploded bottles of Prosecco.

"She loved her Prosecco," Max said.

"Maybe they know something in the village," Sophie said. "We'll stop there on the way to Salerno."

No one knew anything about the Fallaces. The fire had occurred a few weeks after the invasion. The Fallaces hadn't been found. Their car was found parked in the small garage at the base of the stair. It was commandeered by a local government official assigned by the US Army to help with the rebuilding of the village.

"Help with the rebuilding, my ass," Max said, as they drove on the winding road to Salerno. "Since there was no one to stop them, they stole it, the bastards."

They spent the next day in Salerno, where the damage was extensive, but the rebuilding had begun. Even a few restaurants were open along the Lungomare Trieste.

"It is all so different here," Max said, as he looked out into the harbor where the overturned hulls of ships lay on the water. "The land and the people look tired and worn out."

"I know how they feel," Sophie said, as she placed her hand on his. "Let's go home. There is nothing we can do here."

* * *

The C-47 took a long, slow sweep around the airport north of Naples and made its approach. Max and Sophie stood in the rain; the Capodichino runway was wet. Dozens of jeeps and fuel trucks lined the edges of the tarmac. Directly facing them was a squadron of P-48 Mustangs, rain dripping from their bright, almost polished, metal fuselages.

"While not luxurious, it will get us there," Sophie said, watching the transport.

"Luxurious is a dirty word. We'll be lucky if we can get a

seat," Max replied. "It will be a long flight, first to Gibraltar, then over Portugal to England. My ass is already hurting." He grimaced while unconsciously rubbing his butt.

"Poor boy, but when daddy calls, we answer," Sophie said.

"I'd rather go back to the villa and spend the rest of the war there. I can rebuild it."

"We'll come back. I'm sure your friends are alive."

The twin-engine plane rolled to a stop, and three grounds crewmen tucked blocks under the tires as a fuel truck parked behind the port wing. In seconds, hoses were pulled, and the crew began refueling. The plane's hatch opened, and the pilot climbed down the ladder and headed to the cluster of twenty or so people waiting alongside Max and Sophie.

"Wacky-Wacky Airlines here. Captain Flash Gordon at your service. The other guy is Dr. Zarkov. Who's to Gibraltar?"

"You serve food?" a voice asked.

"Nah, too heavy. It's either you or food, make your choice. But whatever you carry onboard don't count, especially wine."

The remark brought a few smiles.

"We are leaving at ten hundred hours—that's 10:00 a.m. for you civilians. Zarkov will get you boarded and strapped in. So, if you'll excuse me, I have to make room for more wine."

The pilot headed toward the base office. Max wasn't surprised to see cowboy boots on the man.

Max and Sophie found that the accommodations were barely a step above the comfort of a Regina Coeli prison cell.

"I wish I'd brought a pillow," Sophie said.

"I don't even want to think about what's coming. It reminds me of my last trip home," Max answered.

Six hours later, they bounced down the runway at Gibraltar. They were given a two-hour layover and a chance to eat hot food before they boarded another C-47 for London.

34

The past six months had been hard; the winter in Italy had been cruel and unforgiving. Max, after his debriefing, was reassigned and sent back to Italy to handle interrogations and translations just miles from the stalled front lines. As the Allies advanced, he followed in their muddy wake. Twice the camp he'd been assigned to had been shattered by artillery fire.

Sophie stayed in London. Max wondered how she rated the assignment. Cynically, he knew it was her father and that he was glad she hadn't had to put up with the winter in Italy.

After the retreat of the Germans out of Rome in June, the Americans took control of the city. Who would liberate Rome was a political hot potato, and through blind dumb luck, the Americans made it into the Eternal City first. Max was a hundred miles to the south at the American base adjacent to Naples' Capodichino airport. Colonel Jones had flown in from London to brief him about the Normandy invasion that had taken place a month earlier. With him was Sophie Norcross.

"You look good," Max said to Sophie. "I missed you."

"Touching. You have a few days before I need you back in Rome," Jones said. "You two can reminisce all you want during the next three days, then you both go north."

"Rome? Why Rome?" Max said. "I'm so tired of Italy. I've had enough to last a lifetime."

"You are beginning to sound like the man I once knew—always bitching and complaining. Are you ever satisfied?"

"Never—my lot in life. What happened to Cattaneo?"

"All I can tell you is that he made it to the States," Jones said. "Beyond that, even I don't know. You will take one of the trains to Rome. They have prisoners for you to interview, as well as chase down reports on Mussolini. It seems he's trapped in Lombardy, and we want him before the communists get to him."

"That strutting monkey—probably prefers us now to the communists."

"He deserves whatever he gets," Sophie said.

"I understand that you know him?" Jones asked.

"Yes, but that was from what seems like a time long ago," Sophie answered.

"Whatever happened to that SS officer, Heinrich Schmidt?" Jones asked. "I never saw a final report."

"We lost him," Max said. "Soon after they began to round up the Roman Jews, he disappeared. We assume he was ordered back to Berlin. Maybe the resistance found him and buried him in some forgotten grave. You might check prisoner lists."

"Not worth the effort," Jones said. "I also have your mail." He handed it to Sophie.

"Typical for your army—they sent all your mail to MI6," Sophie said as she sorted through the letters. "Most are from Chicago; I recognize your mother's handwriting."

Max organized the letters chronologically by their postmarks. Both his father and mother had contributed. They were simple things about the city and the changes in America due to the war. One brought the war too near:

April 3, 1944
Dear Max,
Father and I miss you so much; these daily letters help us to keep you close. We are well, even though your father has a late winter cold. He can be such a baby. Surprisingly, conditions here are getting a little better; maybe it's the optimism about the end of the war. We all read about the fighting in Italy. I hope you were far away from all the "action." We have loved Rome since my first visit there as a little girl; it is such a wonderful city. I cannot even think what it is like now. You remember the Rosenfelts? They left Berlin in 1936 and moved to Rome. I have not heard from her in two years. I hope they are safe.

My weekly lunches with Mrs. Krause, Mrs. Weiss, and Mrs. Jacobs have grown sadder. These occasions have become as much giving them support as some reprieve from the news from Poland. Really, it is the lack of news. Mrs. Weiss has not heard from her family for three years; Mrs. Krause, only one letter a year ago. Dozens and dozens of their family members are missing. I pray to God that they will be found.

And Mrs. Jacobs's son, Aaron, is buried somewhere in Italy. He landed with the invasion force in Salerno; I hope that you know a little about it. He was killed somewhere near Naples. It has been a tough year for her and their family.

Sadly, we have heard that Dwight Loomis was killed in the Pacific. A note arrived from his parents; it happened four months ago at a place called Tarawa. When I have more information, I will send it. We are so sorry; Dominic and Dwight were wonderful boys and good friends. We pray that this war ends soon.

The good news is that Uncle Wilhelm made it to Cuba. He is there now. He says he left soon after you saw him in Paris. He took your advice and fled south to Marseille. He says in his letter that he caught a boat to Porte-au-Prince, then after a few months was able to get to Havana. He is there and is trying to get his papers together to come to Chicago. We are doing what we can to help. Considering what has happened to our friends' families, thank you for talking him into leaving.

The store is doing well. Some days are long. It's hard to find employees—so much different than ten years ago. I mentioned optimism; these young people, even with the war, believe in a bright future. We do what we can to support them.

I want you to tell me everything about this Sophie Norcross; your letters have been a little short on information. Are you serious? When can we meet her? Does she come from a good family?

I have enclosed a letter from Dominic's aunt; we see them a few times a year. We stop for a late lunch. She always wants to talk about you. Seems that a letter came from her brother in Amalfi that talks about you. Why haven't you said anything about them? Then again, I suspect it is due to the war and such.

Write soon.

All our love,

Mother and Father

This last letter in the stack was three weeks old, and inside the envelope was the letter from Dominic's aunt, Renata Rossi. As he read, tears began to build. Sophie put her fingertips on his wet cheek.

"Is everything all right? What is it? Are your parents okay?"

Max took a deep breath.

"They are alive," he said.

"Your parents?"

"Yes, they are well. It's Cesare and Lucia Fallace—they are alive."

* * *

Two days later, Max and Sophie stopped the jeep at the foot of the stone façade that supported what remained of the Fallace villa. Sophie wore an orange and green cotton dress, a reflection of the brilliant summer colors that climbed the face of the mountain above the villa. Max was dressed in his uniform. He carried a dark green canvas bag with his free hand; the bottles packed inside clinked.

As the two climbed the stone stairway, a familiar voice called from above. "Why didn't you call? The phone works again."

"Lucia, we didn't have time," Max said as they reached the terrace.

Lucia, thinner from the years of the war, enclosed Max with her arms and squeezed him so tight that he winced. Happiness poured out of both of them. She kissed Max on both cheeks, and for a long moment looked up into his blue eyes. Tears left damp tracks as they rolled down her cheeks. She then looked around her giant, and smiled at Sophie. "And who is this beautiful woman? Max, she's far too pretty to hang around with a disreputable fellow like you." She looked back up at Max and winked.

"Lucia, may I introduce you to Sophie Norcross. Sophie, this is Signora Lucia Fallace, Dominic's mother, and one of the most special people in my life."

"Delighted and honored," Sophie said and gave Lucia a hug and a kiss.

"Come. Cesare will be so surprised." Lucia took each of them by the hand and led them across the terrace to a large army tent.

"We are assigned back to Rome and were able to take a long weekend," Max said as they walked. "I was able to get the jeep for a few days."

"Who got the jeep, mister?" Sophie said.

"Sophie borrowed it from some Neapolitan friend of hers. I don't ask questions," Max said. "One of many favors she's been collecting."

Lucia stopped and hugged them both again.

"This is the most wonderful of days," she said.

As they reached the tent, Cesare stepped out. He was holding a large spoon covered in red sauce. He handed the spoon to Lucia and hugged Max. This time, Max teared up both from the hug and seeing his old friends.

"Is so good to see you again. After everything we've heard about Rome, we weren't sure what to believe," Cesare said, apologizing, then noticed Sophie.

"Signor Fallace, every time I see you, you're holding either a drink or a spoon—I'll tell you about Rome later," Max said and introduced Sophie. He noticed a slight blush on Cesare's cheeks when she kissed him.

"We prayed you were safe. We hadn't heard anything since—" Cesare said.

"It's hard to remember when," Lucia said, interrupting. "Time seems to have stopped during this past year." She steered them to chairs.

Max explained, "I wrote as soon as I received the letter from Renata. We were so happy to find out that you were safe—I'm not surprised my letters haven't arrived. You, where have you been?"

"Later—much to tell," Cesare said and disappeared back into the tent.

Nicola arrived. The young man seemed to enjoy Sophie's hug more than Max's. Lucia sent him to the jeep to fetch the luggage.

"When Nicola told us that you stopped in late March, we were disappointed," Lucia told them. "Nicola said you were well, but it was mostly about you, my dear. He seems to have developed a crush. I'm sorry we missed you. We returned a few days later. We have prayed for your safety."

"I really can't believe you're cooking," Max said when Cesare returned.

Cesare's face turned melancholy.

"Our cook, Maria—you remember her—was killed," Lucia said. "She'd left here to visit her family east of Campania and stopped on the road to visit a shrine she had prayed at since she was a child. When she approached, a mine exploded."

"She had been with us for more than twenty years," Cesare said, sadness to his words. "She was more than a cook, but a dear friend, a cherished part of our lives. We miss her very much."

Lucia interrupted with glasses of Prosecco.

"This is my last bottle, so drink slowly," she said.

"This is the last of the wine?" Max asked.

"No, no, no, we have plenty of that. The cellar was un-damaged." Cesare laughed. "It's that Lucia wants to celebrate everything since the Americans liberated Rome, so now there's no Prosecco left."

From his canvas bag, Max produced two bottles of American bourbon, two bottles of scotch, and two bottles of Prosecco.

"These are for you. It was a promise I made before I left, don't you remember?" Max said.

"I remember and thank you. Our cellar is open to you. You pick," Cesare said.

Max reached again into the bag and brought out a box.

"And these are also for you. I met a general who offered me this box of Cuban cigars for a favor I did him. It's my small way of saying thanks."

As they waited for dinner, they sat in the breeze that drifted up from the sea. The talk shifted back and forth to those lost and those who lived. Max and Sophie told the Fallaces about Rome. Cesare and Lucia talked about the fearful hours spent hiding in the cave.

"We stayed there another night," Cesare said, accepting a cigar from Max. "Everyone was too exhausted to climb back down the mountain. We had wine and food, and the children were finally settled. Lucia and the other women comforted the old woman and said prayers over the man's body. It was rough—earth-shattering explosions continued all through the night. Everyone was afraid the Germans would come over the ridge and down the valley directly at us."

Lucia refilled everyone's glasses.

"But no one else died that night, thank God," she said. "It was the weeks and months that followed—they were hell. And then the winter—I've never seen so much rain and cold. Hundreds, maybe thousands, in the Campagna died from disease and hunger. Only God has the count."

"It was luck that got the call through," Max said.

"Luck and God," Lucia said. "All of us put our lives in God's hands these days."

"What happened?" Sophie asked, looking at the burnt ruin of the villa.

"With all the destruction and chaos, and the recent eruptions of that evil bitch Vesuvius, the loss of the villa is really nothing," Lucia told them. "I was cooking. I turned away from the stove for a moment to reach for something—I don't even remember what. When I turned back, I knocked the pan full of olive oil onto the stove, and it exploded. From there it caught the curtains on fire, then the flames took on a life of their own. We grabbed what we could—some family pictures and artwork. We'd actually made provisions for this in case the war swept back over us. We stood on the terrace and watched as the fire consumed everything."

"We were lucky. It can and will be rebuilt," Cesare said. "We left and went to the farm in Campania. We spent the rest of the winter there. It was hard, and food was scarce, but we managed. One of your American military units was stationed near us; we received food from them. We made sure others in the area also had food. But it was difficult for the young and very old. We lost more friends to sickness and those ungodly mines the Nazis left everywhere."

"Nicola went to his brother's house," Lucia added. "He said he told you the story."

She looked fondly at the teenager.

"When we returned, we found him in the cottage. We're all staying there—Nicola sleeps in the small front parlor. You remember it, don't you?"

"Of course," Max said. "And the tent?"

"I don't want lightning to strike twice," Cesare said. "We spend our days down here. Many come by to say hello, and now you have come back. My heart is full."

"Spring finally brought some hope; we finally made it into Naples," Lucia continued. "I was shocked at the destruction. I—we—lost so many friends." She kissed Cesare's cheek. "War is never a friend of anyone. We are just grease under the wheels of tanks and war machines."

"Your children, are they okay?" Sophie asked.

Lucia gazed tenderly at Cesare and put her hand on his.

"Yes, thank God. A letter arrived a week ago; it took almost a month to get here. They are in Rome and hope to be home soon."

"Lucia, if we had known, we might have been able to make arrangements for them," Sophie said.

"Thank you for that, but they are well and unhurt. That's all I can ask," Lucia said. "Salerno is recovering and rebuilding. Even the fishing fleet has been able to set their nets and lines again."

Dinner was served on a large plank table. Nicola carried out plates of spaghetti and bread. Max noticed strange cubes of meat in the sauce.

"Your American Spam," Cesare said. "It may not be traditional, but it's not too bad."

"Especially when you have had nothing to eat for a few weeks," Lucia added.

After dinner, Cesare opened one of the bottles of bourbon and handed a cigar to Max. The four friends moved to a cluster of lounge chairs that looked to the south. The last rays of the setting sun flicked off the waves of the Bay of Salerno as if a million little mirrors floated on its surface. Max lit Cesare's cigar and the cigarettes for the women. Lucia poured the bourbon into crystal tumblers.

"We found these when we went through the ruins," Lucia said, holding up her glass. "They will always be reminders of the past."

"Even during the war, this villa was a secluded fairy castle," Max said. "All the craziness and hatred could not breach that surrounding stone wall. It's an island of peace in an insane world."

"Yes, our beautiful prison. We were fortunate, but our hearts are still heavy. Our children are safe, but we miss Dominic," Lucia said. "Even after five years, there is a quiet emptiness in our lives."

"There is not one day that goes by that I don't think of Dominic," Max said softly. "He is and will always be with me. There were times that I honestly thought he was watching over me, like a guardian angel."

* * *

London
Late July 1944

As with all armies, plans change. After returning from Naples to Rome, Max was sent back to London. In late July, Max and Sophie stood at the American Bar in the Savoy, in London. Colonel Jones swirled a glass of rye, two cubes of ice occasionally clanking against the crystal. Max sipped a bourbon, Sophie a glass of Pernod.

"General Donovan sees changes coming, and they are coming fast for the OSS," Jones said. "Now that the Allies are marching on Paris, the war will end this winter or in the spring at the latest. Germany is collapsing. If the winter doesn't throw us surprises, or the Germans kill Hitler first—God knows they've tried—this part, our part, of the war is over."

"Part? What do you mean this part of the war?" Sophie said. "When Germany's done, it is over."

"I think I know what the colonel is saying," Max said. "The Russians are advancing fast from the east—and they are seeking retribution for Hitler's actions. You've read the reports—the way Stalin is pushing his army, who the hell knows what will happen? Hell, they may even reach Berlin first."

"Miss Norcross," Jones said, "your MI6 and other security agencies have watched this for years and will continue to monitor the postwar changes. I've talked with many who believe there will be trouble in the eastern European countries, Vienna, Budapest, the Mediterranean—especially Egypt and Palestine—when the Nazis surrender. And, Max, it's your people that are causing a lot of the trouble, especially in Palestine."

"Colonel Jones, sometimes, begging the colonel's pardon," Max said, setting his drink on the bar, "I should just pop you in the mouth. My people? The Jews? Is that who you are talking about?"

"No, the Zionists," Jones answered. "The political and military side of the effort to free Palestine and Jerusalem from the British."

"We know that Hitler used Arabs and other Muslims to fight in the Balkans," Max said. "I would remind the colonel that the Muslims have been far more militant than many of those in other countries conquered by the Nazis. And they have been pushed politically by Al-Husseini, the mufti of Jerusalem, to continue to provoke unrest throughout the Muslim world. The Zionists may be the only ones to stand against this push."

"I've never heard you speak like this," Sophie said. "You, a

Zionist? Not a popular subject here in London."

"Don't I know it. However, I have seen too much over the last five years not to see that there's a good chance there will be a massive shift in the world's political structure—and that includes the emigration of those not wanted by these damaged countries. Most would be glad to rid themselves of the Jews."

"Sorry, Captain, I didn't mean it had anything to do with the Jews. Nonetheless, the OSS is changing," Jones said. "In fact, the scuttlebutt is that we will be shut down after the war is over."

"You can't," Sophie said. "MI6 needs your resources more than ever."

"You know that, and I know that, but it's politics—plain old American politics. In fact, all the world's political structures are being thrown into an mad vortex of fear and retribution."

"What's the talk?" Max asked.

"The rumor, or so I've heard, is that out of this shutdown a new agency will rise. What it will be I haven't a clue, but we will need smart people, experienced people, to get this off the ground, and I mean off the ground running."

"When this is over, I'm going home," Max said as he lit a cigar.

"Home to Mommy?" Jones snorted.

Max set the cigar gently in the ashtray, smiled at Sophie, then slugged Jones in the jaw, knocking him to the tile floor. He then reached down and helped Jones up.

"I've learned a lot since the last time we danced, Colonel."

The End

REVIEWS PLEASE

Today authors rely heavily on the reviews posted by our readers. As an independent self-publisher this is even more important than traditionally published books. If you have enjoyed this novel, please take a few minutes and post a review on Goodreads and Amazon.

About the Author
Gregory C. Randall

Mr. Randall is Michigan born, Chicago raised and
Californian by choice.
He makes his home in Northern California.
Mr. Randall is the author of fiction and non-fiction
works available through the usual outlets and
Amazon.com.

For more on Max Alder and the other characters in the writing universe of Mr. Randall, please visit his website.
http://www.gregorycrandall.info

OTHER NOVELS BY GREGORY C. RANDALL

The Cherry Pickers

The Max Adler WWII Thrillers
This Face of Evil
Pawns in an Ancient Game

The Sharon O'Mara Chronicles
Land Swap For Death
Containers For Death
Toulouse For Death
12th Man For Death
Diamonds For Death
Limerick For Death

The Tony Alfano Thrillers
Chicago Swing
Chicago Jazz
Chicago Fix
Chicago Boogie Woogie

The Alex Polonia Thrillers
Venice Black
Saigon Red
St. Petersburg White

The Gypsy King Sci-Fi Adventures
Sector 73

Nonfiction
America's Original GI Town, Park Forest, Illinois